A Time To Love

by

Gail Symmonds

This is a work of fiction. Names, characters, places, and incidents are either the product of the author's imagination or are used fictitiously, and any resemblance to actual persons living or dead, business establishments, events, or locales, is entirely coincidental.

A Time To Love

COPYRIGHT © 2008 by Gail Symmonds

All rights reserved. No part of this book may be used or reproduced in any manner whatsoever without written permission of the author or The Wild Rose Press except in the case of brief quotations embodied in critical articles or reviews.

Contact Information: info@thewildrosepress.com

Cover Art by *Rae Monet*

The Wild Rose Press
PO Box 708
Adams Basin, NY 14410-0706
Visit us at www.thewildrosepress.com

Publishing History
First Faery Rose Edition, 2009
Print ISBN: 1-60154-501-0

Published in the United States of America

"It's all right, lass. I've got ye. Stop thrashin' aboot. Yer safe now."

Comprehending what held her, she fought violently to extract herself.

"Let me go you stupid idiot," she screamed at her assailant whilst trying to get back her breath. "Let me go or I'll break your damn nose."

The sound of crunching gristle followed by a howl of stunned pain, caused the vice-like grip around her waist to loosen, giving her a chance to use her legs to push off his and glide backwards though the water. She felt better for putting distance between them, and creating space enough for her to better defend herself.

A man, no, a huge man, stood in front of her with his hand over his nose, and blood running down his chest into the water. It gave her a perverse sense of satisfaction. Euphoric over this victory, she lifted her eyes to his, and felt as though the breath was knocked out of her. Dark, piercing eyes bored into her. His face was without expression, but it needed none. His eyes told the story. He was furious.

She threatened him again, "Don't come any closer, or I'll, I'll..."

"Do what? Break ma other nose?"

"No, but I'll rearrange your balls."

Understanding her meaning of 'balls,' Connor found it difficult not to smile. This woman was as crazy as a wild boar. She was cornered, irrational, and making rash judgements that would lead to her ultimate defeat. Connor began to enjoy himself, curious to see where it would lead.

Dedication

For Dad...
with me every day.

Acknowledgements

To my Mum, Daphne and that other lovely lady, Lynda Taylor, for all the time you gave me in the early stages of this book. You are both remarkable women. Sharon Fowler, the first to read it when half finished and simply said "keep going." Linda Brock, Carolyn Henry, and Sherree Rieger for your friendship and support, and Janine Williams for reading it twice! Suzanne Brandyn for showing me how to add the final polish—you're a gem.

Of course, to my husband Al and the precious jewels in my life, Callum and Bronte. Thank you for understanding when tea was late or I forgot to pick you up from the bus stop.

All of you, friends and family, never uttered anything but positive encouragement which inspired and motivated me to 'the end.' I am so lucky to have you all in my life.

Chapter One

Joanne Dunstan was cold.

Her body refused to wake. The persistent chill continued to invade her consciousness. She was vaguely aware of her cheek feeling uncomfortable and wet. Something tickled her foot. "Lewis, go away," she mumbled. As consciousness returned she could hear the continual squawking of a bird. "Shut up," she grumbled.

As reality drifted to the surface she became aware of daylight creeping under her eyelids and the fact she was shivering. She attempted to roll over and pull the doona to her chin, but met a solid object. Her eyes snapped open.

The severe morning light made her squint for a few seconds before her eyes adjusted.

She faced a tree—a big tree.

Reaching her hand out to see if the tree was real, she began to push up from the ground with her other hand. Immediately her attention shifted from the tree to the ground. It was cold and wet; her palm crushed what looked to be young bracken fern into the damp earth. Standing, using the tree for support, Jo began to survey her surroundings. "What in God's name?"

The forest loomed, dense and overgrown with vines and bracken. Huge trees reached for the sky. Fallen logs were covered in soft green moss and the forest seemed alive with birds. A deer jumped over a log beside her and continued on its way undaunted. "I'm dreaming. I have to be dreaming—don't I?" she said as if expecting someone to answer.

Her body trembled. She knew, even for a dream, she must start moving or she was going to freeze to death. Her baggy, tartan pyjamas held little warmth.

"Hello," she called out.

Silence.

She stepped away from the tree and began to walk. The ground was cold beneath her feet, but worse was the feel of the damp earth pushing between her toes. She shivered with cold.

It was a beautiful place, in a wild and unexplored kind of way.

Her next step sent her to the ground as pain shot through her foot. Wrapping her hand around the arch of her foot she applied pressure as the gash, caused by a sharp stick, welled with blood. Raising her head to the trees she yelled, "Okay, I'd like to wake up now. Pain is not allowed. In nice dreams you don't feel pain."

Silence.

Tears stung her eyes. *No, no, no. This is ridiculous.* Standing once again, she moved through the forest. She didn't know where she was going, but sitting on the wet ground shivering wasn't going to solve any problems.

She hadn't moved far when she found a track. It was probably an animal track but the pathway was clear and Jo figured she was less likely to injure herself if she kept to it. Playing along with the dream she continued to walk, going over in her head her predicament, trying to reason out her situation.

The evening before, she'd dined with June, left at eight, and had a bath at home, followed by an early night.

So what the hell was going on?

Oh, yeah, that's right; it was a horrible day at work. The worst ever. Everyone was escorted to the elevators after being told the international company they worked for collapsed. Bankrupt. They brought in security guards to make sure they didn't take a single token pen or paper clip with them. It was humiliating and really spun her out.

That must be why she was having such a freaky dream!

She walked for ten minutes, ignoring the dull ache in her foot, when she thought she heard noises. She tilted her ear toward the sound and recognised voices. As she got closer the sounds became clearer. Men's voices spoke with a guttural accent she hadn't heard before. When they came into view, Jo stopped dead in her tracks, mouth gaping, as she tried to comprehend the sight in front of her.

On the other side of a fallen log in a small clearing, a group of about twelve men stood around a campfire. Not unusual for a dream she supposed, but the fact they wore tartan car rugs over their shoulders amused her.

An animated conversation took place between two of the men. Their voices became raised and a knife appeared. The man holding it looked fierce enough to turn this dream into a nightmare, and when he lunged at his opponent, Jo couldn't withhold a gasp loud enough to attract the attention of the other ten men whose eyes swung towards her.

The men formed a circle; backs to the centre, ten huge swords drawn and pointed outwards. The two quarrelling forgot their dispute and drew their swords like their comrades, advancing with care, eyes scanning the dense forest on either side of her.

"Oh, shit," was all she could get out, a sheen of sweat breaking over her body, before her trembling limbs refused to hold her any longer and she fainted.

****

Scottish Highlands 1626

He sat his horse like he was born in the saddle. The early morning mist swirled about the damp earth. The chickens still nestled within their coops, hidden away from the morning chill. The stallion beneath him stomped restlessly, impatient to be on his way.

"Whoa there, Thief," came the deep, calm command, "patience is nae your virtue."

The truth was, the man was also keen to make a prompt exit. This village was always the worst. The dwellers promptly paid their rents and were good, hard-working tenants. The problem was, Tallach contained an abundance of young women, and a severe shortage of young men!

So when the laird himself rode into town, normally once a year, he got far more attention than he craved. In fact, Laird Connor MacKay never encouraged any female interest, particularly from within the tenanted farming families. The girls of the village were willing to offer him favours, but he held no interest in spreading his seed that way. It could only lead to complications and regret.

Therefore, the dark, brooding man with the body of a warrior and striking looks that continually turned women's heads, was anxious to leave Tallach and make his way to the next collection point. Connor was a warrior at heart, but as laird, he had other obligations that needed fulfilling. He didn't like some of them, but he did what needed doing. There were seven more villages to go, hopefully returning the party home to Shreave within a fortnight.

Running into a pitched battle with his broadsword swinging was much easier than dealing with the administrative side of lairdship—and the endless line of daughters. It wasn't that he didn't enjoy the pleasures a woman could offer—he bedded his fair share—it was just none moved him, challenged his intellect, or his authority. He didn't want an obedient little puppy. He wanted a real woman.

His friend and brother in arms, Dougal Haig found this kind of marriage. Maeve drove Connor mad with her blunt, outspoken, opinionated ways, but he couldn't help admire the woman. Though he would never, ever, tell her so.

Connor long ago decided women, apart from Maeve, were all the same—deceitful, manipulative, and unworthy. Past experience taught him that lesson well. He was better off alone.

****

"Well Dougal, what do ye make of this?"

"Ah dinna ken, Neill. I canna even tell if it's a man or woman." The group of men gathered around Jo's unconscious body. They'd already scouted the surrounding area to ensure this was no ambush attempt. There were two ambushes in the last five weeks and Clan Sutherland or Sinclair was thought to be the culprit. However, it was hard to ascertain as no plaids were worn and the attacks happened at night.

"What tartan do ye liken it ta be?"

"None I have ever seen," Dougal replied to Neill.

Neill bent closer and gave Jo a poke in the side with his boot.

Jo's eyes fluttered open. Oh yes, she was sure this was a nightmare not a dream.

How could this be possible?

She was the centre of attention, surrounded by a group of bearded Neanderthal men.

Panicking, she sat up and scrambled backwards on her bottom. Pyjamas were not designed for this kind of manoeuvre and she felt the elastic in the back of her pants drag halfway down the cheeks of her behind. She stopped and grabbed the waistband and hoisted it back up whilst rising to her feet in one unladylike movement.

The expressions of gruff confusion on the faces

of the men changed to one of surprise and realisation.

It was obvious she was a woman. There was no hiding a C-cup, even in a sloppy pair of flannelette pyjamas.

Confusion swamped her. Green eyes darted to the faces surrounding her as she tried to ascertain the intention of the men. She felt threatened, but the stunned looks on the faces of her audience told her they were as unsure as she.

With a huge log behind her and a circle of men in front, she decided on a direct approach. "Er, h…hello," she stuttered. If she wasn't so confused the whole situation would be comical. They were gaping at her. Hadn't they seen anyone in pyjamas before? "Er, I'm…I'm having a really bad dream. Do any of you know how I could wake up?" The reaction was more stunned faces, frowns, and blank looks. Finally someone spoke.

"She talks funny. Where do ye think she's from? I've nae seen that tartan around these parts before."

"Maybe the lassie is lost," answered another large blanket clad man.

"I think she may be from MacKenzie way. They have some giant lassies down there," replied another with a short red beard and scar on his left cheek.

"Nae, most of the MacKenzies are with red hair. This lass has nae the look of it," chipped in someone else.

The man called Dougal scratched his chin in thoughtful contemplation. He studied her as if she was a fine specimen of rare insect. The other men in the group began to converse amongst themselves, bickering the origins of this latest find. Jo stood back, mouth agape, watching the deliberations in front of her.

"Don't be daft man. Nellie doesna have the red hair."

"Oh nae, I suppose not. But, her cousin Kathryn does."

Dougal pondered the discussion when a tall man with fair hair chipped in.

"Nae…nae, Kathryn's hair is auburn, nae red."

A young man, who looked no older than fourteen, spoke with reverence. "I've never seen breeches on a woman before."

The ridiculous conversation over her supposed origin stopped. Every man's attention was drawn to Jo's long legs and mud encrusted bare feet, one of which was bleeding. The man called Dougal stepped forward, looking inquiringly at her feet. "Where are yer boots lass? Did ye lose them?"

She held back a hysterical laugh. *Lost boots, no I haven't lost my boots, but I'm losing my bloody mind.*

Her feet were colder than ever and caked with mud, and her pyjamas were wet from her fall to the ground. She also became aware of her surroundings and in disbelief realised this couldn't be a dream.

The smell of the forest was fresh and clean, like after a spring shower; the sounds clear and sharp. The men in front of her were detailed and very much real. A hopeful thought arrived, she must have walked in her sleep, but there were no forests she knew of with this type of vegetation in Melbourne, Australia, not even at the botanical gardens.

As she appraised the situation and the men in front of her, she didn't want to fathom any other possibilities. The men needed dealing with first, and even though not pointing at her, their swords were still unsheathed and their stances told of trust hard won.

Her body trembled, but she didn't feel threatened. The situation reminded her of the tough union negotiations she spearheaded. A direct approach in a hostile environment often worked. Shivering, she folded her arms across herself and faced the man named Dougal. "I didn't lose them. I don't have any...with me. Could you tell me..."

"Neill," Dougal commanded, cutting her off. With an almost unperceivable nod of Dougal's head, the man Jo supposed was Neill left the group, moving off to the horses tethered to branches beyond the clearing.

She glared at Dougal, seeing behind his eyes the strength of leadership. He stared back and Jo knew he was assessing her. He was suspicious of her. There was no need to be wary, she was harmless—unless provoked—and outnumbered twelve to one.

She *was* absolutely sure, for some reason Dougal was uncomfortable with her direct eye contact. He was almost scowling at her. It was apparent he was prepared to extend a courtesy to assist her. She was happy to remain silent until she could get her head around her predicament.

It appeared Dougal would be patient until the time came for explanations. Explanations she didn't have.

Her best plan was to say as little as possible. After all, what could she say?

"You'll come with us, lass." An order, not a question. Turning, he muttered under his breath, but loud enough for her to hear. "Ye'll be Connor's problem."

Jo raised her voice to draw Dougal's attention back.

"Who's Connor?" she asked.

Dougal stopped and turned to stare at her, another frown marking his brow. "The laird, of course."

Neill returned with a heavy tartan blanket similar to those worn by the men and an old pair of leather boots that smelled of stale bread. He thrust them at Jo and walked away.

Wasting no time, Jo pulled the over-large boots

on and hugged the blanket to her chest feeling its warmth. This was no rubber backed picnic blanket, but heavy, woven wool. Feeling the texture with her fingers, she startled at Dougal's silent approach.

Noting her surprise, Dougal said, "Don't play with it lass, put it on." Jo was quick to unfold the length of wool and wrap it around her shoulders like a shawl. Dougal frowned, but said nothing and began to issue orders to the rest of the men who stood, watching in silence. They all moved to untether horses, put out campfires, and pack all their belongings, although from what she could see, they travelled light.

She estimated the men ranged in age from about fourteen to fifty, though it was hard to tell because the majority of them wore long beards, some with thin braids plaited at the side of their faces. They were clothed in long linen shirts with woollen blankets thrown over one shoulder, falling to their knees. It was interesting how the blanket was pleated and belted.

Curious for a better look, but unwilling to get too close to any of them, she held her ground. She suspected the blankets were an older version of a kilt. As the packing continued it appeared she was forgotten. If only for a moment.

She couldn't mistake the curious sidewards glances by the men as they went about bundling their meagre belongings into leather pouches on the backs of their mounts.

One of the men in particular eyed her. He wore long dark hair and a beard similar to the others, but it was his eyes that drew her attention. They were light grey in colour and had a cold, sullen gleam which unnerved her. A chill went down her spine. She'd learnt over the years to trust her instincts. They were often right.

He moved off to pack his horse and Jo

shuddered, but shook off the feelings and tried to put together the events of the previous evening.

Standing like a shrouded statue in the middle of the clearing, she went over all possibilities as to her arrival in this predicament.

She remembered yesterday's events. How could she forget what happened at work? And June, her wonderful neighbour and friend. At seventy-four, the older lady was the mother she never had. Widowed for only a year and with no children of her own, June and Jo clicked. They leant on each other, June grieving the loss of her husband, and Jo getting over a bitter divorce and the death of her own selfish mother. The fact they'd not got on hadn't lessened the grieving.

Last night, Jo had poured out the day's events at work. June simply said, "So, tomorrow is a new day of opportunity." June put her at ease, fed her, and then surprised her with a special gift.

June said, with a twinkle in her eye, "I think it's the right time to give you this, my dear. I've been meaning to for a long time, but you always seemed so busy. I think now you will have...time to enjoy it."

It was an antique gold chain carrying a Celtic styled pendant with a large blood red ruby in the centre. A family heirloom.

Jo was stunned. The women held each other for a long moment and shed a few tears before June placed it around her neck.

Later that night, she had felt like being decadent and wore the necklace in her spa and then to bed.

She grabbed at her throat for the heavy gold chain.

The necklace was gone.

Maybe it came off in bed or dropped to the forest floor. Devastation swamped her. But overriding these feelings was the madness surrounding her.

She fought back tears, knowing she had enough problems to deal with at present.

How *does* one go from such an ordinary life to a dense forest in an unknown place, surrounded by kilt-clad men with strange accents?

She'd worked for Hardwick International's head office in Scotland for three months some years back, and recognised the Scottish accent. However, it was far broader than what she was used to. Sometimes they broke into a language she didn't understand at all.

Maybe this was a dream, but common sense told her it was not. It was something far more extraordinary.

With all horses ready to go, Dougal announced Jo would ride with Neill. He was slightly taller than her, with fair hair, a short-cropped beard, and a pair of dark brown unreadable eyes. He showed no outward sign of displeasure at being chosen to ride double with her. Aware these might not be his true feelings, she said nothing as Neill brought his horse forward and mounted. The chestnut-coloured animal looked solid with its soft, shaggy coat. Neill reached down and hauled her up behind him. Knowing nothing about horses, she surmised the beast was mongrel bred, but sitting behind Neill she felt the sure strength of the animal beneath her. On closer observation, all the horses looked alike, as if bred for strong sturdy work.

The close, intimate contact with Neill made her uncomfortable. But with no option other than walking, she held herself as erect as possible to lesson the contact between their bodies. The horses followed one another in a single file.

Dougal led the way, followed by Neill, with the rest trailing behind.

She had no idea where she was going, no idea where she was.

Her stomach churned.

Her real fear was anxiety. If she gave it permission, it would completely crush her.

In silence, the group moved through the forest, winding their way along the narrow track.

Chapter Two

Several hours later, Jo thought walking a preferred option. Her lower back ached and her rear-end burned from the continuous chafing between her loose pyjamas and the horse's saddle. As the animal began a steep decent, she couldn't help let out a quiet groan. It felt like her lower vertebrae were being crushed from the jerky movements of the beast. Her pelvis ground into Neill's back, adding to her pain and discomfort.

A few minutes later at the bottom of the hill near a small clearing, Dougal gave one of his unperceivable nods, and the horses were guided off the track and brought to a halt. The men all dismounted, including Neill, who walked off and left her still mounted. For the life of her, she didn't think she could move her sore, unbending muscles to enable her to dismount.

Recognising her dilemma, Dougal came up beside her, wrapped his two huge hands around her waist, and lifted her with ease to the ground. He didn't let her go straight away. Somehow he knew if he let her go, she would flop to the ground in a heap. "Have ye gained yer legs back, lass?" he whispered.

Realising he saved her the embarrassment of making a fool of herself in front of all the curious onlookers, she gave him a nod of appreciation. With a barely concealed look of disgust he added, "My Maeve sits a horse as pitiable as ye do!" With his sarcastic chuckle ringing in her ears she walked away trying to bring some life back into her stiff, screaming muscles.

The rest was brief and before she was ready, she found herself mounted and riding again. The landscape began to change over the last half an hour. The trees thinned out and rich green paddocks could be seen dotted over the countryside. The path widened and the men rode two or three abreast talking amongst themselves, and there was a more relaxed feel to the group as if hidden dangers were left behind. Taking advantage of the mood change, she decided to find out where they were going.

With Neill sitting in front of her and Dougal now riding beside them Jo tentatively broached the subject. "May I ask where we're going, Dougal?"

Taken aback by her using his name, Dougal made no move to answer.

Jo recognised a man working on a response. She waited for him to speak.

"Home," came the reply.

Not satisfied with this brief answer, she pushed, "Where is home?"

Dougal turned to face her with a question of his own. "Ye dinna recognise the landscape then?"

"No. I've never been here before." There was far more truth to this than she was yet to realise.

"Where are ye from, lass?"

"I come from Melbourne."

"Mel-bun." Dougal tested it on his tongue. "I've nae heard of it before. Is it beyond Sutherland borders?"

"I haven't heard of Sutherland before. Is it in Victoria?"

Dougal and Neill turned to each other with a blank look. "Victoria," Dougal said. "Where is Victoria?"

Jo was getting confused. For the moment, she thought these guys were in more trouble than she was. "It's my home. It's your home, too. You know, here in Australia, where we all live."

"Lass, I've lived on MacKay land all ma life. Scotland is the only home I've ever known."

A wave of unidentified emotion washed over her. With a blank look on her face she sat there contemplating Dougal's words. Scotland? For hours now she tried to ignore her surroundings and pretend she was dreaming. She took in the environment but had chosen not to look *too* hard at it.

The men she travelled with during the day wore strange kilts, but she hadn't wanted to examine their clothing too carefully. The accent they all spoke with was not something you heard every day in Melbourne and at times they spoke a language all of their own. She chose to ignore this, too. The fact was, she was afraid of the conclusions she may draw if examined too thoroughly.

There were some things, though, she couldn't close her eyes to and disregard any longer. It was the air. The smell. It was the way the sun shone cleaner and brighter than it did at home and the way the vegetation grew lush and green with health. It was the quiet.

There was no sound of vehicles and the traffic of congested freeways or roads. There was no sign of machinery that cleared forest paths and ploughed farmer's paddocks. No jet streams streaked across the sky, left by planes carrying passengers to all corners of the planet. There seemed to be more insects and small animals scurrying about the countryside. But, maybe she was wrong. Maybe this unsettled feeling was nothing but the aftershocks of the previous day's events.

Or maybe it was her conscience trying to make her see.

Forcing herself to speak, she turned towards Dougal who was still riding beside Neill and herself, looking at her. His eyes never left her as if he was trying to read her mind and discover all her secrets. "If this isn't Melbourne then, and you say it's Scotland, then how did I get here?"

"That is one of the very questions I would like ta ask of *ye*," replied Dougal, staring at her. "Ye were found near the border of MacKay and Sutherland land. It is a dangerous thing ta wander unprotected away from home. There are raiders aboot, and being sae close to the border is a risky thing. We found nae horse and nae weapons in the surrounding area where we came upon ye."

Dougal looked down at his hands holding the reins of his horse, a wrinkle of confusion marked his brow. His face told of a man choosing his words with care. It was obvious to Jo he was far from trusting her. He lifted his eyes across the meadows lined with forest, towards the crest of an approaching hill. "Ye are in the heart of MacKay land now. It is ours ta protect—from raiders, from Sutherlands, from MacLeods, Gunns, and if need be, Sinclairs. All of these people have reason ta want our land and some will go ta any lengths ta find a weakness so they can enter and attack our home and take it fer their own. Some of them would send a spy ta pilfer what information they can gather and then use that information ta steal our cattle, hurt our families and our children. We canna allow this ta happen. We *willna* let this happen. So ye understand lass?"

She listened to Dougal, feeling the compassion in his words. He was a man who loved his home, a man who loved his family. But to think she may be a threat to any of them was absurd. She looked him in the eye as he did her. "I understand what you are saying Dougal, but I assure you, I am no threat to you or your home. I can't explain how I got here because I don't know. There are questions in my head even I don't have answers to. I'm...I'm just lost." Yet again, she felt the sting of tears but forced them away. "But I promise you this, Dougal, I mean you no harm."

Dougal stared back at her, his face expressionless. Without another word, he rode off ahead of the group; his back straight and unbending. Her instincts told her Dougal was a fair and just man. A man who speaks with such passion about his home couldn't be all that bad. She hoped.

Adjusting her backside in the saddle to reposition the sorest spot, she groaned, having given up holding herself erect to minimize the close contact with Neill. He'd remained silent the entire journey.

"We're nearly there."

Jo was so surprised he spoke it made her jump. With two hands full of Neill's plaid to stop her falling from the saddle, all she could think to say was, "I could go a latte."

A frown marred Neill's face, although she couldn't see this from her position behind him.

"Ye have a strange way of talking. Ye must be from the Lowlands." Unsure if he was addressing her or talking to himself, Jo explained.

"Everyone talks like this in Australia. Although, latte is Italian, I think."

Neill made no reply to this. Thinking he may remain silent again she prodded for some information. "You said we're nearly there. Where is there?"

Neill raised his arm and pointed towards the approaching hill. "Over that knoll is home."

Waiting for him to say more, and getting frustrated when he didn't, she began to mentally curse all men. Why did you have to prod and squeeze information out of them? Knowing too well men were 'bottom liners' when it came to conversation making, she sighed and fished for more information.

"What do you mean by home? A town? A city? Or

are we talking about a house?"

"Ye ask too many questions."

"And you answer too few."

She felt the quaking of Neill's body as he tried to suppress a laugh.

"Weel lass, we Highlanders aren't known for our intellect, or hadn't ye heard? We're considered feral simpletons. It's all the inter-breeding ye know. Maybe ye should keep ta asking one question at a time…ye know, so I dinna get confused?"

His response delighted her. After being silent for the entire painful journey, Neill not only spoke, but also offered a show of humour, sarcastic humour, but a sense of wit nonetheless. She understood sarcastic humour well, after all, she was an Australian and the Australian sense of humour shared this trait.

"Yes, well, I wouldn't want to tax your brain, and let's not forget it's a well known fact men can only do one thing at a time, so my apologies for befuddling you. How about the first question then? Is home a town?"

Neill glanced at her over his shoulder. "Cheeky one, aren't ye. Nae, home is nae a town, as ye call it. It is Shreave Castle. It is the centre of Clan MacKay land.

"Do you and all these men live in the castle?"

"Nae. Dougal and his family do. My family and most of these men who have family live in the village. The single men live in the barracks."

"Why does Dougal and his family live in the castle?"

"He is like a brother ta the laird and is second in command when Connor is absent."

"Who is this 'Connor'?"

"The laird."

"Where is he?"

Neill turned to look at her with an exasperated look on his face. "That's enough, lass. Cease with yer questions." Thinking she'd pushed hard enough for the moment, she kept silent, although there was still much she didn't understand, know, or could begin to fathom.

The group of riders reached the crest of the hill, and as one, all of them stopped to stare at the sight beyond. The young, freckle-faced boy she noticed earlier in the day wore a relieved look upon his face. The other, older men in the group, all shared similar looks, tainted with pride. Their faces told of ones being gone from home for some time and it was enough for them at this moment to drink in the sight of their beloved castle and surrounding land. It was obvious this was a much-anticipated homecoming.

The view before her was breathtaking. Rolling hills spread before her, edged with the thick, dense forest she'd ridden through over the past hours. The beautiful landscape rolled all the way to a huge lake. On the edge of the lake along a ridge of cliffs, stood a huge fortress constructed of dark grey stone. There were two turrets either end of the castle and three floors of narrow windows in between them. She was in awe of the scene. It was something out of a childhood picture book, the sort she'd seen little of when she was young. A huge outer wall surrounded the castle. Leading to the castle was a road of sorts, which also bore many dwellings along its edge.

Their horse jerked forward, catching her by surprise, and began to snort and prance. It knew it was home. Neill reached out a hand and patted the animal on the neck, "Aye there, boy. It has been a time, has it nae?"

Unable to remain silent any longer she asked, "How long have you been away, Neill?"

"Long enough," was his reply.

An ear splitting cry rent the air. Up ahead, Dougal cried out as he rode hell-for-leather down the other side of the hill. The rest of the group followed suit and all cried out. She couldn't understand what they said as it was said in the guttural language she often heard them conversing in, but she thought it must be some kind of war cry or clan chant.

As the horse began to gallop down after the others she hung on for dear life and cursed all horses and all men as jarring pain and fear brought tears to her eyes. The road widened and people wandered out from mud hut dwellings, waving and cheering. As the riders slowed their horses and she began to breathe again, her pain was soon forgotten at the sight before her.

From the top of the hill it looked like a fairytale landscape and scenery. Now she was almost upon it, the reality overwhelmed her. It was massive. The outer wall stood over seven meters high with a huge wooden gate marking the centre, which they headed for. The people lining the road wore old, worn-looking clothes covered by the tartan plaid similar to her entourages'.

They cheered and someone called out to one in the group who responded with a smile and a wave. She was also aware of the attention she drew. Groups of women whispered to each other and looked at her. With all the long hours spent in the saddle, she never felt uneasy, even though bewildered by her unexpected surroundings. Now she felt unsure and conspicuous and a tinge of fear made her grip Neill's plaid harder.

Sensing her increased unease, Neill leaned his head to the side and spoke quietly, "Rest easy, lass. Nae harm will come ta ye if ye be honest and have naught ta hide."

Given the circumstances, his comment didn't lesson her apprehension, but made her face the reality of the situation. How could she tell the truth? Who would believe her? She didn't even believe it herself but her chafed bottom and aching back could not be ignored and felt all too real. She knew she wasn't dreaming, but the alternative was absurd and the reality bizarre.

But there was still hope she was sane. Maybe this was the biggest hoax ever and she'd been caught up in the middle. Or maybe this was an elaborate movie set and they were filming *Braveheart 2*. She felt a hysterical laugh building inside her. "Beam me up, Scotty," she muttered to herself, still trying to dampen down a sense of incredulity that bordered on hysteria.

Chapter Three

Upon entering through the huge timber gates on the outer wall, the horses plodded toward a long stable. Young boys ran out and gathered the reins as the men began to dismount. Neill threw his right leg over the head of his horse and slid off leaving her still mounted. She knew there was no way she could dismount without falling to the ground. Her legs felt numb and her skin so chafed she was afraid to move and cause herself any more pain than necessary. Neill, oblivious to her discomfort, walked off to greet a young blond woman with a small child in her arms.

It was a warm homecoming for the men as women and children gathered around the group with relieved smiles and hugs for husbands, brothers, and friends. She received her fair share of stares, made worse by her being the last one left upon a horse. Dougal appeared at her side and lifted her from the saddle, once again hanging on to her a few seconds so she could get her balance and feel her feet.

"Ye'll go with Colin. Do as he says." Holding her eyes for a few seconds longer than necessary, she understood the silent message—don't try anything.

Colin, a young red-headed boy, came up to her and prompted, "This way, mistress," and walked towards the huge wooden doors leading into the castle. *'Mistress,'* she thought with some humour. Who are these people? She couldn't shake this disbelieving, hysterical emotion trying to consume her. She wanted to laugh out loud at their stupid clothes and accents. She wanted someone to say,

"It's okay, you can wake up now." She suspected this wouldn't happen. It was all too real. Hobbling off like a woman three times her age, she forced her muscles to move and follow Colin.

Inside the castle, she stopped and stared in breathless wonder. She'd been led into a huge hall that looked like a cathedral with a lofty gabled roof constructed of heavy timbers and high, straight walls with long, thin windows, except the windows weren't the ornate, lead-light kind found in a church. Magnificent wall tapestries depicted scenes of battle with people in plaids swinging massive broadswords. Along the right-hand wall were a series of fireplaces built into the grey stone. At the far end of the hall was a raised platform, almost like a stage, with a long table across it and another large fireplace at the rear. The room would easily hold three hundred people.

"This way mistress," Colin requested. He stood on the bottom step of a wide staircase on the left side of the hall. He'd been observing her whilst she studied the layout of the great hall. He wore a frown upon his face as he scrutinized her attire.

Catching his eye, she looked down at her tartan pyjamas and then back to Colin. "Not very flattering are they?"

Unable to hide a bright red blush, Colin replied, "I'm sorry for staring, mistress, but…"

She didn't think it was possible for the poor child to blush anymore than he already was, but he proved her wrong. "It's okay Colin. I must look pretty strange to you, but let me tell you, all this…" She swung her arm around to indicate the great hall. "Is very strange to me."

Colin looked like he wanted to say more but thought twice about it.

She prompted, "I have been told this is Castle Shreave and it belongs to Clan MacKay. Is this right

Colin?" Colin, needing no more encouragement than this, jumped into the conversation.

"Aye, it is mistress. I've lived here for two winters now. I'm a MacKenzie and I'm fostering here with the MacKays. I'm going ta be a warrior, trained by the laird himself." Colin preened with self-importance.

"Where are your parents then, Colin?" she asked with concern, as Colin could be no older than ten.

"They be at Castle Loch. I've three sisters there, too. Where are ye from then?"

Finding the question too hard to answer with so much whirling around her head, she decided on an honest answer that skirted the truth. "I'm from a long way away from here. I got lost...and Dougal and his friends found me."

"Oh, ye mean the raidin' party found ye? They've been gone fer a time looking fer…" Colin paused, realising he was saying too much to a stranger. "Anyway, that's nae matter ta ye. Tis lucky they found ye then," he said with earnest concern. "There are marauders stealing our cattle. With winter approaching, we canna afford ta lose stock now, can we?"

"But you just said Dougal was in a raiding party."

"Och aye. But only ta get back what was taken from us in the first place."

"I saw no cattle today."

"They be hidden well and good, ta fatten up before the cold weather comes." She thought of her icy feet and wondered how much colder it got here. She hadn't felt warm all day.

Standing on the bottom step conducting their conversation, they became aware of other eyes upon them. Two pairs of round eyes peeped through the railings that ran along the first floor overlooking the great hall.

"Millie, get back ta the nursery. Ye will have Mrs. Moray after ye if ye dinna scarper," Colin yelled, full of adult authority. The two small children ran away, disappearing into the depths of the castle. "Just bairns," Colin proclaimed, shaking his head like an indulgent parent. She smiled to herself as Colin started up the stairs ahead of her.

The steps were steep and her muscles struggled to make the climb. "Where are we going, Colin?" She groaned.

"I'm ta take ye ta the lower rooms and ye are ta wait for Dougal there."

They continued down a long corridor and made several turns before she no longer knew east from west. When they came to a door, Colin opened it and stood aside, indicating for her to enter. She stepped into a small room, containing a pallet in the corner with a washbowl and cloth on a wooden stand. There was no window and she couldn't help notice the heavy lock on the door.

"It has been pleasurable talking ta ye, mistress. Dougal will be along soon."

The door shut and locked and she was left alone in the small, dark room.

****

Melbourne, Australia, Present Day

June Newbury stood at the kitchen window, the kettle boiling merrily. Switching it off, she poured the water and placed a tea-cosy over the pot. She felt uneasy. "I'm sure I did the right thing, Lewis. She seemed so lost—cut adrift. You know her as well as I. She worked too hard. What life did she have? Working eighty hours a week. If it wasn't for her Tae Kwan Do club she'd have been a recluse. It was time for a change. Time for an adventure. She'll find it hard at first but..." June noticed Lewis watching her, his tail swishing back and forth across the linoleum. "Yes, yes, I know I should have told her, but what would she have said? She'd never have believed me. She'd have thought me mad and suggested the old folks home. You know I'd never put her in harm's way, I love her like my own." June's eyes wandered to her fence line and the empty house next door. "She'll be fine...she'll be fine." June tried to convince herself. Jo's cat swished his tail even faster. He felt most put out.

Chapter Four

By the time the entourage approached Skallan word already reached the village that the laird was but moments away. As the heavy carts laden with coins, chickens, sheep, and farm produce rolled into the midst of the community, mothers had their daughters lined up along the roadside, preening and batting eyelashes.

Oh God, thought Connor MacKay, *will it nae end?*

He steered Thief to the hitching post, dismounted, and draped the reins over the rail, unnecessary for a trained warhorse, but it gave him an extra few seconds to fortify himself before the onslaught.

Christ, he mused, *I shouldn't even be here.* Connor had already commenced the annual rent-takings when news reached him about the stolen cattle from the winter pasture.

Having left his loyal and trusted friend Dougal Haig to guard Shreave and run affairs at home, he could not justify returning to hunt the perpetrators. Besides, he'd never hear the end of it from Dougal.

If he'd ridden through the gates of Shreave any sooner than expected, he would have to endure Dougal Haig's merciless teasing. His friend would have instantly known the laird did not ride in to help save the winter stock, but ran away from insufferable girls. Only Dougal Haig, or his wife, would ever risk taunting Connor. Laird MacKay was not a man who endured easy banter.

He was stubborn, pig-headed, some would say

rude, and he seldom smiled. Many a man even feared to approach him for risk of being cut down with the mighty broadsword he carried upon his hip.

But most never could, and never would, know the true MacKay.

****

"Damn strange if ye ask me," Dougal said to Maeve as she put another bowl of food in front of him.

"Well, husband, she sounds harmless enough from what ye've told me. Her dress sounds strange though." Maeve sat opposite Dougal and stared at him with a small grin on her face. This was their first moment of privacy since the men returned. Their castle chamber provided a welcome haven. "I must say it's quite gratifying ta see ye so perplexed."

"Listen here, woman," he chided. "She could be a spy from the Sutherlands or Gunns. It's nae a joking matter. And I'm nae perplexed. I'm...I'm—"

"For heavens sake Dougal, ye canna always pick it. I know ye have a way with people and can pull the truth from anyone, but this lassie sounds different. I think there is a great tale ta be told and all will come out when Connor returns from collecting the rents." Maeve refilled her husband's cup with ale and poured a small one for herself. "I canna explain it Dougal, but I have a feeling about this. It became stronger when ye finally arrived home. Ye know how it is with me."

"Aye, I do ma love. I've learnt well ta trust yer feelings. Yer whole family has that way about them. And I will hold my opinion until Connor has time ta deal with her, but as for thinking he will be able ta sort it out..."

"Ye doubt he can?"

"I do not and never will doubt Connor's ability. I would trust nae other at ma back and would follow his lead nae matter what." Dougal's voice rose with his passion and loyalty. "It's just, this woman…is different." Dougal looked uncomfortable in his seat and a little frustrated. He'd come across no other woman, beside Maeve, who would address and question a man as if it were her given right.

"Oh, my lord husband, this has got ye in a pinker."

"I'm nae pinkered."

Much to her husband's growing ire, Maeve chuckled.

Dougal was one of the most feared warriors in the Highlands and was respected and revered within Clan MacKay as a just man, but a man renowned for swift punishment to those who were disloyal or threatened the peace and safety of those within the clan. It was also understood, Connor and Dougal's fierce allegiance to each other made Dougal's word law when Connor was absent.

Maeve walked around the small table and sat on her husband's lap. His arms rose to hold her buxom body closer. Her long brown hair fell over her shoulder in a heavy plait and her pert nose nuzzled into his neck.

He fell in love with Maeve several years ago after she hit him over the head with a lump of wood. Dougal and a raiding party were drinking at a tavern and Maeve was serving at the bar. She'd gone out back to get more peat for the fire as Dougal went outside to relieve himself. Confusion and misunderstanding prevailed and Maeve, thinking Dougal had randy thoughts on his mind, dented his skull. It resulted in a large wedding followed by three babes a year apart.

"Tell me husband, do ye think Connor will be as pinkered with this woman as ye are?"

"Nae," he reluctantly offered.

"Ah, that would be a great shame then, aye?"

"What is that supposed ta mean, woman? The

lass could be a spy."

Not taking Dougal's concerns seriously, Maeve's hand began to caress her husband's broad chest, having the desired effect on him. He lowered his mouth to hers in a kiss that demanded no argument. With desire ignited, Dougal began to remove Maeve's plaid.

"What I mean, husband," Maeve said breathlessly. "Is Connor sees all women as subservient imbeciles having nae the intelligence ta count ta three. He would allow none ta ruffle his feathers. I would enjoy seeing him challenged by a woman who will not grovel pitifully at his feet and drool over him. But then ye know ma thoughts on Connor."

Maeve, now almost naked in Dougal's arms, returned her husband's forceful kisses with equal ardour. It was no wonder their family brood grew so fast.

"I nae wish ta discuss Connor's lack of social graces. His scars run too deep for ye ta hold judgement. Cease yer chatter woman. I'll nae get inta this argument with ye again. I have more urgent desires needing attention."

With that, Dougal picked his wife up and threw her on their feather mattress and began disrobing himself.

"Ye have been gone too long, husband," Maeve replied silkily while admiring the view as he threw off his under-shirt. "I believe I also have a need ta be attended ta urgently."

Chapter Five

It was dark and cold again. Jo woke from a restless sleep filled with unease and a vague awareness of discomfort. As consciousness crept over her, she began to have flashbacks of thick forests, tartan-clad men, and a long journey upon a horse.

Impossible! She didn't know how to ride a horse. The tumultuous events she *thought* she'd experienced must have been a dream.

Boy, what a dream, the most vivid she'd ever experienced. What a relief to find herself in bed; confirmation it wasn't real. But as she sat up a sinking suspicion invaded her awareness. Why was her room so dark? Why was it so quiet? And cold? She was sick of feeling cold. Reaching across the bed she stretched to switch on her bedside lamp. There was no lamp. There was no table.

A wave of dread overcame her followed by a feeling she'd felt once before in her life, when she confronted Andrew about his unfaithfullness. Following his blasé confession and personal insults regarding her being frigid, she'd gone home, sat numbly on the living room couch where a physical wave of disbelief and despair crushed her senses, leaving her feeling insecure and scared. She'd wrapped her arms around herself in soulless comfort thinking to prevent herself from shattering into a million pieces.

She rose from the bed and groped around in the dark hoping to find the light switch, which she knew wouldn't be there. The cold wooden floor underneath her bare feet was unforgiving and made it painful to walk around. She became aware of her increased breathing as the first stage of panic set in.

No, no, no! This is not happening; it's not real. But when her toes smashed into a wooden washstand, bringing the pottery bowl on top crashing to the floor, she could no longer control the overwhelming emotions scattering her sanity. With an anguished cry she fell to the floor in a heap. Her chest tightened and it was hard to draw breath. On hands and knees she crawled across the cold floor until she hit a wall. Curled up in a tiny ball she shook with fear—fear of the dark, fear of the cold, fear of being alone. She was awake, but the nightmare was real.

****

Dull light speared through the slitted window onto the feather bed. Dougal's snores sounded like a trumpet. His wife slept next to him, oblivious of the racket. They'd not a great deal of sleep during the night. Theirs was a rare love match. The never-ending attempts at peace saw many women married off to opposing clans, with the hope the link would strengthen fragile clan relationships. Often, peace was an illusion soon shattered.

A loud rapping on their chamber door at first went unnoticed. The insistent pounding eventually stirred the slumbering couple. Dougal sat up in bed and cursed the intruder. "Will ye cease yer clobbering? I'm coming, I'm coming." Throwing his under-shirt on, Dougal wrenched the door open with violent energy, the hinges almost snapping with the force. Neill stood on the threshold, a wry grin on his face. "Shut yer clobber," was Dougal's terse command, even though Neill was yet to utter a word.

It was well known amongst those closest to Dougal and Maeve they shared a rather lusty appetite. Pulling his face into what almost resembled a serious look, Neill spoke. "A messenger has come from The Sinclair."

"I'll be down," replied Dougal, and slammed the door in Neill's face. "God wife, why did ye nae tell me I slept half the morning away?" he said, turning to his wife.

Maeve, who'd woken and heard Neill's missive, ignored her husband and stretched like a lazy cat who'd lapped the cream off the top of milk. Her plump breasts rose above the furs, causing Dougal to growl and curse even more.

"The rooster has nae even crowed yet, ma love. Stop cursing. Do ye think the men will think less of ye for lying abed after being away fer so long? Yer sense of duty is above reproach, so remove the frown from yer brow and come and kiss yer wife good morning."

"I willna come anywhere near ye, viper, or I willna see the messenger until noontime." Dougal finished dressing while Maeve gave a soft chuckle. Whilst observing her husband go through his morning ablutions, Maeve decided it was time for herself to rise. The children would be wakening in the nursery soon and there was much to organise in the castle. A celebratory dinner was to be held tonight to honour the homecoming party and successful return of fifty head of cattle.

Maeve took care of domestic affairs in Castle Shreave since Kathryn, the old laird's wife, died of an infection. The old laird suffered after his loss but continued to rule the clan, until he succumbed to a chest infection six months past. The unanimous vote saw Connor, his only son, take the lairdship. Connor proved himself time and again a great warrior and leader.

Maeve believed he needed to brush up on his social skills. Connor was hard to love, but Lord how she tried, for Dougal's sake as much as anything. Brought out of her thoughts by a smacking kiss on her lips, Maeve climbed out of bed and hugged Dougal.

"I will see ye at noontime," Dougal promised, squeezed her bottom, and left.

Maeve washed, dressed, and went over what needed to be done that day. The kitchen needed to start preparations for the nights feasting. There were also rooms to be aired as many of the village leaders would come for the celebration and stay the night. Connor was expected any day now, so his room must be readied and a fire lit. No matter the time of his arrival, it was the laird's privilege to always have a peat fire burning low in his chamber. There were also her children to attend to.

Though they spent several hours a day in the nursery with Mrs. Moray, Maeve loved being with them herself and sometimes resented her castle duties as they took time she would rather spend with the children.

She was also curious about the mystery woman able to pinker Dougal.

She looked forward to meeting her.

****

It was mid-morning when Maeve queried Dougal as to the whereabouts of the mystery lady. Sitting at the high table on the dais, Dougal was in deep in discussion with Shreave's highest ranked warriors. He frowned at his wife and told her young Colin had been attending her. Not wanting to further interrupt their conversation, Maeve sent a kitchen maid to find Colin. He put in an appearance, covered in muck, after being found in the stables.

"Ye be a hard one ta find, lad. What were ye doing? Sleeping in the hay loft?"

Colin's brow dipped with indignation and he puffed out his chest. "Nay, ma lady. I have been helping ta birth the laird's new foal. I was on the ground in the stalls and…"

"Yes, yes, all right lad. I didna mean ta insult ye. I am just a bit harried with all the preparations fer the feast. What I wanted ta see ye about was the lady ye took care of yesterday. Has she eaten well?"

Taken aback, Colin replied, "Ah dinna ken, ma lady. I took her ta one of the lower rooms yesterday and have nae seen her since."

"What do ye mean, ye have nae seen her since? I thought Dougal put ye in charge of her care. Who is watching over her then?"

"I canna say, ma lady," Colin said, looking flustered.

"Dinna fash yerself, lad. I will sort it out with Dougal. Go on then, get back ta yer chores." Frowning, Maeve left the kitchen and returned to Dougal in the great hall. The soldiers were just leaving the hall and Dougal didn't look happy. Maeve hoped it wasn't unfavourable news in the missive earlier in the morning. "Bad news?" questioned Maeve as she watched the warriors retreating backs.

"The sooner Connor gets back the better. There is trouble with more raids. The clans are getting riled and threatening war. Connor willna stand by and see this happen."

"I hope yer right, husband." Maeve didn't want another war. She believed nobody ever really won them. Remembering her reason for seeking him out, Maeve questioned Dougal, "I was wondering, whom have ye put in charge of looking after our guest in the lower rooms?"

"I told ye. I put young Colin ta looking after her."

"He says he doesna know who is ta be watching her." There was a short silence after this comment. "He has nae seen her since yesterday when he took her there."

"Oh, heel!" Dougal swore, and went storming up

the stairs to the first floor housing the lower rooms, with Maeve hot on his heels.

Chapter Six

When Jo heard the lock slide open on the door to her cell, she'd not the energy or the inclination to sit up off the floor and look at who entered. She was cold, so cold. She'd withdrawn so far inside herself, nothing mattered anymore. Her fear and loneliness over the last twenty-four hours caused her to shut down all her senses to protect herself from going mad.

She'd sobbed for hours, calling for help in a small, pathetic voice which had no chance of penetrating the thick stone walls or heavy wooden door of the pitch-dark room. As the hours passed, her stomach grumbled and her mouth became dry and parched as dehydration set in.

Dougal Haig knelt beside her and placed his hands on her shoulders, lifting her into a sitting position. What he saw on her face and in her eyes made him curse. She was his responsibility and although he didn't trust her, had no idea who she was and what her intentions were, there was an unwritten code between the Highland clans.

Prisoners received the benefit of the doubt. They were fed and taken care of with the basic necessities until a decision was made on their guilt or innocence. They might be put to death if found to be guilty, but until then nobody would be accused of barbarianism. Worst of all, in Dougal's mind, was the fact she was a woman. Women were treated far better than this.

Dougal noticed her puffy eyes and filthy, dirty face. He could see the blueness on her lips from being so chilled. She little resembled the plucky lass they found yesterday morning in the forest.

Now in a sitting position she opened her eyes, but the bright light from the torch Maeve held aloft shot sharp pains through her head. Blinking to adjust her eyes to the unaccustomed light, she recognised Dougal's face. At first feeling scared and cornered, her immediate reaction was to flatten herself against the wall in a vain attempt to put more distance between them. Then an emotion overcame her which at first she didn't recognise. As her mind lifted through her half-aware state of despair she began to feel reassured by the emotion. Anger. Pure unadulterated anger.

It filled her, giving her strength.

Dougal must have read it in her eyes and almost pulled back until he checked himself and held his ground. It was too late to move himself off his knees, as she launched herself at him. It was a frenzied attack, using her fists and fingernails to punch and rake at Dougal. He was so taken by surprise, she bloodied his nose and scratched his neck before he overpowered her by locking her in a bear-like grip with her arms pinned to her sides. She tried hard to struggle free but soon collapsed against him in exhaustion. It was then the tears started. She thought she'd none left to cry but her head fell to Dougal's shoulder and she sobbed. She sobbed for being scared and alone in the dark all night. She sobbed for feeling so anxious and frightened. And she sobbed for feeling so cold, always so cold.

As the shudders abated and the warmth of Dougal's body permeated her pyjamas, she moved her head to the side and was shocked to see a woman kneeling beside them.

"Don't be afraid anymore. Nae harm will come of ye," said the woman in a kind voice. "And if ye be thinking of clouting me husband again, save yer energy. I'll do it for ye later!" The voice, so soft and kind, just didn't relate to the look upon the woman's face. Her eyes spoke of great annoyance—directed, not at Jo, but the man she was crying all over. "I think ma husband owes ye an apology. It seems he neglected ta organise for someone ta watch over ye."

Jo pulled away from Dougal and wiped her nose on the sleeve of her pyjamas. Between the abating hiccupping sobs she looked at Maeve and said the one thing she could think of. "I'll help you clout him. I'm sure I can find the energy."

With that Dougal rose, lifting her to her feet. When she winced he couldn't suppress a concerned look.

"Have I hurt ye lass?"

"No," she snivelled, "but if I have to sit on another bloody horse within the next ten years, it'll be too soon."

****

Within half an hour Jo was bathed with a wash cloth, and Maeve rubbed some putrid smelling liniment on her sore muscles. The cut on her foot was cleaned and she was bundled into bed somewhere in the castle. She lost all sense of direction—yet again—whilst being taken to another room. All she remembered was being led up a flight of stairs and down long stone corridors. The journey seemed endless. But now, all tucked up in bed with soft furs thrown over her, she felt the warmest in what seemed like days.

Dougal left Maeve to tend to her, after much discussion that bordered on argument. He was concerned for Maeve's safety and didn't wish to leave her alone with the stranger. Maeve guffawed then kissed her husband and said she would be fine. When he went to further disagree, she gave him an intense look telling him she *knew* she would be fine. Dougal stared at his wife, and nodded in unspoken understanding. Jo was puzzled by the exchange but he kissed his wife, gave Jo a pointed look, and departed leaving the two women alone.

Her new accommodations were little better than before, but at least this room boasted a small slitted window to let in the light and a full sized bed instead of a pallet. The room was still very small with no carpets to take the chill off the cold floors and was about the size of her bathroom at home.

Maeve stood by a small table, piling up the dirty linens used to clean up Jo. She eyed Jo, as if assessing her. Jo wondered what she thought of her body, far taller and leaner than most of those she saw yesterday. She reached up and touched her hair, dark and thick, but short compared to Meave's, reaching just past her shoulders. She'd always thought of herself as plain, but Meave continued to examine her with interest. When Maeve nodded, Jo felt as if she'd passed a test.

"Ye will do nicely," Meave proclaimed.

"Pardon," she asked, confused by the comment, but let it lie when Maeve continued, changing the subject.

"Dinna fash yerself about Dougal," she offered, "he deserved a good clobbering. I'll apologise for him as ye willna get one from his lips." Maeve smiled then continued, "He's a good man. He's very protective of me, and the clan...I'm sorry, but I dinna think we've been introduced properly. I'm Maeve Haig, and ma husband, of course, needs nae introduction."

Maeve's honesty touched her and she responded without hesitation. "My name is Joanne Dunstan, my friends call me Jo, and you're right, your husband needs no introduction." Both women looked at each other and then burst out laughing. There was an unspoken camaraderie between the two and Jo felt herself relax a little because of it. "It's nice to meet you Maeve, and thank you for cleaning me up and helping me pull myself back together. I don't usually, I mean, fall to pieces, you know, and..."

"Enough Jo! Ye have had a trying night and *ye* have nae reason ta apologise. Ye'll need ta be abed for a couple of days. I want ta keep an eye on ye in case the cold night has left a mark on ye. And yer muscles could do with a rest, too."

There was a quiet knock at the door and a young serving girl came in carrying a tray filled with food. The smell started Jo's mouth salivating.

"Put it on the table Fiona, and tell Mrs. MacBain I am grateful."

"Yes, ma lady." The girl gave a quick curtsy and left the room closing the door behind her. Maeve, without delay, went to the tray and poured a large drink. She handed her the goblet, which she put straight to her lips. She didn't know what to expect but she didn't expect the goblet to contain pure, clean, unadulterated water. It was heaven. She gulped it down.

"Aye, I knew ye'd need that. Here, get some of this inside ye too."

Whilst she guzzled water, Maeve filled a plate with bread, cheese, and what looked like cold lamb and some fruit. "Ye'll be eating all of that lot, I think."

Once the edge of her severe thirst and appetite was sated, she looked around her room. She'd questions needing answers and wasn't quite sure how to begin. Maeve, sensing her confusion, sat on the edge of her bed.

"Ye are in Castle Shreave, but I think ye already know this. Ma husband says ye were found near the MacKay and Sutherland borders. He says ye were lost. Can ye tell me, Jo, where home is?"

Jo stopped eating and fought with what to say next. Her instincts told her Maeve was a friend, but she new too little of her predicament to be sure of anything. Hell, she didn't even trust her own reasoning at the moment, but common sense told her she was not in Australia.

The gaps in her memory needed filling and to sort it all out she needed some pertinent answers. Did she trust Maeve enough to seek the answers from? Was she going to sound like a complete nutcase asking the questions she needed to ask?

She couldn't decide if she was more worried about the consequences of them hearing her story or them thinking she was a candidate for the funny farm.

Fiddling with a piece of cheese on her plate, she looked up into Maeve's eyes, trying to read her thoughts and decide if it was safe to trust the woman. She never thought herself a coward, or a liar. So she decided on the thing she felt comfortable with. The truth.

"Maeve." She paused self consciously. "What I'm going to tell you…" She sat up straighter in the bed as if to fortify herself, "I'm not from here, but…"

"Can ye tell me, Jo, where home is?"

Very good. Jo was impressed. The broken record method. She liked Maeve even more. A woman of her own kind. "I come from a place called Australia."

"I've nae heard of it before. Is it in Scotland or abroad? Maybe in the Continent?"

"Maeve I think I need to ask a question of you first."

A cold sweat raced over her body. It was just a question, but...

"Maeve, what year is it?"

Chapter Seven

The laird came home a week after the 'mystery lady' arrived at Castle Shreave. He rode into the courtyard midday along with an entourage of thirty armed MacKay warriors and a scribe. The annual rent collecting was an important part of clan life. Their survival depended on everyone contributing what they could. The income saw to the ruling and defence of MacKay land by the laird and his army of one hundred and fifty trained warriors. It enabled families within the clan to raise their children without fear or threat from bordering clans and promoted prosperity and harmony.

A wooden wagon containing all the monetary rent, in addition to bags of oats, sacks of flour, and the odd goat and chicken, rumbled into the yard surrounded by the laird's men. All were relieved to be home without incident.

Connor dismounted and handed the reins of his black mount to Colin. "All is well, Colin?"

"Aye sir, all is well."

Connor walked across the courtyard towards the castle's main entrance, oblivious to the hero worship in Colin's eyes.

Connor MacKay always was a man of few words. After a childhood running free and wild on MacKay land and with a father whom adored him but spent much of his time in Edinburgh, he'd grown into a strong and spirited lad. There were many who thought he would be far too wild and irresponsible to, one day, lead the clan, but Connor proved them wrong time and again, even from the age of fourteen, when he saved his friend Dougal from a charging boar. His agility and proficient use of broadsword and bow saw him win the annual clan games.

As Connor grew into adulthood, there was just one who could match him in speed, agility, and skill—Dougal. He came close on many occasions to besting Connor. But as unbelievable as it was, Connor was *more* stubborn than Dougal.

Seven years ago, when fierce and bitter feuds erupted between Clans Sutherland and Ross, Connor built a reputation bordering on legend. Fighting side by side with his father, he showed no mercy to those who threatened Clan MacKay. Connor never tried to be a leader. He was born to it. Men older than himself looked to him for guidance even when he was a lad of nineteen. Now at thirty-five years, there wasn't a man on MacKay land who didn't respect and honour his position as laird, although some of them feared the dark, imposing man of few words.

Entering the castle, Connor went straight to the great hall's rear hearth upon the dais where chairs surrounded the fireplace. He was there just a moment when food and ale were bought to him from the kitchens. Dougal appeared seconds later, poured himself ale, and sat opposite his friend. "Nae trouble on yer journey?" Dougal inquired, looking pointedly at Connor.

"Nae. I saw nae sign of raiders. What of yers? Did ye retrieve the cattle?"

"Aye. We caught up with them before the lower pass. The raider's numbers were nae large enough ta move them with haste. Their spotters must have seen our approach and they scarpered. They hid their tracks weel. I dinna like it. This is nae like past raids. Something is amiss." Dougal took another swallow of his ale whilst Connor washed down a mouthful of cheese the same way and pushed the plate towards Dougal.

Dougal began chewing on a bannock as Connor spoke. "I wish I knew. The villagers are uneasy. The raiders have them spooked. We need ta take action, and soon. We are nae the only ones being targeted and it is causing suspicion amongst all the Clans. The peace we have is held by but a thread and it will only take one rash move and war will break out. Now the rents are in, it is time ta act." Connor drained his mug and poured himself another.

Dougal nodded. "I agree." He hesitated before continuing. "We have news from The Sinclair. A message arrived seven days ago."

Connor schooled his face. "What did he want?"

"They are having the same problems as us. They have lost seventy head of cattle ta raiders. They believe it was Sutherland doings." Dougal said with raised eyebrows.

With suspicion lacing his voice Connor replied, "Why?"

"Probably because they hate all Sutherlands as much as ye hate Sinclairs."

It was no secret Connor bore no love of Sinclairs. All but one. He would not dwell on her, for the pain it caused was unwanted.

"Have they seen a Sutherland plaid?"

"Nae. The raids are after dark as they are here, with nae plaids worn." Dougal looked to be choosing his next words with care. The rest of the message was yet to be delivered and he knew his friend well. "Sinclair...he wants ta meet."

Connor let out some colourful expletives and rose, violently shoving his chair back. His jaw and fists were clenched. Anger crossed his face as he walked to the fireplace and rested both hands on the mantle.

Dougal observed his laird with resignation on his face, and gave him the rest of the message. "He wants a meeting with ye ta discuss the raiders. He believes ye are nae responsible, for ye would nae jeopardise peace and cause a dangerous rift between our clans, for fear of Meg. He…"

Before Dougal could continue, Connor exploded. "He thinks I am nae responsible?" Connor yelled at his friend. "Did he have ta contemplate it long before deciding ma innocence?" He walked back to the small table and smashed both hands down upon it, making the last bits of cheese and bread jump from the plate.

Servants preparing the hall tables for the evening meal scurried away like scared mice. Connor was well known for his vile temper, and when he exploded, Shreave inhabitants disappeared before his anger could be directed at *them*. Except for Dougal. He sat unmoving, watching Connor. Connor's eyes were unreadable black pools deep enough to make the bravest of men take a backward step. "That bastard thinks I am nae responsible?"

After some even more colourful oaths, Dougal bided his time until Connor's ranting abated, before continuing. "Ye know as weel as I what he is trying ta say. We need ta uncover the perpetrators of these raids, and we need ta do it together with The Sinclair."

Connor pulled the unreadable mask over his face once again. He knew what The Sinclair proposed was a wise alternative. The raiders must be caught. Connor was prepared to contact Alick Sinclair himself, much to his disgust, upon his return from rent collecting. But the man pre-empted him and Connor admired the move—and resented it. "So…The MacKay and The Sinclair must come face ta face."

Connor's friend looked up at him. "There is one more point within the missive. Meg sends her love. Yer sister wishes ye ta know she is with child and intends ta visit with The Sinclair when a meeting can be organised."

Connor stood back at the hearth, head bowed, arms resting on the mantle in emotional reflection. He fought with his demons and was unprepared to give any concession to Alick Sinclair or his own beloved sister. He looked at Dougal and gave a barely perceivable nod. No other words were spoken. Dougal left the hall to summon a messenger to ride for Sinclair land within the hour.

Feeling a multiplicity of emotions he chose not to identify, Connor caught control of his anger. His and Alick's friction, no, hatred began two years ago when Connor became betrothed to Kira Sinclair, Alick's sister. It was an arranged marriage he'd been reluctant to agree to. Not because he didn't like the Sinclair girl. More so, Connor wasn't interested in being saddled with a wife. Any wife.

After their betrothal, Kira moved from her Sinclair home, Castle Wick, to live at Castle Shreave. Connor tried to get to know the girl before their marriage took place, but Kira resented Connor from the beginning. When Kira fell pregnant three months into her stay at Castle Shreave, there was great celebration. In the Highlands, a betrothal was considered as good as a marriage and her pregnancy boded well for future generations of MacKay lairds.

But unbeknown to Clan MacKay, Connor and Kira's relationship was one of lies, deceit, turbulence, anger, and mistrust. Only those closest to Connor knew there were problems between the couple. Kira wrote to her brother on many occasions, claiming she was mistreated and abused, creating friction between the two powerful lairds.

All ties between Clan MacKay and Clan Sinclair were severed when Kira died giving birth to a stillborn daughter. Connor thought it appropriate the fragile ties between the clans were broken. Life without a Sinclair in it would be fine by him. But then, much to his horror, the old MacKay laird suggested rejoining the two clans by another marriage and offered his daughter to the heir of The Sinclair. Megahn MacKay and Alick Sinclair met once—and fell in love.

Connor sighed in resignation. With the rents collected there was much to be done within the castle. Also, countless tasks to be completed before the bitter Highland winter came upon them. The current mild weather could give one a false sense of security. Hunting parties must stock up on fresh meat to be salted and stored. The clans ate a fair portion of their own beef and lamb, but this was supplemented with what the forests contributed. There were the raiders to deal with and young Colin's training was sadly neglected.

An immediate priority for the laird was to clean himself up before the evening meal. The tables were prepared and the succulent smell of roasting meat wafted from the kitchens. Normally clean-shaven, a thick black beard now covered his face and he felt like two weeks worth of dirt and grime covered his clothes and body. Unusual for Highlanders, Connor preferred a bath every day, and he was looking forward to a good soak. Leaving the great hall he made his way to his chamber.

Chapter Eight

Jo finished building up the peat fire and brushed the soot from her white apron. Dressed in a shapeless grey dress far too short for her height, flat leather boots—the most ugly she'd ever seen, and her hair tied up under a drab, colourless headscarf, she felt like a bondservant portrayed in a TV mini-series.

The truth was, and she was still coming to terms with it, she *was* a servant. Well, almost. She'd been given a list of duties to occupy herself with on her second day within Castle Shreave. Upon recovering from her ordeal, Maeve showed her around the castle and introduced some of the other castle employees. Well, not employees, they received no monetary rewards for their work. They were given food and clothing material for themselves and their families.

It quite impressed her how they all worked together for the greater good. Back home, many lessons could be learned from these industrious Highlanders.

Back home! She would never forget Maeve's words when she'd found the courage to ask what year it was.

Maeve had frowned and asked if she'd hit her head and lost her memory. "Do ye have a wee lump on yer head, Jo? Mayhap ye have fallen and forgotten. It is 1626! Everyone knows that."

Startled by her sudden ashen complexion Maeve became concerned Jo was sicker than thought. Right at that moment she *had* felt quite ill.

After all the clues she refused to see and all the denials in her head, Jo knew some phenomenon moved her from the comforts of her own time to a dense forest in the Scottish Highlands.

But the Highlands of 1626? At first she gave a nervous giggle giving Maeve even more unease. After the initial shock, she'd explained to Maeve the past forty-eight hours of her life.

Through the entire explanation Maeve not once laughed or gave any indication she thought her mad. When blank expressions appeared on Maeve's face (and there were many) Jo tried to explain more clearly, but how do you explain a car, freeway, a light switch, or any form of technology to a woman from the seventeenth century?

At the end of her story, Maeve sat in quiet contemplation on the edge of her bed.

Jo felt like a fool. "It's ridiculous, isn't it? I mean, who goes to bed one night and wakes up the next day in a different century? Nobody, right? Oh God! You must think I'm absolutely insane." She'd rubbed her hands over her face as if to wash away the frustration.

Maeve gently pulled them away. "In my life, Jo Dunstan, I have learned ta nae question circumstance but ta be sure and see all the possibilities."

Jo was silent for a moment. Surely this woman didn't believe her story? Hell, she couldn't even believe it herself. But Maeve stared at her with solemn respect and no hint of ridicule or doubt.

Maeve believed her! After two days, some of Jo's anxiety abated.

The women chatted long into the night, Maeve, like an eager student with endless questions and counter questions and Jo with the same concerning life within Shreave castle. They talked of Maeve and Dougal's children, Jo's friend June, Jo's failed marriage, Maeve's special gift (or *Sight*, as it was referred to), the old laird and the new, and many other topics which initiated further conversation.

Dougal came to inform Maeve the evening meal was ready but she'd asked for it to be bought up to Jo's room. They would eat and continue their exchange of information.

Dougal did not look happy with this arrangement, but let them be. As he left Jo glimpsed Neill outside the door. It was apparent, on this matter at least, Dougal would not bow to his wife's judgement.

Neill was her jailor.

By midnight the women became friends with a depth of understanding that surprised them both. Their mutual respect was as if they'd known each other for years, not hours.

Jo didn't know how long she'd been kneeling in front of the warmth reviewing the week's events. The peat fire she'd been attending now breathed with life again. Maeve gave her the laird's chamber to tend, as he was due home soon. It seemed a waste of peat to leave it going when no one occupied the room, but the laird's fire burned even when he was away.

Maeve was a constant source of support for her and informed her, "Caring for the laird's room is a privilege. One of the top jobs in the castle!"

She knew well enough when she was being duped and whatever Maeve was up to, she would find out.

Castle life during the past week was quite tolerable. Jo took on the laird's chamber and other cleaning duties with gusto. She needed to be occupied. Her high-pressured job at Hardwicks was exhilarating. She was used to being in charge and in demand. To sit and do nothing was alien to her. Recognising this, Maeve soon had her scrubbing fireplaces and changing sheets. At first her back ached and her hands were raw, but she decided to view it from Maeve's point of view. What if, as Maeve pointed out, there was a reason for her presence in 1626? What if she woke up tomorrow back in her own bed in Melbourne? What if she'd been given the opportunity to experience something extraordinary?

With this in mind she got the notion to treat her predicament as a working holiday. This mind-set made it easier to accept the circumstances and apply herself to her chores and castle life with enthusiasm.

Her eagerness did not go unnoticed by other clan members. She won the respect and friendship of others within the walls who delighted in her way-out tales of flying machines and escalators. At staff meal times, taken after the family and soldiers ate, she would sit with the workers and learn to share and revel in castle life. By week's end she blended in just fine; well, until she spoke and was teased about her foreign language.

Rising from the floor, she surveyed the laird's chamber, a dull, masculine room with no appeal. Heavy, dark tapestries hung from the walls and a monstrous four-poster bed surrounded by velvet curtains dominated the space. Heavy timber trunks lined the walls.

A doorway to another smaller room, a study, contained a writing desk covered with papers and documents and yet another fireplace, also lit. Curiosity stirred and she entered the study and leaned against the desk to peruse the documents. The writing was written in what she supposed was Gaelic and there were detailed drawings of an architectural nature. It looked like some kind of addition was being considered for the castle.

Perhaps the laird was a bit of an architect. Also on the desk was an ornate, golden jewelled box. Still curious, she couldn't help herself and reached across and touched the box. It felt warm. Strange. As she squeezed behind the chair to get closer to the box, she leant against the wall and was surprised to hear a dull thud, like when one leans against a door. She assumed there was a stone wall behind the tapestry hanging there.

Intrigued, she lifted the edge and peered behind the tapestry. To her great surprise, there was a small door. She lifted the latch and the door opened. She stood breathless for a moment and couldn't help feel she was doing something wrong, betraying the trust Maeve placed in her. She berated herself for being such a baby, but her honest nature meant snooping did not come naturally.

She checked the main bedchamber, but nobody was there. She had the insatiable urge to add some excitement to her working holiday and couldn't believe her own daring. She closed the study door behind her and moved towards the tapestry. Lifting the heavy wall hanging away she opened the small, secret door.

There was just enough light behind her to illuminate the entrance to what looked like a tunnel. A torch hung on the wall to the right. Now experienced using a flint, she lit the torch and began to follow the tunnel downward until she came to steps built into the stone.

It was a rapid decent and about thirty meters on she smelt an acrid, sulphuric smell. It was unpleasant, but not overbearing. Torch held aloft, she kept moving for another fifty meters or so until she heard the sound of water. Castle Shreave was next to a lake, and she wondered if the castle was built over a river that ran into the lake itself. It would be an advantage to have a continuous flow of fresh water within the stronghold during a siege and she assumed the designers of the castle thought likewise.

She moved forward with care, as the stone steps and walls seemed to be glistening with dampness. To slip and injure herself while snooping would be an embarrassment! Not to mention she didn't want to give Dougal's spy theory any credence.

The tunnel flattened out into a small cave. What she saw took her breath away. Now she knew why the walls were wet. Steam! She was staring at the biggest spa bath she'd ever seen. It was an oval pool, about five meters long and disappeared around a corner into a private alcove. The water was hot and steam billowed from the surface. It seemed to be flowing from right to left and she assumed it came from a hot spring, ran through the pool and then out into the lake.

She stood transfixed. On a rock ledge near the pool, a small array of washcloths, towels, and soap were stored. She assumed this was some kind of private bathing room for the laird. She wondered if anyone else in the castle knew of its existence, or if anyone else besides the laird was permitted to use it. Her skin tingled with anticipation.

She washed every day with a cloth and bowl of tepid water, but she was a twenty-first century girl; with no bath or shower for a whole week, this opportunity was too tempting to resist. She knelt to feel the temperature of the water and couldn't withhold a sigh of pure pleasure. "Oh yes, yes!" It was warm and perfect.

Small, narrow steps were chipped into the stone for easy entry into the pool. Ignoring any further thoughts of guilt or repercussions, she stripped off her drab grey dress and ugly boots and entered the pool.

Chapter Nine

Connor slung his satchel on the floor of his chamber. It was good to be home and done with the rent takings. Dealing with the concerns of the outlying MacKay communities was not hard work, but it could be tedious. Some of them saw the laird on this one occasion each year and took the opportunity to ensure he knew of every issue whether large or small and every new birthing or neighbourly quarrel.

He was often frustrated with these mundane concerns and at times felt inadequate. Connor was never disinterested. He lacked the skill to deal with them. Not that he would ever admit this to anyone.

On many occasions, he watched his father turn people's troubles into triumphs and quarrels into partnerships but felt incapable of such diplomacy himself. He would prefer to fight raiders, disposing of them with his sword, and thus feel he was adequately fulfilling his role as laird.

Removing his plaid and stripping naked, Connor moved to stand in front of the hearth. The fire burned bright, the soft warmth glowed on his skin. Connor often found his bedchamber a lonely, solemn place. He felt more comfortable wrapped in his plaid, sleeping under the stars. Outside there was always Mother Nature for company, and the stars never left you alone. In Castle Shreave he could be surrounded by individuals, but still feel isolated.

Connor was a deep, quick thinker, and well educated, but preferred his own council, lacking any need for idle chatter. The only person he would ever seek an opinion from was his father, and now, only Dougal.

Connor and his father were close. Their mutual respect was strong and though he was now gone, Connor would forever admire the older man's fortitude. It was hard not to show sympathy as he'd weakened with illness, but the old laird viewed this as an insult to the full life he'd led. Connor's assistance, even for the slightest task, was brushed aside and he would be told in no uncertain terms, "I'm nae dead yet, laddie." The refusal of help Connor understood—but not being called laddie!

Smiling at the memories, Connor crossed the room to the mirror and began to remove the beard from his face. Once he finished shaving he walked to the study door and opened it. He froze dead in his tracks.

The hairs on the back of his neck stood up and his senses sharpened as he swung around, trying to ascertain what alerted him. First, the study door was closed, not open. Then he smelt a familiar smell. Sulphur. He was cautious as he lifted the tapestry behind his desk and saw the entrance open. At first he relaxed, thinking the maid was down there replacing the towels, but for some reason his instincts disagreed.

He retrieved his dirk from the bedchamber and entered the tunnel without a sound, not even bothering to light a torch. As a child, he came to the pool with his mother and grew to love swimming. Bath time was fun time under the watchful eye of Lady Kathryn MacKay.

Connor descended the stone stairs with speed and agility. Brushing his fingers along the tunnel wall, he recognised every bump and crevice and took each step with surety. When Dougal and he were young they competed to see who could navigate the tunnel the quickest, without torches, because torches would take the *fun* away. After many scraped and bruised knees, and bone-jarring falls, they soon learned the dynamics of the passage.

Reaching the opening of the cave, Connor heard the distinct sounds of a woman humming. She sounded at home in *his bath*. Rounding the edge of the cave entrance, Connor stayed in the shadows cast by a lit torch, so he could observe unseen the female monopolising the laird's pool. What he saw took his breath away.

There was a pale pink water-nymph swimming in the water. He drew in a sharp breath as he observed the spectacle before him.

He was mesmerised.

Her dark brown hair flowed around her head whilst she floated on her back with arms outstretched. She worked her arms in slow sideways movements, gliding across the pool with effortless grace. This afforded Connor a perfect view of the most beautiful breasts he'd ever laid eyes on. They were silken cream mounds, glazed and shining with the warm water. Her eyes were closed, while an unfamiliar tune resounded softly from her vocal cords. It caressed him.

His eyes blazed a trail down her body to the dark hair at the apex of her thighs, where her long luxurious legs began. He envisioned them wrapped around his body.

As the soft tones continued, his eyes caressed her. When she reached the end of the pool, she stopped and stood. She was tall. Taller than any woman Connor recently met. He knew Clan MacKenzie's women were large, but this one, though tall, was lithe and graceful. She turned in the water and started to move back to the other end, when, without warning, she dove under the steaming waters giving the laird the most tantalising view of her bottom. Expecting her to surface at once, Connor became anxious when seconds passed and there was still no sign of her.

Without realising it, Connor left the shadows and stood at the edge of the pool searching its depths, convinced something was wrong. The water, though not deep, was dark against the stones, and the single torch provided insufficient light to locate the lovely stranger.

Connor raced down the narrow steps, the warm water enfolding his naked body as he dove beneath the surface searching. Frantic.

All at once there was a dull crack as two heads collided in the pool causing both owners to rise, one standing solid and the other floundering wildly. Coughing and spluttering in exasperation, she tried to disentangle herself from whatever it was holding her clamped around the waist. Connor, assuming she was in shock from near drowning, held her close to his chest and tried to sooth her with calming words. "It's all right, lass. I've got ye. Stop thrashin' aboot. Yer safe now."

Comprehending what held her, she fought violently to extract herself.

"Let me go you stupid idiot," she screamed at her assailant whilst trying to get back her breath. "Let me go or I'll break your damn nose." Without even giving said idiot any chance to react or respond, she freed one of her arms, wrenched back her shoulder and elbow, and thrust forward with the heel of her hand straight up and into Connor's nose.

The sound of crunching gristle followed by a howl of stunned pain, caused the vice-like grip around her waist to loosen, giving her a chance to use her legs to push off his and glide backwards though the water. She felt better for putting distance between them, and creating space enough for her to better defend herself. Standing in a right-leg-back Tae Kwan Do stance with her hands raised in front ready to defend, she assessed her assailant with a wary eye, whilst the initial panic receded.

A man, no, a huge man, stood in front of her with his hand over his nose, and blood running down his chest into the water. It gave her a perverse sense of satisfaction. Euphoric over this victory, she lifted her eyes to his, and felt as though the breath was knocked out of her. Dark, piercing eyes bored into her. His face was without expression, but it needed none. His eyes told the story. He was furious.

Determined not to give any advantage by showing fear, she decided anger was a better weapon. Holding her fighting stance she made the first move. "Who the hell do you think you are? And what do you think you're doing attacking me in my bath?"

Connor's anger dissipated a little. He'd many adversaries in his life and knew the look of fear, no matter how hard a person tried to conceal it. His nose throbbed, but he could not help admire the lass who stood there so brave, thinking one lucky shot would be sufficient against his superior size and strength. And the view was quite tantalising.

She stood in naked glory; the water reached her ribcage, offering him every opportunity to ogle at his leisure. The soft curve of her waist and the rounded swell of her ample breast were of particular interest. As were the soft pink nipples, raised from the warm waters, hardened delightfully.

She was beautiful. He'd an urge to run his hand along her cheek.

It annoyed him that with all the luscious flesh presented, it was her face that would draw his caress. His broken nose must have addled his brain. Splashing water over his face to wash away the blood but never taking his eyes off her, Connor took a step forward, hands at his side, relaxed but ready.

She threatened him again, "Don't come any

closer, or I'll, I'll..."

"Do what? Break ma other nose?"

"No, but I'll rearrange your balls."

Understanding her meaning of 'balls,' Connor found it difficult not to smile. This woman was as crazy as a wild boar. She was cornered, irrational, and making rash judgements that would lead to her ultimate defeat. Connor began to enjoy himself, curious to see where it would lead. "Oh, aye, but that wouldna be verra fair, lass. Ye are one up on me already."

His soft, deep brogue didn't seem to suit his size and demeanour. He stood a good head taller than her. The water only came to his hips.

My God! He was gorgeous!

Wet black hair came past his shoulders with two braids down either side of his face. His nose was long, straight, and swollen. His lips were full and would be divine to kiss. *Oh, Christ, what am I thinking?*

His shoulders were broad and his arms, she was certain, could crush rock. Jet-black hair covered his chest, tapering tantalizingly down his abdomen before disappearing into the water. The rest was left to her imagination. Raising her eyes to his face, she could see nothing to indicate his intentions.

"Would ye like me ta get out lass, so ye can finish yer...exploration?" Mortified she'd been caught staring at him, she retaliated.

"I'm pretty sure there's nothing worth seeing."

"Oh. That is a shame then. Because I canna say the same for ye. I would be inclined ta see the rest of ye, seeing as the top half is so..."

"Ohhhh shit, you, you..."

The realisation she was showing off her breasts to this stranger made a flaming blush creep up her neck and face as she hurriedly ducked into the water to cover her nudity.

This slight distraction was all Connor required. He lunged forward through the water and locked her in a vice-like bear hug, wrapping one of his legs around hers in such a way, she couldn't move. She was pinned to his chest. Trapped. Vulnerable. Her heart raced.

She fought valiantly, but Connor just held on until her energy waned and she slumped limp in his arms, her chest rising and falling against his own. With a voice devoid of emotion, Connor asked, "Now lass, if ye have quite finished, I would like a few answers from ye. What is yer name?"

Recovering from her struggle, she managed one word. "Jo."

"Jo? Hmmph. Do ye often steal into others property…Jo, and use it as ye will?"

"No. I…what do you mean?" Aware of his chest hair brushing against her breasts—and *other* parts of him brushing against her stomach, she was finding it hard to string words together. What was happening? She should be feeling terror, anger, any emotion other than, than…lust! *Oh hell! This is insane.*

Yes, she was concerned, maybe a little confused but somehow she knew—knew this man, with all his strength, all his power—would never harm her.

She looked into his eyes, eyes that called to her, and said the only thing she could think of. "I'm sorry I broke your nose."

An apology was the last thing Connor expected from this buxom viper. He held her gaze for what seemed an endless amount of time, their faces but a breath apart, when he whispered, "Who are ye?"

Chapter Ten

Jo stormed off to the castle's second floor, walking along the corridor until she came to the nursery. Mrs. Moray was the castle nanny and she watched over Maeve and Dougal's children for a few hours each day whilst Maeve saw to the running of Castle Shreave. Millie was three-and-a-half years old, Kaitlyn was two, and their latest was a baby boy, just three months old.

Without knocking, she barged in to ask Mrs. Moray regarding Maeve's whereabouts, but found the object of her search in a rocking chair by the hearth, with her youngest babe at her breast. Young Davie had fallen asleep now, his belly was full of his mother's milk. She felt contrite and some of her annoyance evaporated.

Covering her extended nipple with her plaid, Maeve snuggled Davie closer to her chest and spoke in hushed tones. "Ye look like ye have the devil chasing ye. What brings ye here? I thought ye would be on yer way ta help in the kitchens. I was hoping ye would make that tasty sauce again. What did ye call it? May…nays?"

"Mayonnaise," she replied, thrown off track.

"Oh aye, that is it. I've nae tasted anything like it. And so easy ta make."

She sat in the chair opposite Maeve. Whenever she saw Maeve nursing Davie a pang of envy overcame her. Silly really, she'd never felt inclined to have children of her own. She was a career girl, and besides, her mother and Andrew never gave her any incentive to tread that path.

"What has got ye all in a bother?"

"It's like you said, the devil's chasing me—or I thought he may!" Maeve raised one eyebrow in silent enquiry. "I've just met the laird," she explained.

"Did ye now." Maeve wore a wicked grin on her face. "And how did ye both get on?"

"Before or after we were naked in his spa pool?"

The comment surprised Maeve so much, Davie almost slipped from her lap. Maeve took the baby into the next room and placed him in his crib, deciding this conversation was best conducted without whispering. Returning to her chair she sat and stared at her friend. "And what did ye think of the laird?"

"Didn't you hear what I said? I was naked in his bath!"

"Nae. Ye said ye were naked in his *spa* pool? What is a *spa*?"

"Maeve!" Jo raised her voice in exasperation but proceeded to tell everything leading to the 'naked' part. Maeve nodded her head or offered that indefinable word "Mmmph."

Jo finished with, "I told him my name and he said I'd better leave now or he wouldn't be held responsible for what may happen. What did he mean by that remark? He's the most implacable man I've ever had the displeasure to meet." She fidgeted in her chair but Maeve did not need this clue to read between the lines of this tale.

Jo wasn't unaffected by Connor MacKay.

"So what did ye do?"

"Well, when he released me from his boorish hold, I high-tailed it out of there. I wasn't going to spend a second longer in his company if I could help it."

Maeve was delighted. She loved it when she was right. She'd a 'feeling' about Jo the minute they met. When Maeve first suggested Jo would be a challenge for Connor and perhaps the one who might unseat him, Dougal scoffed, disbelieving the premonition. In Dougal's opinion, Connor would not be led astray by a strange lassie, no matter how attractive. Women threw themselves at Connor all the time and he was an expert at evasion. He would no sooner fall for a woman's scheming wiles than a dog would fall in love with a cat. Connor's scars were deep and would take time to heal. So Maeve didn't mention it again, but kept the thought to herself.

"I would say Jo, it was lucky ye did, how did ye say, *high-tail* it out of there—what with Connor's reputation."

"What *reputation*?"

"Weel, I dinna know if ye had chance ta notice but Connor is nae an ugly man. In fact, most of the lassies swoon when he passes. I would not be at all sure, but I would say he is used to, shall I say, err, taking what he wants."

Jo absorbed this information in silence. Of course she'd noticed his looks, and oh my, what a body! It was none of her business how many women he slept with, or bedded as they said here, but why did this piece of information irk her so much? It gave her a funny knot in the pit of her stomach. Ignoring these feelings she stated, "If I never come across him again, it won't bother me. His eyes are black as coal. Have you ever seen him smile? I swear, he's the most arrogant man I've ever met."

"Weeeel...I guess it is a good thing he nae affects ye then, aye?" Maeve replied, all innocence.

"Affects me! That'll be the day. And anyway, if he tries to 'take what he wants' anywhere near me, I'll just break his nose again."

For a moment, Maeve just stared at her, her bottom jaw in her lap. When she managed to get over the shock of Jo's words, all she could do was howl with laughter. Tears ran down her cheeks, her ample bosom wobbled so much her chair began to creak under the strain.

Jo had real concerns Maeve might have heart failure if she didn't get a hold of herself.

Between wheezing, breathless gasps of mirth, Maeve managed to get out "Nose..."

****

The noon meal was being served up in the main hall. Jo added her personal touch to a couple of the dishes, obliging Maeve with mayonnaise and also creating great excitement with seventeenth-century Scotland's first-ever pizza. Mrs. MacBain, the head cook, was at first wary, feeling threatened by her culinary expertise. She laughed to herself. The thought of being considered a master chef was absurd, but to these simple, delightful folk, she was a culinary genius. Mrs. Mac (as she was affectionately called) hung on every word Jo uttered whilst being taught to make stir-fried vegetables. It was a revelation to Mrs. Mac to not boil or roast vegetables, but to put them raw into a hot pan mixed with a few herbs and spices. Simple.

Jo threw herself into the meal preparations with gusto. She needed to occupy her brain; all she could seem to think of was a pair of fathomless black eyes. It was unsettling to feel not-in-control of one's own mind.

After leaving Maeve in the nursery, and feeling irritated at her seeming lack of understanding, not to mention sadistic sense of humour, she went directly to the kitchens hoping beyond reason she wouldn't bump into the laird along the way.

Her cheeks flamed red every time she thought about their encounter in the pool. It wasn't only embarrassment at being seen naked by him; she also felt shame being caught in a place obviously private and off limits to servants. It was the first time since arriving a week ago she felt bothered—no, annoyed—by her situation. She was happy to do the work assigned. It surprised her how satisfying it could be. But she came from a place in time where the privileges of the seventeenth century were available to all citizens in the twenty-first century. Every home in Australia contained a bath or shower. She couldn't help feeling piqued. She was accustomed to bathing every day.

It was an eventful day. Ascending the stairs back to her room, she felt a little wearier than usual. Entering her room she was surprised to find two new dresses and matching slippers on the bed. Stunned, she moved forward to feel the dress fabric. Made of the softest wool, one was lemon, its low-cut bodice trimmed with lace and the other was similar in style, but leaf green. Delighted she stripped off her apron and the dull grey potato sack and tried on the lemon dress. As she slipped it over her head, there was a knock at the door and Maeve entered the room. "Oh aye, that looks lovely on ye. I thought the colour would suit ye, with yer brown hair. Try the shoes, see if they fit."

"Did you organise these for me, Maeve?"

"Aye."

"That's really nice of you. Thanks so much. But the cleaning girls wear grey dresses. I wouldn't feel right in these."

"Oh, dinna worry none aboot that. I have a new job fer ye. Come on then, try the slippers on."

Jo sat on her bed and kicked off her ugly boots and slipped her feet into the lemon slippers. They fit beautifully and were so comfortable. Overwhelmed by the new clothes, she couldn't help feel like she was dressing up for a play. These were the type of clothes you'd see in movies, like *Romeo and Juliet* or *First Knight*.

"Do they fit ye?"

"Oh yes, yes they're great. Thank you, Maeve,"

she answered sincerely.

"Weel, I couldna have ye looking like a common servant around the head table."

Surprised by the comment, Jo tried to clarify the point. "What do you mean?"

"Ye've been promoted." At Jo's blank look, Maeve explained, "Mrs. MacBain's daughter is due ta birth her fifth child. So Eva is going to stay with her in the village ta help with the wee ones fer a while. I need someone ta take her position whilst she is gone. Now young Ellie will do this. She is a good lass and I think she is ready ta move up. This leaves her spot vacant, which will be taken by Shona. That means there is nobody ta look after the head table. Ye see."

Her head was spinning with the explanation and she laughed at Maeve. "Whoa there! You lost me at fifth child."

Maeve looked at her and chuckled. "Ye may have realised I have a tendency ta prattle at times. It annoys Dougal so much. I would hate ta change ma self and spoil the fun."

"Anything that annoys Dougal is fine by me. I still haven't forgotten my first night in the castle." The comment sobered both women.

Taking Jo's hand, Maeve sat on the bed and pulled her down next to her. "How have ye been Jo? I know we have seen each other each day this week, but I have nae asked, ye know. It must be hard. Are ye coping?"

She thought for a moment before answering. "I don't know. Some days, I've felt right at home, and others, it's like I'm walking around in a dream, but everyone's been so kind."

Maeve squeezed her hand. "I think it still best if we nae tell anyone else yer story. I have told Dougal ye are still suffering memory loss. I nae like lying ta him, but...weel, they are nae likely ta believe ye anyway," Maeve surmised.

"Thank you Maeve. I don't know what I'd have done without your kindness. And your support. Don't worry about me though, I'm fine."

"Good, good. Weel then." Maeve stood and walked to the door. "I'm glad ye like the dresses. Ye've the rest of the day ta yerself then, as Mrs. MacBain willna be leaving until tomorrow. Shona will fetch ye in the morning and tell ye what it is ye'll need ta know, aye?"

"I'll be fine, Maeve. And thanks again."

"Why do ye not take a walk outside? It is a grand afternoon. There is a new foal in the stables, quite bonnie I am told." Maeve left the room with a twinkle of mischief in her eye.

Chapter Eleven

The stables were a favourite place for Connor and he often visited there. As a child, he spent many hours with the horses and Old Nick, who taught the laird much about horsemanship and treated Connor like a second son. Nick long since passed and his son Tannan became the stable master.

When Connor had things on his mind he would spend time in the stables, grooming his horse whilst gathering his thoughts. Tannan, finding the laird in the stalls, knew to leave him be. Today, the laird had company.

Connor leaned on the stall railing, admiring the beautiful new colt wobbling around its mother's legs. He won the mare, Mia, some years ago in a game of chance. This was Mia's third foal after mating with the laird's new stallion and the result was very pleasing.

Colin was in the stall giving Mia an enthusiastic brush down. Dougal sat on the saddle rack observing the boy. "If ye brush much longer lad, she'll nae have any hair left." Colin's cheeks flushed bright red causing Dougal to chuckle, adding to the boy's discomfiture.

Connor gave no sign he noticed Colin's embarrassment, and instructed him to finish the mare and give Thief the same treatment and some extra oats. Rushing off to do his laird's bidding, Colin left the two men alone.

"If that laddie could die fer ye, he would," remarked Dougal, "Ye couldna say he lacks enthusiasm!" Connor managed a grin, but it was obvious to Dougal the laird's mind was elsewhere. "We should be hearing from The Sinclair any day now," prompted Dougal, earning Connor's attention. "What do ye think he will propose?"

Connor pushed away from the railing and filled a bin with oats for Mia. "He will nae be proposing anything. He will do as I suggest."

"Keep the watches up?"

"Aye. We nae have enough men ta cover all MacKay borders. Joined with Sinclair men we can cover them all. We will catch these raiders and soon have answers." Connor gave Mia the oats and closed the stall door to leave her and the foal in peace. Turning to Dougal he said, "I heard ye had an altercation with Brian again on the way back from recovering the cattle."

"I dinna like him."

It was one of the things Connor most liked about his friend. He never minced words, and you always knew his position on things.

"Aye. I'm aware of that." Connor could not suppress his grin, which raised Dougal's ire.

"He is trouble, cousin or nae."

"Stop worryin' aboot him. He is nae bother ta us."

"I know ye give him leeway fer yer mother's sake. But I still canna say I like it."

Knowing this conversation would go around in circles, Connor changed topics. "I hear ye picked up a passenger on yer travels."

Dougal, busy with organising a messenger to The Sinclair forgot to mention Jo. "Aye, I suppose Neill filled ye in." At Connor's nod, Dougal explained the circumstances of finding her. "The lassie is a mystery. I havna ever heard her accent before. Ye'll know I have Neill keeping watch on her. Dinna tell Maeve though. She and the lass have become friends."

Connor was tempted to rib Dougal about Maeve. She was the only other person he knew who could get the upper hand with Dougal Haig. Instead he probed for more information about the lass whose naked image kept him awake for most of the night. He told none of the encounter at the pool.

"Keep Neill on her," commanded Connor, more out of annoyance than anything.

"Aye. Until her memory returns we have naught else ta do."

Not missing the suspicion in Dougal's voice, Connor said, "Neill says she has worked hard ta earn her keep, and not done anything ta be suspicious aboot. What is it bothers ye?"

With a familiar stubborn look on his face Dougal replied, "Not knowing is all." Then with a smile, "but I've always been a suspicious old bastard, aye?" Both men laughed and Dougal pointed to Connor's swollen nose. "What happened?"

Connor looked away saying, "Thief and I had a close encounter. Tis nothing."

Dougal said no more, but he'd a sneaking suspicion there was more to it than Connor admitted.

At that moment a shadow fell across the entrance to the stables, causing the men to look up. Taking Maeve's suggestion, Jo came to view the new foal. This was her first real walk beyond the castle since entering it the previous week.

Needing a few seconds for her eyes to adjust to the darkened building, she walked slowly along the stalls, her eyes likely adjusting to the dimness. The stable was huge with over a hundred stalls. Nearly all contained at least one horse, many of whom thrust their noses over their gates to curiously view the newcomer. Unaware the two men were observing her, she reached out her hand to stroke the soft velvet muzzle of a large roan.

"Hey boy...or girl?" She bent her head and looked between the railings. "Girl. Aren't you beautiful?" The horse snuffled her hair then tickled Jo's face with her soft nose, earning a delighted laugh.

From the other end of the stables Connor could not take his eyes off her. He vividly remembered their 'wet' encounter and could not help undressing her with his eyes, knowing what lay beneath the becoming yellow dress. He'd felt a pang of regret as she raced from the cave, and he berated himself for not being as chivalrous as he should have. However, self-preservation came first and if she'd not attacked him he would have let her leave unhandled.

But would he have? Women frequently offered their bodies to him but never did one so vehemently rebuff his attention. It was quite a unique situation and he could not decide *how* he felt about it. There was no doubting she was a beautiful woman. As she petted the roan with affection, he could not help but imagine how it would feel to have that attention directed at him. If she ran her hands over his body and whispered soft words in his ear. Blood rushed to his groin and he cursed, angered at his lack of control.

Dougal also watched the woman and called out, interrupting her private conversation with the horse. "Hey, lassie! Dinna go handling the horses. Some of them will take yer hand off in spite of yer kind words."

She spun towards Dougal's voice but locked eyes with the laird. *Oh, drat.*

Apart from their embarrassing meeting, she knew little of the man other than what Maeve imparted, but she found his eyes hypnotic. They drew her. His hair was tied back showing his strong, powerful neck, emphasising his broad shoulders. As he looked she felt a blush run up her neck. *Oh, double drat.*

She rarely blushed and found this most annoying. Deciding attack was better than defence, she walked towards the men with a confidence she didn't feel.

"I'm sorry. I hope it's okay to come into the stables. Maeve said I should come. Apparently there's a new foal worth looking at?"

Dougal gave an indecipherable "Hmmph" and pointed into the stall they were leaning on.

She advanced and looked inside and couldn't contain her "Ohhhh!" This was enough for Dougal and he walked off but stopped, returning for introductions. Or so he thought.

"Connor, I nae believe ye've met our…guest? Lass, this is Connor MacKay, Laird of Clan MacKay." With the introduction made, Dougal hastened from the stable. Much to her relief.

Each time she and Dougal passed each other over the previous week he walked by frowning. She wondered what it was about her that seemed to bring out the worst in him.

"Dinna fash yerself about Dougal, lass. He is like that with everyone."

Unaware her expression was so readable, she turned to Connor and replied, "I don't normally have this effect on people, you know. Usually they find me quite nice, even friendly."

Touching his nose for effect, Connor countered, "Nice, ye say? Friendly, ye say? I havena had the pleasure of seeing *that* side of ye, lass."

She felt his taunt unjustified, after all, he grabbed her unexpectedly from the pool, and scared the life out of her. How did he expect her to react? She reasoned he thought all women were the same and would fall into his arms willingly. Well, she had news for him. "Maybe if you hadn't snuck up on me, I wouldn't have had to defend myself. And by the way mate, I'm not your lass and I'm not your lassie. I have a name. It's Jo. Okay?"

Why did this man irk her so?

It seemed Connor didn't like being put in his place. He took two long strides, blocking her exit. With her back pressed against the rails of Mia's stall he reached out and wrapped his hands around the top railing on either side of her shoulders.

She felt threatened and became defensive, planning another attack. Prepared this time, Connor grabbed her wrists, startling her with his lightning-quick reflexes. He pulled her arms together in front of her so they rested on his chest.

She was furious. "Let go of me."

"Nae."

"Let go of me you son of a bitch." She struggled vigorously.

"Are ye aware it is most unbecoming for women ta use such foul language? I believe I heard some of yer more colourful dialogue yesterday, in *ma* pool." Connor's emphasis on 'ma' ensured her anger, or rather *embarrassment,* even further. He eyed her blush. "Furthermore *lass,* in Scotland lassie or lass are terms we use for a girl or female. It is nae an insult. And I know yer name is *Jo*, as ye told me yesterday before ye ran like a coward from the cave."

She put more effort into her struggling. So now he thought she was a coward! His hands felt like steel grips giving her no chance of pulling out of his hold, or using her legs, as there was no room to move between him and the railings.

"Another point I would make, *Jo*, is if ye'd like me to be your *mate,* I can be quite obliging, when an offer is made," he finished offhandedly.

Taken aback she stopped struggling and looked at Connor in disbelief. "You think..." she stammered. "You honestly believe I would throw myself at you like you were some, some..." Lost for words she struggled with an array of emotions. His arrogant presumptions stoked her anger, but she became aware of the warmth of his body infusing hers through her soft woollen dress. She also felt the hard planes of his thighs against her own legs. It unsettled her.

Now angrier with herself than him, she turned her head away as she felt another blush creep up her face, thwarting any pretence she was indifferent to his company. Connor, not missing any clues, struggled not to show pleasure at her squirming.

It wasn't just that she blushed so readily around him that gave him pause. He could not help but notice how green and beautiful her eyes were and how long the lashes. He was also very aware of her perfume. Lavender; soft, subtle, and mixed with her own female smell. Annoyed and confused at his wayward thinking, Connor stepped away, giving her space to move away.

She remained motionless with all but three feet separating them, as if waiting for something to happen. He continued to stare at her, watching the play of emotions flit across her face. He enjoyed seeing the subtle confusion played out by the movement of her eyebrows and the soft tensing of her lips. The thought came unbidden. *Lips that would be so soft and pliable to kiss.* He knew she'd no idea how easily he could read her. Her brief hesitation told him she was unsure of herself and he almost felt sympathy for her. It was not the first time Connor's stony demeanour confused an opponent.

She was annoyed at the way he again entrapped and outwitted her. At each meeting, they seemed to end up angry at each other. What did it all mean?

She wasn't used to *not* having the upper hand in a confrontation. The long and difficult workplace negotiations with the unions during her time at

Hardwicks never left her feeling unsure of herself.

Taking a deep breath, she tried to end the awkward stand-off. "I should be going back to the castle. I'm sure Neill is getting bored having to wait to follow me."

His eyebrows rose at the dig.

Then more sincerely she added, "I don't...I'm usually not...I'm sorry, it's just, you irritate me. Do you do it on purpose?" She thought he wasn't going to reply, but he took a step closer, forcing her head back to look up at him. She looked into his eyes and a shiver ran down her spine.

"Only if someone irritates me first," he replied.

She released a breath and giggled. He didn't know she was laughing at the absurdity of this whole situation, and of her own confused feelings.

His brows dipped into a frown as he turned and left, leaving her alone in the stables.

Chapter Twelve

Of all her tasks over the past two weeks, Jo decided serving at the head table was by far the chore she disliked the most. She hoped every day Eva Mac's daughter would send her mother home and start caring for her own children, new baby or not! Then the chain of command would be returned to normal and Shona could have her job back at the head table.

It wasn't that she found the work hard. Heavens! Anyone could do it. The laird attended each meal served in the great hall and it was *this* she found awkward.

It seemed a battle of wills ensued for the duration of most meals. Maybe it was her imagination, but she got the impression Connor MacKay enjoyed having her serve his meal and fill his ale tankard—and it irked her to have to do it.

Damn the man.

She felt no qualms serving everyone else, but either way, there was no doubt—she was a useless waitress.

Two days previously, the priest of Shreave Chapel came as a dinner guest. Maeve ensured correct protocol was followed within the castle and asked Father Michael on *behalf* of the laird. The meal was going well until Jo was required to carry out a large server of roasted meats. In hindsight, the platter was far too heavy for her over the long walk from the kitchens to the hall.

As she stepped onto the dais, her arms gave way and the food slipped off, landing on the rushes beneath the table with a wet thunk. The diners on the dais peered over the edge of the table in shocked silence. Father Michael was the first to react and rose to assist, inquiring if she hurt herself. She replied honestly. "Only my pride, Father." This caused the young priest to chuckle, but it was the look in the laird's eyes that annoyed her more than anything. If prizes were given out for the darkest frown, Laird Connor MacKay would be grand champion.

"My apologies for the girl's carelessness, Father Michael," Connor said with sarcasm. "She is new ta the job and has much ta learn. Go back to the kitchens, lass, and get some more, or do ye expect our guest ta eat off the floor?" he inquired, tone surly.

She looked up from the mess and glared at the laird. She wanted him to *feel* her anger because her own good manners would not allow her to cause a scene before all in the hall.

Picking up the ruined meat from the rushes, she returned to the kitchen. A fresh, though smaller, platter was quickly prepared for the table. Whilst no one watched, she prepared a special one for Connor.

Giving Connor her most innocent smile, she placed his meal before him and left the hall.

She missed the look on his face as he chewed roasted lamb encrusted with grit and straw. None noticed his amused expression as he smiled to himself and washed it down with ale.

****

Later that evening a message arrived from Laird Alick Sinclair, indicating he and his entourage would arrive at Castle Shreave on the first of the month for discussion concerning the Highland raiders and what could be done to eliminate them.

This inspired much commotion within the castle, particularly for Maeve, as Shreave's chatelaine. The preparations placed so much stress on Maeve that Jo offered to assist with her duties. Occasionally, this involved her picking up the children from the nursery and taking them for a walk.

The day before the Sinclair entourage arrived, she took them to the stables for Millie's riding lesson. Millie, though only three-and-a-half years old, rode well, but Kaitlyn, just two, was Jo's biggest concern.

Baby Davie was, as usual, no bother, sleeping contently in a nursery sling tied over her shoulder, nestling the small baby against her chest. However, she couldn't take her eyes off toddler Kaitlyn for a second or the child would walk up to any horse, trained warhorse or plough pony, and pat it.

On the way she noticed the increased activity in the bailey. Extra supplies were being brought in from the main storerooms in preparation for the special meals in honour of the visiting Laird Sinclair. But many castle inhabitants, particularly Maeve, were looking forward to seeing Laird Sinclair's wife, Megahn.

Maeve told her about Meg and Connor growing up together at Castle Shreave; with Meg as much of a hellion as her brother in their early years. Growing up, Meg rode as well as any of the boys, including Connor and Dougal, and could shoot an arrow as straight and true as either of them. The old laird was criticised for not placing a sterner hand on the girl. Lady MacKay however, delighted in her daughter's abilities, leaving the laird no chance of turning his only daughter into a lady.

Meg grew into a beautiful woman, with hair as fair as her brother was dark. She turned down many betrothal offers from neighbouring clans hoping to secure beneficial alliances with the powerful Laird MacKay. When love and marriage took her to her new home at Wick, she was missed by all.

Jo admitted she looked forward to the appearance of Megahn Sinclair.

As she and the children reached the stables a friendly voice called out, "Is that our little angel here for her riding, then?" Tannan came from the stables and Millie raced towards him and was quickly picked up and given a warm hug.

"Hello, Tannan. I don't think we've been properly introduced." She reached out her hand to Tannan. "I'm Jo. And you need no introduction. Millie has told me all about you," she said with a twinkle in her eye.

Tannan looked a little bemused as he took her offered hand. He obviously was not used to shaking a woman's hand. The stories he'd heard of her forthright behaviour within the castle must be true. He smiled. "I hope she has only told ye the good things aboot ma character?"

"All very good. She also informs me she's going to marry you one day."

Tannan laughed but a slight blush could be seen in his cheeks. She estimated Tannan to be twenty years old.

"Oh aye, I'm sure when she's old enough, she'll nae take a second look at the old man that runs the stables." With his hand over his heart in mock jest he said, "How will ma heart ever survive?"

With the formalities over and Millie taken into the stables to help saddle her horse, she took Kaitlyn's hand and started towards the main gate, but the small child had other ideas and pulled her around the side of the stables towards the east side of the castle. Although Kaitlyn was only two, Jo was surprised by her single-minded determination.

Deciding to let the child take the lead, she followed. It wasn't long before their destination became clear.

She could hear dogs barking and realised the

kennels housing the hunting hounds was ahead. The shed stretched long and narrow with a low, thatched roof. Kaitlyn headed straight for the door on the end and banged on it demanding entrance. Jo noticed the latch was high up and thought it was a good idea or else this little girl would be sneaking off to the dogs whenever she was able.

She was unsure what to do. Maeve hadn't mentioned the kennels as an idea for an outing with the children, but Kaitlyn gave the impression she'd been here before. Deciding to have a peek inside to make sure all the dogs were tied up, she carried the child on her hip, careful not to squash Davie, and reached for the latch. She pushed the door inwards and peeped inside.

"I would be careful if I was ye. The hounds nae take kindly ta strangers."

She jumped in fright. Kaitlyn almost slid down her hip to the ground and Davie stirred. Settling them down, she turned to glare at Neill. A grin marked his face.

"Ye would nae have jumped so if ye were nae doin' something ye shouldna."

"I didn't know I was doing something I *shouldn't* have. Kaitlyn brought me here so I thought she came here often. I wasn't going to go barging in there with two small children if it wasn't safe to do so. What do you take me..."

"All right, all right, lass. Dinna get yer breeches in a knot. I was jesting."

"Well in future, when you're following me, could you not sneak up like that, okay? I'm used to having a shadow that *doesn't* talk."

This made Neill chuckle and he opened his mouth to retort, when another voice interrupted.

"Is there a problem here?" Connor watched her jump as he spoke.

"Nae, ma laird," replied Neill. "I was just

cautioning them aboot entering the kennels alone."

Connor nodded in understanding, gave a slight, dismissing nod, and Neill turned back to the stables leaving them alone.

Jo became defensive. "I told Neill I wouldn't have gone in there without making sure it was safe. What is it about you men? Do you think all women are stupid or something? Do you think I would put these children in danger? I'm sick of being followed everywhere. I'm sick of not being trusted."

Restless at being held back from her goal of entering the kennels, Kaitlyn almost wriggled free. Jo struggled to hold onto the child but Connor stepped forward and took Kaitlyn from her arms.

This surprised her. She hadn't expected this man to be considerate of domestic difficulties, particularly (going by previous encounters) when she was involved. What came next shocked her even more, as the child wrapped her arms around his neck and gave him a kiss on the cheek. Connor kissed the child back and whispered, "Aye, ye wee rabbit. Ye are up ta mischief again, nae doubt."

It was obvious Connor MacKay felt great affection for the child. He held her safely in his arms, dwarfing her with his physical size. Jo couldn't help feeling envious, knowing his warmth and strength. Feeling disturbed at being jealous, yes jealous, *of a two-year-old*, Jo hmmphed.

Connor moved towards her and she noticed the smooth, supple, and soundless grace of his gait. No wonder he'd been able to sneak up on her that day in the pool. She blushed—it didn't pay to remember that particular encounter. He surprised her yet again when he reached out and placed his hand on Davie's downy, soft head. His large, strong hands, calloused with hard work and swordplay, were gentler than she would have imagined.

He stared at the baby, showing no visible sign of

emotion, and then said, "I am their godfather."

She observed his face, understanding it hid a multitude of secrets. "All three of them?" she asked.

"Aye."

"Well," she grinned, trying to make light of the unease she felt by his close proximity, "I hope Dougal and Maeve live long healthy lives then."

Before she could offer another, nervous jest, Connor leaned in and placed his lips on hers.

She was startled by the intimate touch and knew she should object to his advance, but the only thing she could think of was how warm his lips were. The kiss was tender and she found it hard to believe a man like Connor MacKay could offer it.

But, what did she *really* know about this man?

Nothing.

Connor had longed to place his hand over the baby's tiny fist as it rested on Jo's chest, and feel the warmth of both beneath. A yearning deeply buried surfaced unwanted to conscious thought. He frowned and banished it back to the depths.

Seeing Jo and Neill in discussion bothered him. It was ridiculous, as Neill had a wife and child of his own he doted on. But he didn't like Neill speaking to or laughing with her. He'd only thought how much he wanted to taste her lips, wondering if they would be as soft as Davie's downy head. Before he knew it instinct moved him towards her. It seemed a natural thing to do. Her teasing and honest smile built an invisible bridge between them.

The taste of her lips was like nothing he experienced before, like a comfortable warmth that told him he was home, and that it was right.

Connor drew back and then advanced again before she could utter a word. His hand slid up under her hair, his warm palm caressed the back of her neck, drawing her closer. This time the kiss deepened as he began to move his lips over hers.

She sighed and by doing so gave Connor the opening he desired, sliding his tongue into her mouth where she tasted of warm spring rain.

"I dinna suppose ye two have seen Davie or Kaitlyn?" Maeve appeared. She wore the most satisfied look upon her face. "Oh, weel!" she exclaimed with mock surprise. "There they are. I would never have noticed them squished between the two of ye like that, aye?"

Stunned, Jo tried to get her senses back in working order, whilst quickly stepping back like a guilty child. She needed some distance between herself and the laird. What the hell just happened? Once again, she blushed profusely. There must definitely be something in the Highland air.

Kaitlyn tried to wriggle out of Connor's arms. He let the child go and she toddled off and latched onto her mother's skirts. Bending to pick her up, Maeve kept looking from one to the other thoughtfully. "Mmm," she muttered in a satisfied tone.

Connor's face was expressionless, while Jo blushed enough for both of them. He didn't seem the least bit perturbed at being caught doing...what?

The toddler pointed with determination at the entrance to the kennels.

"Have ye nae taken yer godchild ta see the hounds, Connor? Ye know she always loves ta go with ye. Do ye have the time fer it?"

He walked over, lifted the child from her mother's arms, and swung her up onto his shoulders. "Aye. I have the time," was all he said before disappearing into the kennels.

"Here Jo, let me take Davie from ye. He'll be needin' a feed before long and I have done all I can to set the castle ta rights before our visitors arrive."

"It's all right Maeve. Leave him. I'll come back with you and take him up to the nursery." As she moved in the direction of the castle Maeve reached out and stopped her.

"Nae, nae, if ye wouldna mind? That is, I would appreciate ye bringing Katie up when she has finished with her Uncle Connor?"

"Oh well, I…don't, that is."

"Ye canna tell me nothing ye blush doesna, lass," Maeve said jovially.

"Yes, but he just…just…"

Maeve squeezed her hand, her expression becoming serious. "Listen, Jo. There are some things I canna explain. Ye are one of them, there is nae doubt. But there are other things I can. He is a lonely man. And I see him watching ye. Oh, I dinna think he even realises he watches ye. But I see." Maeve paused and smiled at Jo's dumbfounded expression before continuing. "He is the most stubborn man I have ever met. He is powerful, strong, and many fear him. But there are things in his past that have left scars, nae just physical scars, but emotional ones."

Maeve paused again, letting go of her hand. "Connor and I have shared some quarrels, but he is a good man. I dinna know why ye are here, Jo Dunstan, and we dinna ken fer how long. But I believe ye were sent here for a reason. And I think Connor is it."

Jo finally found her voice. "How could you possibly think that? I mean it's just absurd. Everything. This whole Scottish, castle thing? The seventeenth century and me, from the twenty-first. Some days I actually still believe I'm dreaming."

"Jo, I am sorry. I am nae trying ta confuse ye or burden ye in any way. I know it must be difficult. But…I just see what I see." Maeve took her hand again and gave it another squeeze and smiled questioningly. "We are nae so bad, are we?"

She squeezed Maeve's hand in return. "It's not

you, Maeve…it's me." Jo began methodically rubbing Davie's back as he stirred in his sling. "Some days I feel perfectly normal and the next day someone comes into the castle with a bloody sword wound, dripping all over the fresh rushes, and no one bats an eyelid. That just isn't normal from where I come from, you know."

Maeve began to laugh. "I dinna imagine it would be any easier if the tables were turned and I were in your time."

"I don't know how I feel sometimes. And him." She nodded towards the kennels. "I just don't get. He confuses and frustrates me. And I can't read him. I just can't work him out."

Maeve reached behind her and began to undo Davie's sling. "Stop trying sae hard, Jo. It doesna have to be something ye 'work out.' Why do ye nae follow and trust yer own feelings? Ye canna control some things. They just have ta happen." Maeve smiled, took her child, and left her to ponder their conversation.

Jo stood at the entrance to the kennels, trying to bolster her courage before entering. She thought long and hard on her friend's words. Maeve made a tactful point. Maybe she should just let things be. Maybe she did try to control her life too much. She became a regimented businesswoman who organised and controlled her work, her life, and those who worked for her. Her steady lifestyle, combined regular interests conducted on certain days of the week.

As the minutes ticked by, she began to realise what her life had become. How she protected herself from hurt or harm with order and regulation. Never stepping outside her boundaries. After the hurtful end to her marriage, without realising it, she'd built a barrier around herself.

It dawned on her that her life was mundane, or

had been. She also realised that in the past she never took risks or ventured into the unknown having always done what was right, what people expected of her, never considering stepping outside her well-ordered regime.

As more revelations washed over her, she moved to the side of the kennels where an old tree stump stood, testament to seventeenth-century progress and expansion of the castle and grounds. She sat heavily upon it not even noticing if it was dirty enough to mark her new dress. She was unaware of how long she sat, consumed with her own thoughts, consumed within memories laced with regret.

The kennel door banged, drawing her attention, and she saw Connor coming out with the young girl sitting high on his shoulders. She made no sound, preferring to observe the two. Kaitlyn grasped two handfuls of Connor's hair whilst she hung on, his long strides causing her to rock from side to side.

Smiling to herself, Jo made an instant decision. Maeve's words made a lot of sense. Jo realised this was an incredible opportunity—the chance to live another life and take a different path. All she needed to do was follow it. Not race down it hell-for-leather, but she would stroll, and see where it would take her.

"Connor!" she yelled out. The man in question turned back unaware she sat around the corner from the kennel entrance. She rose from the stump and, feeling light of heart, started to follow her 'new path.' As she approached, Connor took the child from his shoulders, gave her a kiss on the cheek, and handed her to Jo, then turned and headed for the stables, leaving both staring after him.

"Well, young lady," she said to the child. "If you have any tips on male psychology or personal anecdotes on males in general, I'd appreciate the knowledge. You've obviously got it in spades!"

Jo turned towards the castle as Neill peeled away from the side of the stables, intending to follow her. She didn't notice Connor's brief shake of his head as he passed Neill.

She no longer had a shadow.

Chapter Thirteen

Before noon the following day, a Sinclair messenger rode into the courtyard to inform Laird MacKay that Laird Sinclair was but an hour away and there were injured men in the entourage. They suffered an attack on route.

Connor and Dougal arrived in the great hall at the same time, where the messenger waited to provide additional information sent on by Laird Sinclair. The Sinclair was ambushed within two hours ride of Castle Shreave by a band of hidden assailants armed with bows. The fifty-strong entourage were better armed and trained than any bandits, but the attack served its purpose. Two soldiers were dead and five wounded. The laird and his wife were unharmed.

The messenger was sent to the kitchens whilst Connor and Dougal mulled over this startling information. "The attack has occurred on MacKay land," Connor spoke, almost to himself. "How could they know The Sinclair would be travelling here taday?"

Connor's fists were clenched and he looked every bit the warrior he was as rage swept over him. "Will they stop at nothing ta cause friction amongst the clans?" He turned to Dougal. "Double the boundary guards and see that extra watches are posted on the walls. If anyone enters or leaves the castle the guards are nae familiar with, I want ta know."

Dougal gave a nod and left. Connor was glad to have a moment to himself as his fury was only just contained. A man who would endanger Connor's sister was a man with a short time to live. But his anger was also directed at Alick Sinclair. He should not have brought Meg along. She would have been safer at home surrounded by walls and castle guards.

Though he knew Meg would never have agreed to stay behind made no difference to his reasoning. Her stubborn streak was enough to rival Connor and Alick's combined. But a man should be in charge of his wife and not be dictated to. Connor thought this proved Alick Sinclair to be a weak man, regardless of fighting prowess and reputation.

Some minutes later Dougal returned, having relayed Connor's instructions to the guard master. He joined Connor at the head table and called for ale.

Folding tablecloths in the linen room, Jo heard Dougal's demand. Her job at the head table was quite a trial. It still dumbfounded her she could do the PR for a corporate merger but found the task of serving a meal awkward. What annoyed her most were the manners, or lack of, from some of the diners. Connor rated high on this scale, but Dougal topped her list. The two men seemed to believe common courtesy did not apply to them.

"Ale, woman!" Dougal shouted at the top of his voice again.

Throwing down a tablecloth, Jo stormed out of the linen room, fuming with indignation and found Connor and Dougal in deep conversation at the head table. She stopped in front of the men with her back to the main hall entrance. Both looked down at her questioningly; Connor, unreadable as ever and Dougal with a grumpy frown.

"Where is our ale, lass?" Dougal asked curtly.

Angered beyond care, she swore if anyone called her lass or lassie again, or forgot their manners, she would scream. The only lassie she'd ever known had a tail that wagged. She was also a firm believer that despite one's station, forgetting your manners was unacceptable.

She was aware Connor observed the flow of emotions cross her face; clearly she was angry. Her body language remained relaxed but her eyes blazed with intensity, like the stillness of a spider prior to pouncing on its prey. However, Dougal, caught up in the conversation with his friend failed to notice her ire. "Ale, lass, get the ale."

"It's on the side table," came her tart reply.

"Aye lass. Ye need ta get it then do ye not?"

"Don't your legs work? Are you so feeble you're unable to pour it yourself? Would you like me to drink it for you as well?"

Now she got Dougal's full attention. He rose from his chair and leaned over the table towards her with an intimidating glare.

"Ha." She laughed. "Nice try, buddy. But that won't work on me. I've dealt with arrogant, rude men before. They use loud voices, verbal abuse, or their size to intimidate people—particularly women. So sit your *arse* in your chair and let's have a little chat."

Robbed of speech, Dougal sat, dumbfounded.

"Many of you here need a lesson in manners. If you want ale…say please. If you wish to address me, my name is Jo. Do you understand?"

Dougal's face was red with anger. "Who do ye think ye are, *lass*? Yer job is ta serve. It is considered *rude* ta talk ta yer superiors in this way. Maybe Maeve didna explain ta ye how it works here, but ye will nae…"

"Oh, pipe down, Dougal." She raised her voice. "I can put up with serving at the tables. What I object to is the way you talk to me, and the other serving girls. They work hard over long hours and deserve to know they are appreciated, not yelled at like a slave.

If your own children spoke to you in such a tone, I'm quite sure you'd be the first to tell them off. So why do the common courtesies not apply to you? And you," she added, looking pointedly at Connor. "When the soldiers eat in your hall, they are at times rude and often intimidate the serving girls. They grab at their skirts and laugh and joke at their expense. You sit back and let it happen. It's not good enough. When they've drunk too much they act like a bunch of lecherous perverts. It starts with you. Leaders should lead by example. Learn some manners. And get your own bloody ale!"

She turned and marched back toward the servant's entrance, leaving two of Clan MacKay's most powerful warriors staring after her, one with a look of outrage, the other, admiration.

****

"The mighty Laird MacKay gets dressed down by a servant! I had nae idea ye would be providing entertainment for us, MacKay."

Laird Alick Sinclair stood inside the heavy wooden entrance to the great hall. He witnessed Jo's twenty-first century display of feminism and was obviously delighted to be one up on his archrival Connor MacKay.

The Sinclair entourage had barely arrived and were in the bailey stabling their horses. So intent was the 'dispute' in the hall, Connor and Dougal failed to hear the clamour outside.

Before Connor could reply, a terse reprimand came from behind Laird Sinclair. "Alick! We are guests here and only just arrived. Please behave." A beautiful woman stepped around Alick Sinclair, whose face now wore a slight scowl, as she marched, head held high, through the hall directly to the head table. Her long, fair hair was braided and lay over one shoulder, her eyes glowed a startling blue, and her nose was dusted with freckles. She wore the

Sinclair plaid in obvious deference to her husband's clan. Muttering under his breath, Laird Sinclair followed his wife into the hall.

Connor, a grin on his face, watched as she approached. "It seems Alick," he called out, looking over her head, "some men have trouble controlling their head-strong wives."

Megahn stepped up to the dais and stood before her brother. "I do hope ye two will try ta get along for once. Ye are like two children in a schoolroom squabbling over toys." Turning she added. "Hello Dougal…and nae add into their arguments either."

Dougal, a huge grin on his face, moved first to give Meg a bear hug. "Well lass, ye know me, I just do as I am told, or Maeve will tan ma hide." Dougal and Meg laughed like the old comrades they were. They grew up together at Shreave and were close friends.

"And how are Maeve and the bairns?" she inquired.

Their banter continued oblivious to the tension between the lairds. Alick stepped up to the dais and gave Connor the curtest of nods, returned with a cold stare. The two men were a striking pair; one as fair as the other was dark and equally matched for size and strength, both earning their places as clan leaders.

Knowing these two men should not be left to their own devices, Dougal bellowed "Ale!" and then indicated the comfortable chairs surrounding the fire behind the dais.

"Come, brother," coaxed Meg, guiding Connor away from her husband. "Tell me all the news of Shreave." Then as an afterthought, she turned to Dougal. "Ye may want ta add a 'please' after the 'ale' part Dougal, else we may never get anything ta drink. My throat is particularly parched."

Dougal rolled his eyes and called out loud and

clear, "Ale. Please."

A flurry of activity began with the entrance of three servant girls bearing platters of cold meats, fresh bannocks, and wedges of cheese. Jo brought the ale and Dougal ignored her, disgruntled.

Connor appeared indifferent. He would never show emotion before Alick Sinclair. He was also becoming aware of how this annoying woman drew his attention whenever she was about, whether he wanted to or not. But there was one person in the world he could never deceive—Megahn.

The siblings were always close, but since Meg married The Sinclair the relationship with her brother was strained. Meg knew well Connor loved her but his stubborn MacKay pride would not allow him to bend. Following Connor's disastrous betrothal to Kira Sinclair, Meg was in a very awkward position, forever standing between the two, trying to keep the peace.

As food and drink were served, Meg watched her brother watch the woman, who seemed unaware of his scrutiny. "That is a beautiful dress ye wear...I'm sorry, I dinna think we have been introduced." She looked at the well-dressed woman, curiosity plain on her pretty face. "My name is Megahn Sinclair. Ye must excuse the men. Ye are quite right. They have nae manners."

Jo stared at Connor's sister, liking her forthright manner. Without thinking she stuck out her hand, and was surprised when Megahn took it. Memories of the twenty-first century flashed through her mind. Shaking hands was routine in the business world. She never realised until now, how much she missed the simple gesture that put each person on level footing.

The handshake was firm and she knew she was going to like Megahn Sinclair very much. "It's a pleasure to meet you, Megahn. You must be very tired after your long journey. Can I show you to your room, so you can rest and freshen up?"

"Rest, no. Freshen up, yes please."

Without a word to the men, the women disappeared up the staircase heading for the third floor guest apartments, their laugher floating behind them. "Ye have the most unusual accent, Jo. Ye talk faster than a Scotsman."

The three men watched the quick camaraderie between the two women with interest. Their pained expressions indicated all three fostered immediate reservations but were unprepared to verbalise them.

Connor was envious of the comfortable conversation between them. It was something he desired but found difficult to accomplish. Each opportunity to talk with Jo ended with him unsure and confused. He'd never felt unsure around anyone before, and he didn't like it. It frustrated him.

He knew Dougal would be feeling dread as he observed the women ascend the stairs. It was enough Maeve and Meg were headstrong and bossy. Now Jo was displaying the same characteristics. He must ask Maeve if she knew any more information that may help to establish the girl's origins and motives, if any, for being within MacKay boundaries when found. He'd a suspicious feeling Maeve was keeping something from him.

As the two woman disappeared from view, Connor struggled to contain a grin as he watched Alick stare after his sister. He was overprotective of her. She was four months into her pregnancy, and he doted on her to the point, at times, of driving her crazy. Connor spoke little of Megahn, but he listened well, always keeping his ears to ground for news from Castle Wick. Meghan corresponded with Maeve regularly, something he was too stubborn to do.

Left to themselves, the uncomfortable silence was broken by Connor. "Ye were attacked on the way. Where?"

Alick faced his brother-in-law. "Two hours from here, near the western gorge. There were about twenty of them. They were poorly positioned and I think they were just trying ta make a point."

"What point?" asked Dougal

"Ah dinna ken. Seven of my men were hit with arrows. Two fatal. But I think if they waited till the end of the gorge where there is nae protection it would have been a more serious ambush. I nae think they knew the area well."

"Mercenaries," Connor said quietly. "But for what purpose?" He looked questioningly at the other two men.

"If its nae Sutherlands, then The Sutherland is either paying mercenaries or it is someone else with something ta gain by clan warfare," Alick surmised.

"Or a grudge." Connor looked at Alick.

"What are ye suggesting, Laird MacKay?" The tone of Alick's voice turned to ice, the equal of Connor's.

Meeting Alick's stare, Connor replied, "I'm suggesting we look at all possibilities. That is all." A silence hung over the three men; the tension strung like a bow, ready to fire.

Dougal, stepping into Meg's usual role of mediator, made a suggestion. "We should convene this eve, after the meal, ye two and yer highest-ranked men. Each may have something ta offer at the table. Between us all, we shall form a plan."

With a curt nod from either laird, the time was set for the first discussions.

As they left the hall Conner heard Dougal mutter to himself. "It will be a miracle if they dinna do damage ta each other before the day is out."

Connor agreed.

Chapter Fourteen

Jo left Megahn's room over an hour later and went to find Maeve. She was surprised Maeve didn't welcome the visitors, but Meg informed her Maeve was a skilled healer and would be in the barracks tending to Laird Sinclair's injured soldiers. Jo understood little medical knowledge, but compared to seventeenth-century medicine, she felt there may be some useful, basic information she could pass on to her friend. After all, Maeve was the one person who would listen and take her suggestions seriously.

She walked towards the barracks in high spirits. She believed some progress in relation to 'manners' within the castle was made. Progress Meg promised to support whilst visiting. She enjoyed getting to know Connor's forthright sister, and was surprised how free Meg was with information, particularly when it came to her pigheaded brother. Jo was intrigued to hear the ups and downs, triumphs, and war stories surrounding him. Maeve had demonstrated her loyalty and sense of place by not revealing the finer details of Connor's private life and failed relationship with Kira Sinclair. But Meg proved more forthcoming. Perhaps she sensed a connection between them.

Approaching the barracks, Jo became aware she was attracting a good deal of unwanted attention. Some of the Sinclair soldiers stood talking around the entrance to the building. They ogled her, making her feel uncomfortable. She was not unused to men's appreciative looks in her own time. She was a tall, stunning woman, although she could not see it herself. The soldiers did not conceal their lust and it made her falter as she approached the main entrance.

"There are times when a man gets it where he can…if the woman's willing." The comment came from one man in a group of five other soldiers. "Dark haired is ma choice…and long, long legs. The kind that will wrap around ye so ye can sink yer hilt all the way like."

The men were laughing whilst leering at her as she walked towards the doors leading inside the barracks. To gain entrance she must walk between them and the side wall, with just enough room to fit without brushing against the crude gathering. As she almost reached her goal the one with the voice reached out and clamped his right hand around her upper arm in a fierce grip.

"Take your hand off me," she said with a calm intensity she didn't feel. The soldier grinned maliciously as she repeated her request. "I said: Take. Your. Hand. Off. Me. Now!"

The Sinclair soldier increased his grip around her arm, causing a numbing pain to shoot to her fingers as the blood circulation was cut to her hand. He then moved in like lighting and cupped her breast with his left hand, squeezing painfully.

She was shocked by the intimate assault and her first instinct was to struggle free and back away from him. She could smell his putrid breath as he released her arm only to wrap it around her back pulling her hard against him.

"You want it, do ye not? Dinna play coy with me, bitch. Servants spread their legs fer anyone."

She raised her eyes to meet his. It was time to defend herself. The man was strong and able to inflict pain but he was a seventeenth-century man who thought less of women, showed them little respect, and would never believe in a woman's ability to defend herself.

With a smooth, practiced motion, she pulled back her right shoulder, raised her hand and gave the man a 'Connor MacKay special.' The heel of her hand caught the soldier hard, under the nostrils, the upward thrust breaking his nose with a crunching sound. His howl of pain as he buckled was loud enough to draw attention from further afield, across the bailey. The other soldiers standing with the offender skulked away, not wanting to be seen with the perpetrator, should there be ramifications.

She stood motionless for a second, arms relaxed by her side, facing her assailant, expecting him to retaliate, and she wasn't disappointed. He was bested, and insulted by a woman, and any common sense he may have was driven away by the desire to hurt. She could feel his anger as he wiped the blood from his nose with the back of his hand, looking at it in disbelief, his eyes streaming with tears from the painful impact.

The anger became rage as he took two giant steps towards her with his fist drawn back, ready to knock her senseless. For once in her life she was grateful to Andrew Malkin. If her ex-husband hadn't turned her life upside-down she never would have taken up Tae Kwon Do.

As the soldier drove his fist towards her head she side-stepped him, captured his arm as it sailed past, and used his own momentum to drive him to the ground, twisting his arm in such a way he fell hard to his knees. She maintained her hold, her own controlled anger masking the real danger she placed herself in by besting the man in public. She immobilised him and need only twist his arm a fraction to break it. And he knew it.

"Don't *ever* touch me again, or next time I'll break it," she whispered in his ear. "If you touch any of the other *serving* girls, I'll find out. Do you understand me?" Perspiration was dripping down his twisted face, but his belligerent eyes told the true story. This wasn't over. He would not take defeat lightly nor would he ever forget her.

She gave his arm a painful twist, just short of breaking and pushed him to the dirt with her foot. She backed away towards the door hoping beyond hope Maeve and some MacKay soldiers would still be inside. Her heart was racing and her breathing rapid as she ran through the building in search of help.

She spotted Maeve and Neill in a large room containing a dozen pallets, five of which were occupied by the injured Sinclair soldiers.

Maeve looked up as she entered, noticing her friend looking in fear over her shoulder. Concerned, she stood. "What is it Jo?" she said, dropping the patient's hand she was stitching. "What has happened?"

Before she could answer, Neill raced out of the room the way she came in. His boots making haste towards the entrance of the barracks.

Maeve took her hand. "Has someone frightened ye? Ye look like the devil himself is after ye."

She hadn't acknowledged her fear until Maeve mentioned it. She clasped Maeve's hand. The solid link calmed her nerves and her breathing began to slow. "It's…it's, I'm okay. I'm okay," she stammered, unsure if she was trying to convince Maeve or herself.

"Here, sit. Ye look like ye could use a stiff drink."

Subdued, she agreed about the drink and began recounting her altercation with the Sinclair man.

"Would ye recognise him again?"

"You bet. I'm not likely to forget and besides…he has a broken nose!" she replied a little sheepishly.

"Ha. Ye should have put yer knee where it hurt.

That would have fixed him. I will tell ye now, The Sinclair will hear of this—guests or nae. It is unacceptable. I must say though," she continued with a twinkle in her eye. "I wish I could have seen ye in action."

Maeve chuckled and she couldn't help but join in. It was short lived though as she remembered the look on the soldier's face. "He would have hurt me, Maeve. There was something in his eyes."

Neill returned and continued to collect the injured soldier's weapons to hang in the armoury until the men were ready to travel back with the rest of their party.

"Well," inquired Maeve impatiently, hands on hips. "What did ye see?" Jo was also staring at Neill, waiting for a reply.

Did the soldier disappear once she entered the barracks? Or was he still spitting blood in the dirt?

Neill grinned. "Ah dinna ken what he did ta ye, lass, but I think it be fair ta say he got what was coming ta him, ye ken?"

This didn't make her feel any better at all. She assumed her assault was seen as just punishment for his offensive behaviour. Neill failed to even ask what the man did. Now she would be looking over her shoulder, waiting for payback throughout the Sinclair's visit. Instinct told her the soldier wouldn't forget the incident any time soon.

****

She spent two hours with Maeve in the barracks that afternoon, discussing twenty-first century remedies. Maeve hung on to every bit of information she enlightened her with and although sceptical at times, believed in her friend enough to apply some of the remedies discussed—even if she did think it a sinful waste to pour good whisky on a wound.

After leaving Maeve, Jo experienced an uncomfortable afternoon. She kept receiving strange looks from people within the castle. At first she thought maybe her dress was tucked into her stockings or there was a dirty mark on her nose.

On the way to her room before the evening meal she passed Fiona, the young serving girl, near the top of the second floor stairs. The girl lowered her head as she passed, only glancing at her from the corner of her eyes. Frustrated at being the object of other people's notice and not understanding why, she stopped the girl.

"Fiona! It is Fiona, isn't it?" Jo questioned, halting the girl in her descent down the stairs.

"Y...yes, Lady," she stammered.

She was confused by the salutation. Nobody ever called her 'Lady' before. She ignored it though, thinking the girl must not know Jo's position within the castle—whatever that was.

"Fiona, I'm sorry to bother you, but I was wondering if you could help me?"

Nervously, Fiona looked up and down the staircase. When assured they were alone, she replied, "Lady, I dinna think ye should be asking me. It is nae ma place ta serve ye. It be Maeve ye should ask. She will be sure ta help ye."

The young girl was quite flustered, confusing Jo even more as to what was going on.

Exasperated, she countered with, "Fiona, you don't even know what I was going to ask. Why would it be something Maeve should answer and not you? Has it got anything to do with the altercation with the Sinclair soldier this morning?"

Fiona's face spoke volumes. Her eyes were as round as saucers and she looked at Jo in awe. "It has everything ta do with that. Do ye not know, Lady?"

The sound of footsteps coming down from the third floor sent Fiona scurrying off leaving Jo open-mouthed, looking after her retreating back. More confused than ever, she wondered if injuring a visiting soldier of a powerful laird was a terrible crime. Feeling the beginnings of a niggling headache, she rubbed her temples, eyes downcast as she ascended the remaining few steps to her second floor room.

On the landing, she smacked hard into what felt like a brick wall. The breath was momentarily knocked from her. When she raised her head she stared into a pair of belligerent eyes. They turned her blood to ice.

The man she heard called Brian grabbed her by the shoulders to keep her from falling. He stared at her for a moment as if contemplating some decision.

She knew one push would see her tumble down the stairs. As if he read her mind he leaned her backwards whispering, "Ye'd best be careful, lass. Ye never know when an accident can cause harm." He grinned as he shoved her to the side and continued down the stairs without looking back.

A cold shudder passed through her and she hurried into her room bolting the door behind her, grateful for the solitude. She sat on the bed, breathing fast and realised her legs were trembling. She was frightened.

It seemed ridiculous, but although she was physically threatened earlier in the day, she never felt the same extent of fear as now. There was a coldness about the man on the stairs and she sensed he wished her serious harm.

She started to shake, unsure if it was fear or the cold in her room invading her body. For the first time since her arrival at Castle Shreave, she felt scared and alone.

She raised herself from her bed, unbolted the door, and headed for the third floor.

Chapter Fifteen

Jo stood, staring at Connor's chamber door. Instinct led her to his room, but she couldn't decide why. Indecision surrounded her as she stood on the threshold and wondered what she hoped to achieve by seeking out the laird. *Oh...hi there, did you know you have a strange man in your castle?* Or, *I think a man was thinking he might push me down the stairs. Ridiculous,* she thought. Yet still she didn't move from the door. Mustering her courage she knocked on the wooden panels. No reply. She knocked again. No reply. She opened the door.

The laird was nowhere to be seen. She thought herself a fool. For coming to his chamber in the first place and for thinking he would be here at this time of day. He was a busy man who would unlikely dally in his room. But it didn't matter. The moment she crossed the threshold a sense of calm returned. She felt safe, even though alone.

The peat fire burned low in the hearth and she knelt beside it. The warmth soaked into her woollen dress, giving comfort. A thick fur pelt lay beneath her on the floor and content with a moment's peace, she sat, contemplating happenings that led her mind in circles. She lay down on her side; the warmth and a feeling of safety within the chamber made her sleepy. Her reflections of the day dwindled as the security of her location lured her into slumber.

****

"If ye draw attention ta yerself again, I'll have yer throat slit."

"Who's ta do that, then, aye? Ye or yer

mercenaries?"

"Don't turn yer back on me. Ye may find a knife in it."

"What of them, then? Ye have nae control over them. They're berserkers. They do what they want. Tis lucky I were nae killed along with the others."

"Tis lucky MacKay didna do it for ye. Ye fool. Leave the woman alone."

"How long are we going ta play this game?"

"Till the time is right—till we can strike at the heart of the two clans. I will have ma revenge—and all the wealth and power. Bide yer time."

****

A noise disturbed her. Jo was unsure of her surroundings but the intrusion broke her bliss. "Lewis, go away. I'm tired."

Realisation is at times slow to surface, when it does, however, it can be quite a rude awakening. She became aware of the soft fur beneath her cheek and the subtle smells of a peat fire burning close by. She sat up, eyes flashing around the room. His room! *Oh God, how long have I been sleeping in here?* It was dark in the room. The sun already set and only the soft glow of the fire enabled her to see the shadows of the chamber.

The hairs stood on the back of her neck. She was not alone.

"Do ye often fall asleep in other people's rooms?" asked a deep voice.

She swung around to see Connor sitting in one of the chairs by the fire, his feet but inches away from where her head lay. His fathomless eyes, as usual, gave away none of his thoughts. How long did he watch her sleep? "I'm sorry…I…it's just…it was warm and I was scared. Oh, never mind." She stood to leave the room, mumbling and shamed to have been found sleeping on the floor.

Connor stood to block her path, reaching out to

steady her as she wobbled. Fear marked her face and annoyance flickered on his, although not for the reasons she thought.

"Ye nae have ta be afraid of me," he said tersely.

She replied, "I'm not afraid of you." It comforted her to know she wasn't. Even standing here, caught out trespassing in his chamber *again,* she felt no fear. "If anything, I'm embarrassed. You always seem to catch me at my worst," she said, while trying to flatten down strands of hair, wisping around her face, tickling her nose. Her dress showed the creases of a long, undisturbed sleep.

Reaching his hand towards her, he tucked an errant strand of hair behind her ear and said quietly, "I would nae say ye were at your worst when I last caught ye out. I would say ye were at first, at yer best, before ye knew I was there. I thought ye were a water nymph." He flushed, obviously not intending to be so honest.

Her face flamed at the thought of the pool incident. "Please, I'd appreciate it if you wouldn't remind me of that meeting. I'm sorry I hurt you, but you scared me and..."

"I dinna want yer apology," he said angrily, raising his voice. "I want...never mind." He dropped his hands and took a step back, giving her ample space to leave the room. She didn't.

"What is it you want?" she asked, her eyes never leaving his. He was so handsome. Every time she looked at him it gave her stomach butterflies. His hair was loose, with just the two small braids edging his face. She longed to run her fingers over the five o'clock shadow on his chin.

Why was it every time they spoke, they fell towards argument or discontent? "Tell me what you want Connor, because I'm tired of feeling uncomfortable around you. I'm tired of people staring at me. Today was the worst of all. I feel lost and..."

Before she could utter another word, Connor closed the space between them, cutting off her rambling. He held her face between his massive hands like she was a precious gem. "Do I make ye feel uncomfortable?" His soft tone and breath caressed her face.

"Yes," she whispered. "I don't know what you're thinking when you do this to me."

"Do what?"

"Touch me."

"Is it important ta know what I am thinking?" The pad of his thumb ran over her cheek. His eyes searched the fine details of her face.

"Yes. You're a walking contradiction and..." Before she could utter another word, Connor dipped his head seeking her lips. Raising her head in response, she took what he was prepared to give, yearning for the warmth of his body against hers. He kissed her with slow intent.

Everything around them ceased to exist. His lips tasted and plundered hers, drinking in her very being. He nuzzled his way to her right ear, breathing in and out on her neck, creating tingling sensations down her spine. He sought her scent, and cemented it firmly in his mind. Connor kissed his way down her neck, revelling in the taste and texture of her skin.

She let out an involuntary sigh that made him smile. She was enjoying this as much as he. Connor was gratified.

His hands rested on her shoulders, his warm touch a kind of foreplay in itself. She drew her head back to give Connor better access to her neck, her hands rising to rest on his chest, clinging onto two handfuls of MacKay plaid. Her breathing became heavier as her whole body reacted to the intimate onslaught.

"Lavender," came his whispered voice. For an instant, she wondered if she heard it at all. Her body was reeling with a hundred sensations.

"What?" she whispered.

"Lavender, ye smell of lavender." Connor pushed aside the shoulder of her dress, exposing pale skin. He caressed it lightly, following his finger with his lips.

She closed her eyes and let the sensations overcome her. She forgot the strength a man possessed and the feelings of safety, when his arms circled you as Connor's did now. He crushed her to him, and lowered his mouth to hers to claim another hungry kiss. Their tongues met on equal ground as they duelled, tasting, savouring the flavour of each other.

She raised her hands to his hair, running her fingers into his thick, dark locks. She felt his arousal hard against her soft belly and realised where this was leading.

Connor sensed her hesitation and pulled back. "What is it?"

"I'm not sure..." She pulled away from his warmth, creating a space between them. "I don't understand this. I'm confused. I don't understand you. You seem so different here, now, in your room, but out there." She pointed towards the door. "You don't acknowledge my presence. I'm invisible."

Connor took a deep breath, ran a hand through his hair, and stepped back. He shook his head, letting her know he was unprepared to analyse his own behaviour at the moment, and turned towards the fire, leaning his arms out on the mantle.

She was unsure what to say or do and felt she couldn't continue without a better idea of where he was coming from. It was like she was chasing a shadow—impossible to catch.

Her instinct was to reach out and run her hands

over his back to soothe whatever emotion he was feeling but the contact seemed too personal, like crossing a boundary yet to be charted, a ridiculous notion considering the contact between them over the last few minutes.

But there it was.

There lay the problem.

A cavern separated them, an unknown hole that should be filled with understanding, knowledge, and details of each other. It was like they skipped all the inbetween stuff and raced to the finale.

"What was it ye said ta me earlier, when I first came inta the room?" Connor pushed away from the mantelpiece and turned to face her. The impregnable mask, like Jekyll and Hyde, slipped over him again. She sighed, feeling wearier than ever, despite her impromptu nap. Rubbing her hand across her forehead she tried to recall what she said earlier. "That I'm tired of feeling uneasy around you."

"Nae. Not that."

"That I'm sick of people staring at me. I don't suppose you can enlighten me on that score can you?" she prompted, resigned to the fact they were back to square one.

"Nae," was the curt reply

Her headache from earlier was coming back with avengeance. "I can't remember, Connor." She massaged her temples, trying to alleviate her tension. Connor took a step towards her and reached for her hands. She went to pull away but he took a firm hold and lowered them to her side. He resumed where she left off, stroking his thumbs over her temples.

Another change—the man was a walking contradiction. She'd never figure him out. As the headache subsided with his gentle massage, her legs became like jelly. All she wanted was to curl up in a ball, shut her eyes, and go back to sleep. But Connor prompted for an answer.

"Ye said something about being scared?"

This made her remember her encounter on the stairs. "Oh, that. It's probably nothing."

"Nothing aye? What was it, Jo-Anne that scared ye so? Sending ye ta ma chamber?"

She was surprised by the use of her full name, but liked the way it rolled off his tongue. She told him about the incident on the stairs.

"Would ye know him again if ye saw him?"

"I would. But there's no need for a line-up." Connor looked puzzled at the remark. "I've heard others in the castle call him Brian, Brian Doubios."

Connor's face turned to stone and his hands dropped, having worked magic on her headache. "Are ye sure of this?"

"Yes, why?" The intense look on Connor's face gave her pause.

"Tell nobody what ye've just told me. Do ye understand?"

She nodded. "Should I be concerned? Does he have something against me?"

"I nae can tell. But I will find out." His chilled tone made her shudder. Connor moved to the door but stopped short and turned towards her. "If ever ye feel scared, for whatever reason, it nae matters—ye come ta me. Do ye understand? If ye canna find me, ye go ta Dougal. If nae Dougal, ye come ta this room. Nobody would search for ye here." He stared for a long moment, his eyes holding hers, then left the chamber, leaving her staring at the closed door.

Chapter Sixteen

Jo returned to her room in a state of confusion. Laird Connor MacKay befuddled her emotions. But she was certainly drawn to him. Their relationship seemed part of some mysterious jigsaw puzzle with the pictures yet to be drawn on the pieces.

It was quite some time since she felt the tingling of desire spiral through her. If she were honest with herself, she would admit Andrew never kissed her in such a way or made her feel like a real woman. It was a sad thing that at thirty-four, she perhaps still hadn't experienced real passion.

Still mulling over their encounter when she entered her room on the second floor, she was surprised to find new clothes yet again laid out upon the bed. There were five dresses in all, with matching wraps, underclothes, and soft leather shoes. She fingered the soft fabrics. They were of even finer quality than the previous two dresses Maeve provided. What on earth was going on?

Never one to look a gift horse in the mouth, she changed into a teal green garment that fell softly to her ankles. The low cut bodice showed off her bosom quite daringly. She slipped on the matching shoes and gave her hair a quick brush, wishing for a long mirror to see the complete picture. She hadn't any idea how attractive and desirable she looked. Longing to try on the other dresses but aware of the time and her duty to the high table (and the need for an urgent conversation with Maeve), she reluctantly left her room and went down to the great hall.

As she entered, Maeve met her at the bottom of

the stairs. "Oh, aye, ye look beautiful in the green. I knew it would suit yer eyes. Ye'll turn heads when ye…ooohff."

Jo grabbed Maeve's arm and manoeuvred her into the linen room out of sight of the Sinclair and MacKay soldiers filling the hall. The evening meal was but minutes from being served. Maeve couldn't contain an exasperated giggle as Jo dragged her into the enclosure.

"What's going on with the clothes, Maeve? What are you up to?"

"I nae know what ye mean, Jo. What is it ye think I've…?"

"Don't give me that. People have been staring at me as if I've grown horns. They're whispering about me but I don't know why. Tell me what's going on before I blow a gasket. I've put up with enough for one day. Attacked at the barracks, pushed down the stairs, well almost, and Connor…Connor, oh, I don't know."

She slumped against the wall after her speech, running her hands across her face. Maeve stepped towards her friend and frowned. "Who pushed ye down the stairs?"

"Almost. Almost pushed me down the stairs."

"It matters nae. Who was it?"

She was about to answer Maeve when she remembered Connor's instruction to tell nobody.

"It's unimportant. Connor knows about it. Just keep it to yourself. Anyway, that's not what's got me so riled up. Why am I drawing so much attention?" She flapped her arms around in exasperation. "Fiona almost panicked when I asked her."

Maeve pulled her over to a wooden bench along the opposite wall of the small room and made her sit down. "Ye haven't heard, have ye?"

"Heard what?" She paused then said, "It's about the Sinclair soldier isn't it? Was I supposed to let him get away with being such a pig? Let a man treat me with such disrespect? I wouldn't put up with this at home and you can't expect me to put up with it here."

Maeve started, "The Sinclair soldier..."

"I knew it! I should have just kept my hands to myself." She rose and paced the small enclosure. "I'm in trouble aren't I? I should have walked away but I couldn't. He would have gotten away with it."

Maeve shook her head. "Ye have no idea, have ye? Ye..."

She cut Maeve off again. "Am I expected to apologise? I won't. Not to that creep! Or is it Laird Sinclair that I've offended in some way?"

"For the love of our Lord, will ye shut up!"

Maeve's outburst got the desired response. Jo shut up.

"It's nae ye, fool. Whatever made ye think *ye* did something wrong, never mind, dinna answer that. It nae matters." Maeve walked over and stood in front of an expectant Jo and continued, "It be what Connor did. Not ye, although I must say," Maeve added light heartedly, "What ye did caused quite a stir aboot the castle. It's the soldier. The one ye totted. Connor saw the whole thing from the lower rampart. Connor was already on his way down, when ye raced inside the barracks. Fiona was the one who saw the look on his face as he stormed through the great hall and outside. The poor wee lass nearly wet herself."

Maeve chuckled to herself. Jo was still coming to terms with the fact she wasn't in trouble. "Anyway," continued Maeve, "Connor finished the man off for ye." Maeve stood quietly, waiting for Jo to comprehend her meaning. However, she was still unsure what Maeve implied.

"What do you mean? He finished him off?" Then, "Oh, my God. You mean he...?"

"Aye. Connor left the man unconscious in the bailey. He was carted off on a litter. Laird Sinclair was fuming over the attack and they say there was a huge argument. But Dougal explained ta Alick. Meg was furious. She was heard to say 'I told ye so' to her husband."

Mixed emotions whirled through her. She was relieved to hear the man was dealt with, but she was unsure how to react to the fact that Connor publicly defended her. Would he do this for any female within Castle Shreave? He was laird after all and ultimately everyone's protector.

But she'd a sneaking suspicion this was not the norm. Connor's actions wouldn't have raised such a stir if it was something he would normally do. She'd no idea about discipline procedures, but she believed the laird didn't go around dishing out punishment every time someone was threatened.

Maeve spoke again, interrupting Jo's thoughts. "Do ye now realise why there has been so much talk within the walls? Connor defended yer honour. He would nae do this personally if he was nae making a claim on ye."

"I don't understand. What should I do?" she asked.

Maeve smiled, tucking a loose lock of hair back behind Jo's ear. "Ye dinna have ta do anything. Just be yerself. Let fate guide yer journey." Maeve paused, as if pondering her next words with care. "He's a good man, a hard man, but ye can trust him. Try trusting yerself, too."

Jo sighed and hugged the other woman with affection.

"Ye look a picture tonight in that gown. There will be more than one set of eyes on ye this evening."

Jo pulled back, looking down at her dress. "About the new dresses, Maeve; there was nothing wrong with the others you made for me."

"Aye, I know. They will do for someone else now. These are far more appropriate for sitting at the head table."

Lost for words, Jo stared incredulously at Maeve.

"Ha, I can tell that bit of news has surprised ye. Nae me though."

"Why would I sit at the head table? Everyone will stare at me even more. If this is a joke, it's a bad one. Come on Maeve..."

"Hold yer horses. Ye have been invited ta sit there."

"By who?"

"Meg. She insisted."

"Oh no! I'm not up for this, really I'm not." Jo's head wagged back and forth in denial.

"Ye'll be fine. Ye'll sit near her so dinna worry. She be a fine lass. Ye know that already though. She told me ye both chatted fer a time."

Feeling a little better, Jo smoothed down her dress and tucked the errant strands of hair back behind her ears.

"Ye nae need ta do that. Ye look beautiful."

"Oh boy, oh boy…it'll be fine," she whispered to herself in an attempt to calm her nerves and bolster her courage.

"Aye, now. That be more like it," encouraged Maeve. "Oh, by the way, what's a gas-ket?"

Confused Jo asked, "What do you mean? What gasket?"

"Ye said it before. Ye said, 'tell me what is going on before I blow a gas-ket.' " Jo didn't recall saying it.

"Oh, a gasket? It's er…cars have them and…oh, not now Maeve," she blustered, pacing nervously.

The sounds from the great hall rose. Loud cheering indicated the two lairds took their seats.

"Come then, Jo. We are late." Maeve stepped

back to allow Jo to lead the way.

"So, I just walk out there and sit at the end of the table next to Meg?"

"Nae, Jo. Meg sits at the centre of the table."

A feeling of dread washed over her. "Umm, Maeve. Who will sit on the other side of me then?"

"Why, Connor of course."

****

To ensure a male, female ratio on the head table, Jo sat in the place of honour on Laird Connor MacKay's right and Meg on his left. Laird Alick Sinclair sat on her other side. She felt dwarfed by the two giant warriors. Despite needing to lean slightly across Connor, conversation flowed easily between her and Meg.

Connor barely uttered a word during dinner. If not for the presence of the two women chatting amicably, tension between the two lairds would have been far more palpable. Dougal engaged Alick in conversation, with the assistance of Maeve. However, Father Michael, seated on Meg's other side tempted Meg into a conversation on theology. This left Connor and her with no one to converse with but each other.

Breaking an uncomfortable silence, she opened up the conversation. "I believe I need to thank you." Unable to meet Connor's eyes, lest it evoke warm memories of their encounter in his chamber, she directed her words towards her plate. Throughout her chat with Meg she'd been aware of his presence—aware of his roughened, masculine fingers, as they tore meat from the bones on his trencher. A trencher she was obliged to share. Mesmerised by his lips as he drank from the goblet, she could not stop herself imagining what they would taste like flavoured with claret. She admitted to herself she found Connor extremely desirable.

But more than this, she wanted him to want her

in ways she didn't think he could.

Maeve said to trust her own feelings and follow them. She decided it was time to do just that. Heck, the man turned her to molten lava each time he so much as looked at her.

"Thank me for what?" asked Connor, turning to face her.

"I believe you finished a job for me this afternoon." Sensing Connor was watching her, she forced herself to turn and look at him. Taking her meaning, he wasn't able to suppress a grin.

The breath stopped in her throat.

She'd never seen him smile before. With his white, even teeth and smile lines around his eyes, he was beautiful. His hair fell roguishly across one eye, but it failed to hide their sparkle.

"Yer welcome. But I would have said, Jo-Anne, that ye finished the job quite nicely by yerself." His gaze never left her eyes.

"I...I was afraid I would have to watch my back. I didn't think he would forget what I did."

Connor's eyes became hard and his smile vanished. "Ye would nae have ta watch yer back—I would have."

It was spoken so adamantly, a lump formed in her throat. Without even thinking she reached under the table with her left hand and grabbed a handful of his plaid, squeezing it hard in her fist.

Feeling it, he lowered his right hand and placed it over hers, gathering her petite fist in his large one, gently squeezing back. "Yer welcome," was all he said.

****

With the meal over, the entertainment began. There was singing and dancing with a set of bagpipes being put to great use. There were small groups where MacKay and Sinclair soldiers mixed well together while others remained with their own groups, their loyalty to their lairds foremost.

The piper was about to strike up a new set when young Colin came racing into the hall, anxiety written across his young face. All conversation ceased as he jumped to the dais in front of his master.

"Laird MacKay, it is the village of Drumfold. It has been burnt ta the ground. The survivors have just arrived in the bailey." Turning to Maeve he said, "There be plenty hurt, Lady. They need ye."

Without another word, the diners at the high table rose and exited the hall, followed by the soldiers of both clans. They made haste for the bailey, Maeve diverting to her chamber to retrieve her herbal kit.

In the coming hours the full story became clear. It was the raiders.

Drumfold village, two hours ride east of Shreave Castle, was attacked after dark. All cottages were torched, catching many by surprise. Some, unable to escape, were incinerated within their homes. Many were children asleep in their cots. Some were still unaccounted for, whilst others would bear the physical and emotional scars of torture or rape for the remainder of their lives.

Litters were set up in the barracks to hold the injured whilst soldiers ferried them in from the horses and carts used as transport. Trancelike, Jo moved from cot to cot. There were several cramped rows filled with pain and suffering. Young, old, male, and female, it made no difference to the raiders. The majority of the injuries were burns. She'd never before smelt burnt flesh. The scent would be with her for the rest of her life. With no antibiotics, and Maeve's limited medical knowledge, Jo knew many wouldn't survive. Those who did would be maimed for life.

She explained the traditional method of

applying butter to burns would cook the injuries further and Maeve was grateful for the advice. She followed Maeve's orders as best she could, dressing wounds with clean linen and placing cold compresses on the lighter burns, attempting to ease some of the pain. Maeve was kept busy with her herbs making poultices, creams, and sleeping drafts. Father Michael, also known as a healer, tended to those he could help.

As the hours passed, Jo walked along the cots with a kind word here and there, or holding a cup of water to another's lips, assisting Maeve with a variety of surgeries when required.

She came across a young woman no older than seventeen who lay on her side facing the wall. She squeezed in to offer her a drink and saw one of the girl's eyes was swollen shut, her lip torn and bleeding. But it was the vacant look on her pale face that concerned her most. She sat next to her, reached out her hand to move a stray hair from the girl's face, then offered her the cup. "Hey, there," she said softly. "Are you thirsty?" No response. "My name is Jo. Is there anything I can get you?" Nothing.

On closer inspection, she saw her torn clothes. Her bodice was ripped down the centre and she wore only one shoe. Feeling helpless, she decided to fetch a cold cloth and at least bathe the girl's battered face. As she stood she heard a soft voice. "Nae. Dinna go."

"I won't be long," she replied to the girl, relieved she spoke. "I'm just going over there." She pointed across the room. "To get a cloth to bathe your face, okay?" The girl nodded and Jo hurried back and placed the soothing cloth over the girl's eye. "Tell me your name."

"Christine."

She was sixteen years old.

Jo spent some time bathing her, then placed a clean sheet over her for a modicum of privacy. During the time the girl was silent, resigned to her ministrations. Jo tried hard not to show her horror as she wiped the blood from the bite marks covering the girl's bruised neck, breasts, and nipples. She also washed between her legs.

Christine cried with the stinging pain of the soft tissue injuries and simply said, "I dinna think Robbie MacBride will want ta marry me now."

****

It was close to dawn when Father Michael ordered Jo to her bed, but she argued, "If Maeve can keep going, so can I."

Maeve shook her head. "No, Jo. There is naught ye can do now. Most who can are resting. I'll be up ta see Dougal myself in a trice." Maeve picked up a bucket full of bloodied rags and walked over to her. "Ye can be of no help tomorrow if ye nae get some rest. Tell Dougal I am on ma way, too."

She agreed, left the barracks, and took her first clean breath of air. It was cool, crisp, and filled her lungs. She felt like a junkie, having a long awaited fix. She witnessed horrific scenes in movies. It gave the illusion 'movie things' never happened in real life. But tonight it was all too factual. The gore, the uselessness, the pain and suffering, the heartache of holding a hand as the life slipped from its owner, the helplessness of never being able to do enough.

In her time, painkillers could do wonders. Here, the pain killed. She tried to swallow down the lump in her throat, but the tears began to fall—tears of sorrow and horror and tears for a time and place away from the carnage of the Scottish Highlands.

She longed for the regulated existence of twenty-first century Australia. She longed for the simple safety rules of pedestrian crossings, traffic lights, local by-laws, and the stricter ones that punished arsonists, murderers, and rapists. She missed the safety of her own home.

Her sobs began in earnest until above her tears she became aware of footfalls nearby—a soldier heading for the ramparts. She sneaked away seeking solitude, and found the stump at the side of the kennels. She sat for a long time in the silence, just breathing, looking at the stars and trying to organise her thoughts. It was some time later she began to shiver despite the heavy cloak she wore. The faint glimmer of pinks and oranges brushed the sky as dawn bloomed on the horizon.

As she dragged her weary body across the bailey back to the castle, all was quiet. Extra guards patrolled the ramparts, but apart from this there was little movement outside. She entered through the main hall door where a smattering of soldiers talked around the fires along the sidewall. Others lay sleeping amongst the rushes on the floor, their plaids wrapped around them for warmth; their beds in the barracks, being used by the dying or injured.

As she neared the steps to the second floor, she walked past a torch, burning in a wall sconce. The torch cast its light over her and she looked down at herself. She could see the remnants of a nightmare evening, making her stomach turn over and bile rise in her throat. Her hands and fingernails were encrusted with dried blood. There were numerous dried patches on her new gown—blood of the victims—and if she breathed through her nose she could smell the stench of death.

She thought she'd no tears left, but was mistaken. As they ran down her face she was caught by an uncontrolled sob as she stood like a statue, arms out to her sides, unsure where to hold them. Her shoulders shook and she walked up the stairs, unaware of what she was doing, her mind numbingly vacant and bone-deep weariness taking hold. Approaching her bedroom door she heard hurried footsteps echo along the corridor. The shadows came closer, and then out of the darkness two faces appeared. Connor and Neill stood, breathless, staring at her. Wearily she wondered why they were running.

"Where have ye been, lass?" It was Neill who spoke, searching her face for an answer. "Maeve said ye left the barracks long ago. We have been searching for ye."

Trembling, she replied, "I've been breathing." She turned from Neill's confused expression and focused on Connor who missed not a single detail of her physical and emotional state.

He nodded at Neill, "Tell the others." Neill departed to seek out Maeve, Dougal, and a host of others in the search party.

Connor's panic abated. She was here and she was safe. He stepped towards her, placing his hand on either side of her face, noting her red nose, swollen eyes, and the grey circles beneath them. Her arms dangled limp at her sides.

The dark shadows of the hallway made his wide shoulders seem even larger.

"Are ye hurt, Jo-Anne?"

"No."

"Has someone bothered ye?"

"Yes," she said fervently. Connors hands tightened on her face. "It bothered me when I saw a four-year-old child get his leg amputated. It bothered me when I peeled the blisters off a face that will never be recognised again." Her face crumpled as she told each tale. "It bothered me I couldn't do anything in this godforsaken time that could make a difference. And most of all," she said loudly, "it bothers me the animals who did this are still out there, running free." She breathed heavily, her grief and anger escalating. "Where I come from, Connor, I feel safe. It's nothing like this...this carnage."

He did not comprehend all she said, but he knew her grief was real. It mirrored his own. This, and other emotions he gave no time to dwell upon. He and Dougal spent most of the night meeting with The Sinclair and his captains. A plan was formed to hunt down the killers and preparations were being made as he spoke. Most of the MacKay and Sinclair soldiers would be mounted and gone by the coming nightfall. "We will find them. They will pay."

She didn't doubt him for a second.

As her sobbing subdued, she was aware of the warmth of Connor's hands on her cheeks. Drawing on his strength was all that kept her from falling to her knees. "Connor, hold me."

His arms embraced her, pulling her to his chest, like bands of steel about her back. He'd never felt this way before. Never wanted to hold another woman the way her wanted to hold her. And once he held her, he didn't want to let go.

Without warning, he lifted her into his arms and carried her to the third floor. He did not stop in his chamber but strode through to the study and entered the tunnel behind the tapestry.

She cuddled, exhausted, in his arms until the sulphuric smell assailed her nostrils.

Connor lowered her feet to the floor of the cave and steadied her before letting go. She looked at the warm pool and burst into tears. "Thank you."

Connor lifted the hem of her ruined dress and eased it over her head. He removed her underclothes, stockings, and shoes and picked her up again as if she were but a feather. He lowered her into the pool and watched as she sank into the depths, disappearing under the churning water, shadowed by the dim light from the wall sconce.

As before, an instant of panic licked over him. He waited, ready to jump in and search for her, when she surfaced at the far end of the pool. She stood in the water looking at her hands, shoulders trembling as the tension and sorrow washed away in the water. Engrossed in cleansing herself, she was unaware of his dark eyes following her every movement.

Connor stepped back to afford her a scrap of privacy, but he kept watch. He knew he should have left and waited for her in his chamber. But once she was within the pool, he was at first concerned about her state of mind, unprepared to leave her alone; but as she moved through the water her every curve, every movement, mesmerised him. He wished for nothing more than to enter the pool along side her, enfold her in his arms, and wash away all the heartache of the night. The yearning rose from so deep within his soul it unnerved him.

He could see numbing tiredness enfolded her, but hoped some of the grief washed away with the swirling waters. She needed comfort, contact, the warmth and company of another. She turned to find him, sitting with his back to the cave wall, watching her.

Her words when they came were quiet. "Come join me."

Connor took a deep breath, knowing what it was she offered. The temptation was great. His body wanted nothing more than to enter the pool and couple with her. But he would not take advantage of her this way. Not tonight.

As he spoke, he hardly recognised his own voice. It lost volume and came out in a hoarse whisper, "Nae tonight."

She nodded in understanding. "You won't leave me here alone?"

"Nae. We shall go when ye are ready."

Chapter Seventeen

"Ye stupid fool! What happened?"

"It was nae ma fault. They were told ta torch a few huts."

"Torch a *few* huts! Now we shall have the combined clans after our hides. Ye messed all our plans ta hell, ye stupid son of a bitch."

"Do ye think ye could have done better? Yer berserkers—they do what they like, when it suits them."

"The clans shall be stronger than ever now. They were supposed ta hate and fight *each other*." The man paced back and forth beneath the shadows of the castle wall which concealed them from soldiers patrolling the ramparts. "I have bided ma time long enough. I want my revenge."

"What do you suggest we do then? Burn down the castle…ha, ye would never get out alive."

A calmness overcame the other man and he stopped pacing. His face showed an evil grin and surety of conviction.

"What? What are ye thinking now?"

"If I can nae burn the castle…I will take from it all that makes it their home."

"What the hell do ye mean?"

"I will strike out at the one weakness they have."

"Ye be making nae sense."

"I've always fancied splitting a *lady* or two with ma cock. Ha, they took mine…I'll take theirs."

****

"Dinna give me that, I was more than capable of

helping. Ye would wrap me up and lock me in ma chamber until spring if ye got yer way."

"Aye, I would lass."

"For the love of heaven, Alick, I am pregnant, I dinna have the festering plague." Meg strode back and forth across their chamber, furious Alick forbid her to assist with the wounded villagers. He assured her there were more than enough able bodies to cope with the casualties. Then Meg discovered Maeve hadn't returned to the castle until almost dawn, and Jo, after going missing for over an hour was exhausted, and Father Michael worked until the rooster crowed.

"What sort of a husband do ye think I am, letting ye work yerself ta the bone? I am laird."

"I don't give a bleeding pig..."

"That's enough." Alick raised his voice. "Ye should mind yer words. Ye sound like some tavern harpy."

"Oh, and I suppose ye know what one sounds like, aye? And if ye intend ta chastise me fer ma tongue, I would suggest ye lead by example."

"Oh, hell, Meg...arrg." Alick realised he proved her right by swearing himself.

"Ha! Got ye."

Alick laughed. His wife, with a mind of her own, drove him crazy sometimes. She would bow to no man—including a laird. It was the thing about her he loved the most and the reason for most of their arguments. He loved Megahn MacKay from the moment he saw her pert nose, freckles, and long blond hair, all presented as a voluptuous, assertive women.

"I love ye, Megahn Sinclair," Alick said. "I will nae see ye become ill from overwork when there are plenty of able bodies ta do it for ye."

Meg walked into his arms, reaching her own up around his neck. "They are my people, Alick. As a bairn I rode ta the village of Drumfold with Connor and Dougal. The people there are part of ma clan; a part of me. I *need* ta do something ta help. Do ye nae see?" Anguish flooded her voice.

Alick did see. She knew it. Her loyalty to Clan MacKay was strong despite swearing fealty to him when she made her vows and became his wife. A woman of strong passions who knew her own mind; she loved Clan Sinclair but would never deny her past.

He dropped his head to her lips and gave her a long possessive kiss.

"What was that fer?" she asked, running her hands through his thick blond locks.

"Part payment...fer ma leniency."

"Part payment? Oh! Well then, what else can I do for ye, Laird Sinclair?" She grinned, running her hands over his chest between his plaid and the shirt beneath. She wanted nothing more than to strip him to allow her better access to his entire body.

"I can think of many things that would serve yer laird well right now." He picked her up and placed her on the bed and ran a hand lazily down her heavy breasts and the soft swell of their unborn child.

"I would be honoured ta serve ye all ye like, Laird Sinclair. I will do ma duty by ye with as much enthusiasm as I can manage." Meg's face was alight with mischief and passion. It felt good to escape the sadness of the preceding night, even if just for a stolen moment.

With that said, Alick threw her skirts over her head causing her to laugh and giggle. Neither heard the discreet knock upon their chamber door. The servant went to knock again but heard the noise within and decided later may perhaps be a better time and left, chuckling to herself.

****

After a fitful rest Jo went down to the great hall

at mid-morning. She suffered a restless sleep, but it was to be expected. The tumultuous events of the night left a shadow over her heart. She was scared by the stark horror of seventeenth-century life and its lawlessness. She longed for June's practical company and the stability of a twenty-first century career, with superannuation, sick leave, and holiday pay; knowledgeable doctors and hospitals with radiology departments and maternity wards; supermarkets, fresh fruit, and vegetables, toilet paper, toothbrushes, and running water—so many things once taken for granted.

She also wondered at Connor's intentions. Did he have feelings for her other than curiosity or lust? A servant on the stairs bobbed a curtsy and said, "Lady." It was a title of authority and rank. She deserved neither, so what were the thoughts of other castle residents? Did they know something she didn't, or were they as unsure as she about her status?

In all honesty she thought she at least knew the answer to one of these issues rattling around her mind. Connor demonstrated his honourable intentions the previous night. He wanted her, she could see so in his eyes. She wanted him, too, and he could have taken advantage of her but was grateful for his courtesy. He threw extra peat on the fire and tucked her up safe and dry in his own bed. She'd no idea where he spent the night, or if he got any sleep at all. She desired nothing more now than to find and thank him.

In the great hall, tables were cleared and fresh rushes covered the floor, while a few servants swept the hearths. Feeling hollow in the stomach, she decided on breakfast before searching for Connor. Perhaps one of the kitchen staff would know his location.

As she followed the narrow corridor to the

scullery, she wondered who designed the building with so many twisting corridors and passageways. A further extension, overlooking the lake was planned (she was still unable to navigate the existing building without directions) and she was surprised that Connor designed and drew plans for the new wing himself. Architecture—another snippet of information proving how little she knew the laird.

She still found it hard to believe, her once ordinary existence had turned into such an extraordinary, and at times frightening, escapade. Would she ever get used to all this and how long would she stay? Forever?

In the kitchens she was surprised to find Meg chatting to Mrs. MacBain at the large weathered table dominating the room. Mrs. MacBain was giving an excited narration on her daughter's birthing of a fifth child. Not wishing to intrude, nor feeling like company, she stopped at the entrance but before she could turn away Meg saw her and beckoned her to join them.

"Mrs. Mac, could we have another goblet of this wonderful brew for Jo please?" To Jo, Meg explained, "It be heavenly, warm, spiced mead. I have nae tasted it in such a long time. I have missed Mrs. Mac's cooking soooo much."

Jo sat on the bench opposite Meg to sip the delicious brew herself, and broke apart a fresh bannock spread with lashings of butter. "I didn't realise how hungry I was until now. It's lovely food, Eva. Thank you."

Eva MacBain smiled and crossed the room to fuss about the pots and pans, giving the two women some privacy.

Meg studied Jo, annoyance and concern on her face as the shadows beneath her eyes and the pale skin told their story. "I heard ye had a long night. I am sorry I was...unable to assist ye. My brute of a husband thinks pregnant woman should be closeted for the entire nine months."

"It was a tragic, sad night but there was nothing more you could have done, Meg."

"Aye, but I *wanted* ta be there."

"I understand. They are your people, Meg. I'm going over to the barracks myself after I've eaten. You could walk over with me if you like."

"Aye. Thank ye. I will come when ye have broken yer fast."

The two women gave thanks to Eva and headed to the barracks to tend the wounded. If comfort was all they could offer, then it was better than nothing.

Chapter Eighteen

One month later on a cool, starry night, Jo stood on the ramparts staring at the moon-lit horizon. A heavy woollen shawl lay across her shoulders, keeping the chill from her skin. The moonlight shimmered like diamonds over the water of the lake. Each breath produced a plume of condensation cascading before her, and wisps of hair tickled her face as the slight breeze pinked her nose.

She'd discovered this spot—her spot—on the ramparts quite by accident. After all was done for the sick and injured following the Drumfold siege, she needed solitude. She wandered about the castle exploring, getting lost more often than not, until she found another secret door in Connor's chamber leading to the rampart.

She bathed every day in the laird's pool, entering his chamber with care to avoid problems with propriety. As the onset of the winter penetrated the castle walls, she also slept in the laird's chamber, believing it a waste for a fire to burn with nobody to benefit from its heat. She curled up on the fur rugs before the blaze every night, the warmth of the burning peat soaking into her bones. What she wished for more than ever was for Connor to come home. She never forgot how it felt to be held in his arms; to feel the warmth of his body close to hers. Most nights, he invaded her dreams.

Connor, Alick, Dougal, and a band of fifty MacKay and Sinclair warriors left Castle Shreave the morning after Drumfold fell. The initial plan was to salvage what they could of Drumfold crops, rebuild huts, and deliver the necessary items for residents to survive the fast approaching winter.

Then the well-armed war party would go hunting. Their sport involved the raiders who attacked the Sinclair entourage as they travelled to Castle Shreave, followed by the callous murders and destruction at Drumfold.

Standing on the rampart, content with her own company, her thoughts turned to the previous weeks and how she'd flourished within the protection of the clan.

Connor's abrupt departure saddened her. At first with regret to realise he left without her having the chance to thank him for his kindness, but as the days moved along, she was grateful for the space to sort her feelings and settle down after her initial confused entrance to this century.

Things moved so swiftly and her perception cleared easily without Connor's brooding presence—yet she eventually realised the castle felt empty without him.

Meg and Maeve became her close friends and she cherished their support. As her pregnancy advanced, Meg desired to return to Castle Wick, but there was little time to escort her following the Drumfold burning. She was safe yet restless. Though surrounded by her own people, Castle Shreave was no longer her home.

She smiled as she remembered a conversation with Meg a few weeks ago. She'd asked, "Meg, are you sure you're not having twins? You look to be popping out quite a lot for five months?"

"Well...I would say I am probably six-and-a-half months."

"But I thought you said..."

"Aye, I did, I did. But ye see, and if ye breath a word of this ta Alick, I will have ye burned at the stake... I lied." Following her confession a soft blush crept up Meg's face.

"You *lied*?"

"Well, I knew Alick would sooner wrap me up in furs and tuck me away for the nine months, or at least the months I was showing. So, I told him I was six weeks pregnant when I was three months." Meg waited in silence for her response, hoping she would not be judged too harshly for the deception.

"Why, Megahn Sinclair. That is the most devious thing I've ever heard. You go girl!" The two women laughed, strengthening their friendship.

"Ye do say the strangest things at times," Meg added.

During their many conversations Megahn told of her day to day activities at Castle Wick. She taught some of servant girls to defend themselves with a dirk and was in the process of teaching them to raise their heads and say *no* with confidence when the soldiers gave unwanted attention.

She admired Meg even more for the gift bestowed on women who saw it as part of their low station to put up with things they need not.

For its freedom to teach self-defence, Meg would love the twenty-first century. Males of the seventeenth-century believed it their duty to protect women; therefore Meg's teachings implied they were incapable of it. A real insult.

Jo also explained the ancient Korean art she learned, avoiding too many details of the how, when, and where, and how she would be delighted to teach Meg and Maeve the defensive skills.

So the weeks passed with work and merriment as the women became accomplished in the basics of Tae Kwon Do. Jo needed no instruction from Meg on how to use a knife for defence, but Jo realised her passion to wield a broadsword. The ancient weapon fascinated her. She was in the armoury on a number of occasions, viewing the weapons and feeling their weight. Already knowing a Highlander used two hands to wield it, she was still surprised when she could hardly lift the claymore off the ground.

Her interest in swordplay developed quickly and on a dark, heavy day that bore an icy wind and the first dusting of snow. She sought assistance. She found Maeve issuing orders to a group of burly youths stocking the main storeroom with the last of the season's produce. Jo asked, "Maeve, have you got a minute?"

"Aye, Jo. What is it?"

"I was wondering..." She hesitated, unsure what Maeve would say to her unusual request. "I want to learn how to fight with a sword. Would it be possible to have one made for me?" Maeve's eyebrows rose in query, causing her to add, "It would be like a hobby. You know how useless I am with a needle and thread."

Maeve smiled, well aware of Jo's propensity for disaster in connection with any new quilt or dress produced in the bower.

"Aye, lass. Our smithy is a good man and should be able ta assist with something light enough for ye."

As she continued looking out at the stars, she smiled and touched the light-weight broadsword hanging comfortably at her waist, hidden by the folds of her cloak.

She longed to sit in June's comfy armchair and talk of life in her new home—the characters she'd met and grown to admire and events experienced during her time at Castle Shreave.

She would tell June of the sword-fighting lessons, given by Tannan in the quiet behind the stables and of besting him on two occasions. The special bond between herself and young Davie, Maeve and Dougal's youngest child, and of the yearning she felt to give birth to a baby of her own. She'd explain to June the way huge meals were prepared every day to feed the masses in the great hall and how she began riding a horse, though felt she'd never be an accomplished horsewoman. And how she missed a man she didn't really know. And how she felt deeply the loss of the beautiful necklace June bestowed on her. Melancholy closing in, she made her way back into the laird's chamber. She would not let the homesickness creep in and cancel out the many good things.

****

On a bleak day with an inch of snow covering the ground, seven weeks after they left, the men returned to Castle Shreave. They were tired, cold, and frustrated. For all the skill of their trackers, the raiders eluded them time and again. They felt defeated without having fought a battle.

She listened to the thunder of hooves clatter through the main gate, and observed the powerful men dismount their horses. She couldn't help reflect on scenes from her own time. Seventeenth-century men practiced swordplay for fun, and in earnest to defend their home, family, and livelihood. Twenty-first century men played sport for fun. But come game day, the battle was to win.

She surmised if men of her time, particularly the football players, came here, they would be the warriors, defenders of the weak, of home and hearth. And she became grateful for the peace and safety of her country and home. She was happy the men of her time *did* play sports and weren't required to give their lives for their families. In years gone by many men gave everything.

From the front steps of the castle she stood by Meg and Maeve, who waited patiently for their men to dismount so they could greet them. Alick was the first to embrace his wife, unmindful of the surrounding observers and the dried mud encrusted on his plaid. He ran his hand over his wife's extended belly, kissed her, then took her hand, leading her into the castle, and Jo was sure, straight to their chamber.

Dougal's greeting was far more robust as he swung Maeve around, her feet flying through the air. Jo saw the lines of tiredness and stress around his eyes, failing to be hidden by his overgrown beard. "Come," said Maeve, and led him inside.

Envy sparked in Jo at the special bond shared by two people in love. She searched the seething mass of horses and soldiers, her eyes locating Connor. At first she didn't recognise him. His huge form stood out amongst the throng, but she hadn't seen him unshaven before. His dark hair was longer, and ratty around the edges, testament to weeks in the saddle. His beard fell past his chin and was dark with just a scattering of grey hairs. His eyes, like Dougal's, looked tired but the set of his jaw told of his frustration, having spent fruitless weeks chasing the raiders.

Feeling a little obvious standing alone on the steps, she turned and entered the great hall, disappointed Connor failed to notice her. But what did she expect? A few kisses shared in private constituted—what? Just because she thought of him endlessly over the weeks didn't mean Connor had lost any sleep over her.

Inside, servants stoked hearth fires to warm the frozen soldiers. She readied the jugs of ale and placed them on the tables for the noonday meal, hoping Eva's stores provided ample cured ham and baked bread to feed the unexpected, but welcome, arrivals.

She placed the last of the jugs at the head table and turned to see Connor striding through the hall. His face looked like thunder and the servants scurried out of his way.

His plaid was covered in mud and his boots

made a sodden squelching noise as his feet trod a direct path towards her. The breath caught in her throat when his eyes bored into her with an intensity that froze her to the spot. Concern flooded her at his condition.

She could tell he suffered a head cold, maybe the flu. Below his red-rimmed eyes were dark circles, his nose was red, and his lips chapped. Judging by his condition, she decided he'd been sick for some time. Influenza was a common cause of death in earlier centuries; fright instantly replaced her concern.

Without thinking, she stepped to the edge of the dais and looked down at him. His eyes did not move from hers. "You're ill," she whispered, placing a hand on his cheek, the coarse beard rough against the palm of her hand.

He made no move to touch her, but continued to stare, taking in the curve of her cheek, softness in her eyes, pink lips, and the way they moved as she spoke. Her cloak hid her body from him, but for all the weeks without a woman, his eyes sought only her face.

He'd dreamt of her features for weeks and feared she would look different from his memories once he was able to look upon her again. But she looked as he remembered.

He noted her standing with Meg and Maeve as he dismounted and hoped she waited for him but when he turned to acknowledge her she'd retreated into the hall. Gut-wrenching disappointment twisted inside him. Seven weeks was time enough to think hard about his life.

The strange woman from an unknown place seeped into his being. There was much he didn't know about her and much he wanted to learn, but the shadows of the past haunted him.

Following the repairs at Drumfold, he realised he was being a coward. The great, mighty Laird

MacKay was frightened to trust again, thanks to Kira's actions; but if he let these emotions ride him, Kira would win. Her scheming and deceit would be her posthumous revenge.

"Connor, talk to me?" she begged, unsettled by his silence and the distance in his eyes. She placed a hand on either cheek.

Connor returned from his musing and placed his hands over hers, pulling them down from his face. She gasped at his touch. "Connor, my God, you're freezing!"

She took his hand. "Come," she said. She went to walk away and her arm almost popped out of the socket; it was like trying to move a huge boulder. She supposed one didn't order a laird to *come* and expect him to follow like an obedient puppy. "Connor, please come. Please."

He stared for what seemed like minutes and then followed her to the third floor of the castle, a rasping cough tearing at his throat. At his chamber door she hesitated for a brief moment. He looked down at her, his face a collage of emotions. She understood them as if she always was attuned to his soul, but it was the vulnerability in his eyes that surprised her. Surely this powerful, mighty laird never felt vulnerable.

He wanted her, but like Jo, he was unsure. Unsure if he would look foolish. Unsure if his feelings over the past seven weeks would be returned. He felt weakened by these feelings, but then he smiled, looking down at her with open longing.

He wouldn't be weakened—but *she* would become his greatest weakness.

As Jo drank in every nuance of his features, a soft smile breaking his lips, she found it hard to speak. "Wel...welcome home, Connor," she whispered and reached up to place a passionate kiss on his chapped lips.

He led her into the chamber, bolting the door behind them, the taste of her lips still lingering on his. He dreamed of those lips constantly over the past weeks. Before she moved a step he pulled her into his arms and crushed his mouth to hers. The kiss was the most possessive she'd ever experienced.

He plundered and took everything, tasting the warmth within her mouth and bruising her lips with his passion. She hung on to his plaid or she would wilt to the chamber floor. He tasted of man and beast all rolled into one. She felt a sudden tenseness within his chest, and he pulled his face away as a racking cough took hold of him.

"Connor, you're sick." She pulled him towards the fire. "Sit," was all she said, half pushing him into the chair. She bent and pulled off his sodden boots. His feet and toes beneath were white and wrinkled with moisture. She felt a burst of stupidity as she realised she liked his feet as she folded the fur rugs around them, rubbing to increase the circulation.

Trying hard to remain focused she said, "I need to get you into the pool."

Connor's eyes closed and his head leant against the chair back. "Nae." He croaked, "The beard first. Itchy."

She realised his throat must be painful. Once settled in the pool she would race and get some of Eva's warm mead to soothe him.

She collected Connor's sharp shaving blade, soap from his chest, and a bowl of water. It would be less scary with a twenty-first century electric razor, but right now she would settle for a cheap, disposable one.

She'd seen someone shaved like this in a movie once. She knew she needed to cut off the excess hair first. It took some time to do and Connor remained unmoving in the chair. She thought at one time he might have drifted into sleep.

As she lathered up his face, Connor's eyes opened and he looked at her.

"Do you really want me to do this part?" she asked. "I should warn you, I've never shaved a man before."

He smiled. "I have nae been shaved by a woman before." Her eyes widened in surprise, but she said nothing.

Managing to get his face clean of hair, with no nicks or cuts to mar his strong features, she gave his knee a gentle push. He'd drifted off to sleep. "Connor. Do you want to go straight to bed or down to the pool?"

He opened his eyes and stared at her. "Weel, that is quite an offer, Jo-Anne," he rasped. "But I nae think I am up ta pleasing ye in bed just at this minute."

She blushed but was grateful his sense of humour was still intact. "Okay, smart aleck, on your feet."

Leading the way into his study, she reached behind the tapestry and lifted the latch. She did it with a practiced ease. Once down in the cave she paused, wondering what to do next, but Connor felt no such qualms.

He disrobed, throwing his plaid and undershirt on the ground in a heap and walked naked to the notched steps, lowering himself into the warm waters. She stared at every firm muscle of his body. His long, powerful legs curved to perfection and his bottom begged to be grasped. His shoulders were wide and the dark mat of hair on his chest tapered down to a flat, muscled stomach. As she glanced at the rest, flames of desire heated her skin. It tingled.

But she then noticed the dozens of scars covering his arms, legs, and torso. She felt a sense of horror as she stared at the different sizes and shapes—probably inflicted by a sharp blade. It gave her a real jolt. Here lay the significant difference between the football heroes of her time and this seventeenth-century Adonis. The scars on the football players were purpose-built to fix knee and shoulder injuries. Connor's scars were earned through battle and some of them must have given him great pain.

"I must look bad ta cause ye ta look so troubled."

"Oh, no. No. It's just the...scars. You have a lot. At home, men don't have scars like that. I mean, they don't fight...with swords," she corrected.

He looked at her intently. "Ye must tell me about yer home."

Realising it was perhaps a bad idea to speak of home, she changed the subject. "I'll go and get you some warm mead. It will help your throat."

"Nae."

She stopped, startled by the vehemence of his command.

"Nae, dinna go," he said more softly. "Stay with me. Please."

Connor was a strong man with an overdose of pride and ego. She knew what the request cost him.

'I'm not going anywhere, Connor MacKay." And she *would* stay with him, but hoped that whatever bought her to the seventeenth century would not take her from this place before she'd a chance to love again.

She slipped off her cloak and sword, pulled her dress over her head, and peeled off her stockings leaving herself almost naked in a thin shift. She went to the back of the cave for soap and towels. She entered the pool and sat on the steps, the water swirling around her waist.

Connor stood still, eyes following her every move, his jaw clenched, holding back restrained emotion.

"Come here and I'll wash your hair," she offered.

Connor walked over, his eyes never leaving hers. Then he turned and sat before her on the steps. She placed his head in her lap and repeated, "I'm not going anywhere, Connor MacKay." She needed to believe it was true as she began to undo the plaits binding his hair.

****

As the warm air soothed Connor's throat and gentle hands massaged his scalp, he couldn't remember the last time anybody did him such an intimate kindness. Tavern wenches from the surrounding villages were always more than happy to accommodate a laird; well, any man, as long as he paid the coin. But he'd not felt such tenderness since he was a small child. He remembered his mother, on many occasions, kissing a hurt or cuddling a nightmare away, but growing into manhood he came to believe affection was a weakness.

She worked the lather through his tangle of hair and ordered him to relax. "You're so tense, Connor," she murmured, almost to herself.

He laid his head back in her lap, draping his arms over her knees. He felt her skin caress the underside of his arms. The slight contact was arousing in itself. "If I relax too much, I will likely fall asleep," he mumbled, eyes closing, revelling in the sensations racing through his body.

"Would that be such a bad thing?"

"Aye. It would. I would nae be able ta look at ye."

She stopped and looked down. His eyes were open and focused on her face. She became molten lava when he looked at her like this.

"You need rest and sleep. Close your eyes."

Connor gave a heavy sigh and did as she asked. "I see ye have spent too much time over the weeks with ma sister and Maeve. I am nae sure I like bossiness in a woman."

"Well sir, it comes with the package," she countered as she rinsed the soap from his hair. "In *my* time, women are strong minded. There was nothing Maeve and Meg could teach me I didn't already know."

He sat up and washed the soap from his eyes, his wet dark hair falling well past his shoulders. She wanted nothing more than to run her hands over his back, feeling every contour and texture. But a reserved shyness prevented her from doing so.

"Ye said that once before ta me."

"What?" Jo frowned.

"My-time. Ye said 'in My-time.' Is it the name of the place ye come from? Has yer memory returned?"

Relaxed and absorbed in tending him, she let her tongue slip and cursed herself for a fool. "Oh! No, not really. Occasionally bits and pieces come back."

"What do ye remember?" Connor turned sideways on the steps, his back now resting against the edge of the cut-out, arms draped across his raised knees.

She couldn't help notice the contrast of skin and dark hair covering his body as the water swirled around him. He was looking at her and she saw no suspicion in his eyes to warrant caution. She decided to be as honest as she could. "I remember football, er, our warriors play it. My friend June—I think of her often. I remember the warm weather and eucalyptus trees."

She told Connor many things but was careful not to reveal too much. As she explained details the gulf between them narrowed. Connor listened, liking her dry sense of humour and the way she used her hands as she talked.

He shook his head in cynicism as she explained about the men from her home. He thought they sounded like pampered princes. He asked several questions, but it irritated his throat to speak, so he listened more than spoke.

"But of course," she continued, "the bank would give you a loan to build the house, and you would pay it back with interest—you know, pay extra back."

He frowned. "I think it strange that where ye come from, a man canna provide fer his family without having ta become indebted ta another. "I think yer men need a lesson in pride." He shook is head as he spoke, rose, and walked into the depths of the water.

He seemed so comfortable with his nudity. Jo, never promiscuous, thought she may soon make up for lost time. All she wanted was to step into his arms and feel him press against her. She seemed short of breath and her skin tingled again with desire as she watched Connor duck below the surface to wash away the grime from his body and soap from his hair.

She remembered Maeve's words and decided for better or worse, to be a risk taker. She entered the pool behind Connor.

Her hands worked on his back, the silky smoothness of soap gliding across his shoulders. He groaned as her fingers worked the soap into the back of his neck, massaging his shoulders. His head fell forward; his tight muscles loosened with each breath. She felt as aroused as she could ever remember being and couldn't believe just touching him would invoke such a potent response.

"Duck down. Rinse the soap off," she said while organising her emotions back in check.

Connor ducked as ordered, the soapy bubbles washing away with the current moving though the pool. He rose from the water and turned to face her, his eyes flaming. Wet hair was slicked back as the water cascaded down his torso. "If ye keep touching me like that, Jo-Anne, I will not be able ta contain myself much longer, ye ken?" His arms were by his side. He looked as if all his energy was being channelled into restraint.

"Connor. I don't want you to contain yourself. I mean... Oh hell! Connor, I've been restrained all my life. Right now, right at this moment—I don't want to hold back. I'm sick of doing the right thing or what's expected of me. It's just you and me here." She lowered her eyes, unable to meet his as a flush of embarrassment stained her cheeks. "I thought of you the whole time you were away," she continued, mindful of a possible rejection, mindful he may not think the same way. "The castle didn't feel right without you in it." He still made no move to touch her and a heavy feeling was building in the pit of her stomach. When she found the courage to look up she found Connor smiling down at her, ripping a hole clear through her heart. "Connor," she asked, "did you miss me at all?"

He stepped closer. His chest touched her breasts, the wet cotton of her shift the only barrier between them. He cupped her face between his calloused hands, his nose almost touching hers. "Ye were in ma dreams every night. I wished for the sight of ye every day. Aye, Jo-Anne. I *missed* ye."

The smile that lit her face was stunning. "Connor, I know you're not feeling very well and all, but, would you like to...have sex with me?" Her face flamed again. *Did I really just say that?*

She thought her request was rather blunt but Connor gave no indication it bothered him and he answered, "Nae, Jo-Anne." Connor's hands left her face and slowly opened the laces on the front of her shift. "I can have sex with a tavern harlot whenever I like. With you, lass...I shall make love."

She closed her eyes and let his words roll over her. She felt the sting of tears behind her eyelids.

Then she looked at him and said, "I would be honoured to share my body with you, Connor MacKay."

"Did ye think I'd let ye leave here until I'd had my way with ye?" he rasped. She began to laugh but stopped as Connor peeled the wet shift from her body. Naked before him, all her bravado left with her shift.

"I have wanted ye this way fer so long..." Connor stopped as a cough seized him.

"Connor, you're too ill. Maybe we shouldn't..."

"Like heel!"

His mouth claimed hers in a breathless kiss. She clung to him, holding back nothing, her body unable to get the closeness it desired no matter how hard she pressed herself to him.

His hand cupped her breast; she relished the heat of him hefting its weight to sit comfortably in his palm. He ran his thumb over her extended nipple. She whimpered in his arms as potent savagery rolled off him in waves. His tongue sought the textures of her mouth, mating with hers as she returned the challenge.

Their breathing became rapid and mingled into one. Connor lifted her into his arms and she wrapped her legs around his hips, his hardness a contrast to her softness. Unaware they moved through the water, she felt cool, damp stone, beneath her bottom, a sharp difference to the warmth of the water as she was sat on the edge of the pool. Once positioned, Connor began an instant assault on her breasts. He tasted her flesh, his teeth almost painful, with his arms around her back, ensuring there was no retreat.

She grasped Connor's damp hair in her fists, using it to lever his head to her mouth for another heated kiss.

Connor stopped and pulled his head back to look

at her. Droplets of water clung to his skin while his chest rose and fell rapidly. She leaned into him, bereft at the loss of contact, but Connor held her at bay, his eyes roaming her body, as her legs clung possessively around his hips.

Out of the water, his gaze swept over her body. Appreciation settled across his strong features as his eyes lingered on her breasts, belly, and hips. "God couldna have made a woman so perfect for any other reason than ta please a man," he groaned.

She was his, belonging to no other.

As his intent gaze travelled down her body, his eyes saw dark brown hair at the juncture of her thighs. His hands glided up her long legs to her hips, his forehead resting against hers. Connor whispered, "Ye are beautiful." He pulled back enough for her to clearly see his face as he stated possessively, "And ye are mine."

He kissed her already bruised lips and then began to work his way down. As he tasted her breasts again and moved down to her belly, Connor jerked her forward by the hips. The movement caused her back to arch and he took advantage of the movement by putting a hand on her chest, pushing her backward. When his hands cupped her bottom, she realised his intent and could only form one coherent breathless word. "Please."

Connor needed no further permission. Did he ever need it? He lowered his head and gave her the most erotic kiss she ever experienced. Sensations spiralled through her body to coil tightly in her centre. She could not escape—did not want to. Her body seemed to ride above her, out of control. From somewhere she heard a cataclysmic groan and was shocked it came from her own vocal cords. Panting, her body tense, she was aware of Connor's tongue exploring places never before charted. The sensation was so intense she began to spin out of control.

When her release came she felt like she was shimmering away into a thousand different pieces.

As she floated back to earth, she realised she lay on her back, rough stones digging into her skin and a sheen of sweat covering her body. An un-ladylike position! Raising her own head, she saw Connor's head nestled comfortably on her stomach, his eyes closed. Thinking of his illness, she became contrite, feeling embarrassed and selfish for taking his last remaining strength.

"Connor...are you okay?"

His head rose like a serpent awakened from a deep sleep, his eyes pools of darkness. "Nae, woman." His hands ran over her ribs to cup her breasts. "I have an urgent need that only ye can attend ta." He rose slowly, reaching for her hands and raised her to a sitting position. "If ye think ye have recovered enough?"

She laughed and wrapped her legs around his waist again, her arms circling his strong neck. "Well, sir," she bantered huskily, "I believe I feel quite...content, at this present minute." She made a liar of herself as she looked into his eyes.

She wanted more. She felt her body respond. The hairs on his chest scratched against her nipples causing desire to sweep through her once again. The playful smile disappeared and was replaced by a look of intense need.

Connor lifted her from the ledge, carried her up the steps, and across to a pile of drying cloths at the back of the cave. He lowered her to her feet; his arm still circled her back, holding her against him. "When I take ye Jo-Anne, I shall nae even have water come between us." He wrapped a cloth the size of a small blanket around her, clasped her hand, and led her from the cave.

Embers of the fire cast a warm glow across the chamber when they entered. The Highland winter was upon them making the room cold compared to the cave's steaming warmth; the fire's heat beneficial only if standing close to it.

She shivered, the dampness on her skin cooling her body rapidly. Connor showed no sign of being even slightly chilled. He began to cough as the cold air entered his throat.

He led her to the fire, laying her on the furs, collecting additional furs from his bed. He covered her shivering form and crawled in beside her, gathering her into his arms. His warm body heated her skin and her shivering slowed as sparks of arousal surfaced again.

Her face was buried into the tickling softness of his hairy chest, and her arms fastened around his middle. The hardness of his erection left an imprint in her stomach as his hands leisurely began to explore. Her hips pushed towards him, demanding his attention.

His hand squeezed her bottom then ran along her thigh, lifting it so her leg draped across his waist. In one practiced movement he flipped her to her back, letting out an audible groan as his hardness touched her centre. She didn't hesitate and wrapped her legs around his waist, seeking the ultimate closeness.

As her need grew she writhed beneath him, but he did not take his advantage. She opened her eyes to look at him. His face was a mask of restrained desire, an electrical storm bursting with power.

"Connor?" she questioned. "Don't stop. Please don't stop." She found it difficult to string the simple words together, such was her own passion.

Connor's head dropped to her chest, he took a purposeful deep breath then looked her in the eye. Jo allowed him to see her desire; she watched control waver in his eyes. But this would be her last chance. She understood he would have no honour if he didn't give her the opportunity to back away.

"I will take ye now should ye wish it. It is the only chance I will *ever* give ye ta walk from me. Do ye understand?"

She answered with action rather than words and reached between their bodies to cup his balls, heavy with seed. She enclosed her hand around his shaft, her palm running the length of it, and placed the tip at the entrance to her centre. "I've waited my whole life for you."

Permission granted, Connor thrust into her. A groan escaped him and she matched his voice with a gasp of her own as she clung to him, his fullness completing her.

Connor slid smoothly outwards, his whole body turned to iron, his muscles, his whole being, screaming for release. He plunged in again and began the rhythmic dance.

She thought her body would explode the pressure mounting within was so great. Connor continued his possessive onslaught and hooked one arm around her leg, opening her to him even more, ensuring he touched her womb and her soul. Her head fell back and her neck arched almost to breaking point as her climax peaked.

"Look at me," he demanded as his tension came close to fruition.

She opened her eyes and stared into his, her passion and feelings for him clearly visible. "Connor... Connorrrrr." Her release came like a tempest.

Jo felt Connor let go of all self-control. He made his final play and erupted violently within her, his eyes never leaving hers. His seed pulsed within her and she knew it was where it should be—inside her and no one else.

Connor's weight sank languidly onto her body. Neither spoke; words were unnecessary to express their feelings.

She didn't know how long they lay there, when a cough racked his body. She pulled the displaced furs over his exposed back. "Connor, you need medicine, or something," she offered, feeling concerned yet again, now that the passion finished clouding her judgement.

"I only need ye," he replied and rolled off her, gathering her close to his body. "Ye are all I need, woman."

It took but seconds for him to fall asleep and only minutes for the tears to build behind her eyes. She now understood what was missing from her life.

Connor's head rested comfortably between her breasts, his breathing even and warm against her skin, while her arms held him. She thanked God for the gift he gave her. Her tears were silent as the wonders of their joining settled into her memory. She felt more blessed than she could have ever hoped. She gently ran her fingers through his damp locks, never believing she would one day hold this mighty, powerful laird against her naked body.

As her own eyelids became heavy, she came to accept her reality. She now knew, more than ever, she was in the right *place*; in the right *time*.

****

Waking from heavy slumber, she saw the pale light creep through the slitted windows of the chamber. Moving her head, she became aware of the warm body tucked behind her own. Her bottom was nestled in the most manly of groins, a solid leg crossed possessively over hers, and an arm the size of a small tree trunk wrapped tight around her middle.

Careful not to disturb the slumbering giant, she looked over her shoulder and saw Connor's eyes remained shut. His breathing, even and deep, carried no hint of a rattle or infection.

He looked beautiful in sleep; long, dark lashes brushed his cheeks, lips soft and pouting, and a stray piece of hair hung boyishly over one eye. *God, he is gorgeous.*

How could Kira have never loved him nor wanted his passion, his possession?

She flushed as she recalled their uninhibited and very intimate assault on each other. She felt carefree with this man and cast aside all reticence.

Wanting to watch him slumber, she rolled carefully to face him. He mumbled in his sleep, his arm did not release her but slackened enough for her to move. She lay motionless, staring at him until his breathing became even again. She tucked the stray hair behind his ear and pulled the furs up to cover his shoulder. Looking down their bodies into the small cavity between them, her eyes soaked in his perfect body. Even with his manhood slumbering, nestled amongst hair darker than night, he aroused her. She continued to drink in the sight of him and she wondered at the hour of the day. They must have slept the afternoon away, for light glancing through the archer's slits was not dawn, but sunset. The rest of the castle would *all* know by now the laird had been ensconced in his chamber for the better part of the day—with her. Once again a flush stained her cheeks. Too late for regrets now.

She gave one last glance beneath the covers and was surprised to see a dramatic change in the condition of his anatomy. His erection grew before her eyes.

"It is yer fault," said a muffled voice.

Her eyes swung up to see a pair of dark, intense ones looking back. "I thought you were sleeping," she whispered.

His eyes took on a heated look while his hands roamed lazily over her hip. "Did ye find what ye were looking for under there?"

"Oops! Caught spying," she replied guiltily. Within seconds she was on her back again, his body pressing her into the furs.

"Connor, you need rest and food and…"

"I already told ye what I need."

The evening meal was being served in the great hall when she finally left his chamber.

Chapter Nineteen

It was one week after the unsuccessful return of the hunting party.

"They knew where we were, what we planned, and the direction of our travels before *we* even knew them. It canna be anything else but a spy amongst us," Connor stated.

There was silence around the table. Such was Highland loyalty, nobody wanted to think this possible, but it was the only explanation for the dismal weeks they spent fruitlessly searching. The Shreave and Wick warriors always found themselves just a day, or on one occasion, a mere hour from trapping their quarry.

Connor paced the dais in front of the hearth, a cup of warm mead in his hand. Dougal, Alick, and the guard captains also participated in the discussion. To leave enough space for the men to conduct their business on the dais, the women sat at one of the side hearths, talking quietly amongst themselves.

Jo felt a bit miffed to be left out, as did Meg, despite knowing their men would tell them everything later. Jo grumbled about "Men and their ways."

Maeve said, "Ye know well enough by now, Jo, that I agree with ye and think we could contribute here, but we do get ta have our say. We need ta be under the furs ta make our point." The three women laughed together, trying hard to subdue their shared mirth and not to draw attention to their banter.

The MacKay and Sinclair soldiers were

becoming restless, wanting revenge for the stolen cattle, attack on the Sinclair entourage, and justice for the people of Drumfold. It was the beginning of the cold season; the Wick soldiers were keen to return home to make final preparations for winter and only a few weeks remained where the snow would be thin enough on the ground to allow another search.

Meg was a good seven months pregnant and ready to ride home to Wick alone if necessary. She told Jo she knew she was being unreasonable, but couldn't help it. Her yearning to nest and prepare for her baby's arrival was strong.

During the weeks the men were away, a reluctant respect developed between Alick and Connor. There was still an element of tension, but considerable improvement, evident by the catches of conversation drifting from the dais.

"Connor, I dinna think it could be from within. Mayhap…"

"Alick, I know it is hard ta comprehend…but we have ta stop ignoring the facts. Their attacks have been well planned, organised, and so far successful. If ye have any suggestions as ta how they could accomplish this with us licking at their heels, I'd be grateful for the notion."

The men around the table sat silently, watching the two lairds, who stared at each other. Neither man spoke for a while.

"What of neighbouring clans? Do they have grudges?" Alick suggested. "And do they have reason ta hate ye and me?"

"At this stage they may hate whoever crosses their paths. But I doubt it."

"Damn them. What's ta be gained?"

"That, we shall find out," finished Connor.

Maeve and Meg spoke at length on the subject and pieced together circumstances leading them to conclusions. They hoped eventually the two lairds would soon see the truth, too.

Much to the delight of the cross-stitching ladies beside her, Jo sat sharpening her sword; they thought she was an advanced woman to have armed herself. Jo covertly listened to the conversation on the dais. She wanted to tell Meg and Maeve about Connor's cousin Brian, but she promised him she wouldn't discuss it. She hoped he wouldn't ignore the incident on the stairs that happened some time ago, or forget about it. She made a mental note to remind him in bed tonight—if there was time. Happily, the man was insatiable!

She looked down at the heavy Celtic ring on her finger. Connor gave it to her last night after making possessive love to her once again.

His face serious, he slid it on her finger then kissed her knuckles. "This was ma mother's. My father gave it ta her when they became betrothed."

Words failed her as she looked at the beautiful, intricately designed ring.

Connor said nothing else, but his eyes said more than words could. It was that simple. She accepted his betrothal gift with neither hesitation nor doubt. Parts of the jigsaw puzzle were still incomplete, but the pictures on the pieces were slowly being drawn. They would make their own present, past, and future, and they would do it together.

"If ye keep staring at that ring ye'll end up going cross-eyed," teased Maeve.

Jo looked up at her friends whose faces both wore an annoying, knowing look. Meg and Maeve, delighted she and Connor finally made a claim for each other, ribbed her unmercifully since she came down from Connor's chamber the day the men returned from the hunt.

As expected, Castle Shreave inhabitants seemed to know what was going on. Jo at first thought they were heartless, more concerned about the goings-on in the chamber than the health of their laird. But she soon realised it would take a thunderous bolt of lighting to lay the Laird of Shreave prostrate for long. And as his health improved over the week, his virility astounded her. A Highland betrothal was seen to be as good as marriage, until other permanent arrangements could be made. She blushed, thinking of the ways Connor took full advantage of this tradition.

"Oh, come now Maeve," Meg chipped in. "What difference could it make if she stares at her ring? She will already be going blind from all the sex!"

Jo gasped at the crude quip and then her chuckle developed into a good belly laugh. "And I thought you were a lady," she managed, the laughter taking her breath away.

"Only if absolutely necessary. I must say Alick does prefer me not ta be in our chamber."

This caused more fits of giggles, drawing looks from some of the men.

Lowering their voices, Maeve added, "Nae, it isna the blindness. It be obvious when it hurts ta walk!"

Two of them snorted with laughter and the other held her face in her hands, trying to subdue the shaking hilarity, in vain. Deciding to exit the hall so they could continue unrestrained, they staggered from their chairs and up the stairs, their shuddering shoulders obvious to the frowning men. When their faces crumpled as they tried to curb their humour and contain their hysterical laughter, Jo tripped on the stairs and bumped into Maeve, who hung onto the railing for support. This made Meg laugh even more and she indelicately passed wind—a problem in her advanced state of pregnancy. The three collapsed in a heap on the first landing. Jo tried to stand but kept kneeling on her voluminous skirts, sobbing with laughter she attempted to crawl away. Maeve gave up all hope of containment and lay flat on her back gasping for breath, her ample bosom quaking beneath her plaid, while Meg held her tummy, trying not to wobble the baby too much, her face red with embarrassment—all traces of 'ladylikeness' gone out the arrow slits as she snorted once again.

The men ran up to the landing, at first grumbling with annoyance at the disrespectful intrusion to their serious meeting, but calling out with concern when they heard the thump as the women fell on the stairs. The girls sprawled above them, laughing like uncontrolled harpies.

The three women became aware of the audience and the astonished looks upon the men's faces. This only made matters worse causing them to laugh even more. As tears rolled down their cheeks, Connor, Dougal, and Alick stared at them.

With a look of disbelief on his face, Dougal asked, "Have ye all been drinking?"

"Meg?" questioned Alick. His face showing he found it hard to believe his wife would drink to excess in her advanced condition, he queried "Surely ye have nae consumed alcohol?"

This again caused the women's hilarity to raise a notch taking them beyond the point of self-control and rational thought.

It was Connor who saw the lighter side of the moment, and as a slow smile crept to his lips, a deep rumble in his chest became audible. He squatted beside Jo, who was trying to crawl to the stairs leading to the next floor.

"I think it would be easier, lass, if ye walked ta our room. I think yer knees may take a beating by the time ye get ta the third floor—although," he continued, whacking her hard on her backside, "your derriere looks quite fetching, swaying side-to-side as ye crawl."

Realising she was being far from ladylike, she flipped over to sit on her bottom, her skirts twisting around her.

Meg slid sideways from her sitting position, her head thunking as it connected with the floor, her shoulders continuing to shake.

Alick joined in the hilarity, laughing at the ridiculous scene before them. "Weel, men. I think we may need ta cart these harpies off ta bed, they nae seem capable of getting there themselves."

And the women were carted off to bed. Not one of them able to make the journey alone, but all relieved, if only temporarily, of worry.

For each woman knew her man must return to the hunt.

****

Two days later, as dawn crept through the arrow slits, Jo rolled over in the huge bed in the laird's chamber. Something was not right. As she reached out for Connor, she found the space beside her empty. Surely he would not leave without saying goodbye?

She sat up and noticed his naked shadow standing by the dying embers of the fire in the freezing room. He never appeared to feel the cold. Connor turned and smiled, melting her heart with the simple facial expression.

"I nae wished ta wake ye," he said in his deep voice, still husky from sleep, or lack of.

"You weren't going to go without saying goodbye, were you?" she asked sleepily.

"I felt guilty keeping ye awake most of the night."

"Did I complain?"

"Nae ye didn't. I nae think I could have stopped even if ye did," he answered with honesty.

She flung the furs back on his side of the bed

and patted the mattress. "Come back to bed, Connor. It's too early even for the stable boys."

Connor slid back in beside her and gathered her to him.

"Ooh, your skin is like ice."

"And yers is like warm honey."

He wrapped his own legs around hers, making her feel like a fly caught in a web. His skin warmed her, infused her. But uncertainty shadowed them.

She had to know and decided to broach the subject she'd avoided all night. "How long will you be away this time?"

"Ah dinna ken. The weather will dictate that."

She felt safe and warm and didn't want her anxiety to spoil the moment, but reality would not be quieted. She would let him go—she'd have no choice. But how she wished things could be different.

If they were in her time…

Much discussion occurred over the last week and a half, until it was decided the full party of MacKay warriors including Connor, and half of the Sinclair party, most of them single men, would continue the search. The other half of the Sinclair party, the betrothed or married ones with family commitments, would escort the Lady Megahn back home to Castle Wick.

Connor provided an additional twenty men to escort his sister.

By combining their forces to chase the mercenaries, the two clans would form a powerful alliance both lairds were mindful of, but still uncomfortable with. It was much easier to hold on to anger than it was to forgive.

Alick would stay with the hunting group, but promised Meg, on pain of a severe tongue-lashing, he would return well before the birth of their first child. He was unlikely to be gone any longer than three weeks. The Highland winter was fierce, and the lairds both agreed the mercenaries, no matter how much their pay, would want to be inside during the frigid months.

"I'll miss Meg terribly when she goes. I feel so close to her." Jo sounded wistful, but Connor did not reply. "You're lucky to have a sister like her." Still no comment. "What? You don't think you're lucky, Mr. Silent?" Jo asked pointedly.

"It nae matters."

"What *nae* matters?"

Connor rolled to his back, his eyes focused on the ceiling and some unseen memory. "We drifted apart. Tis all."

"Why?"

It was a question with an easy answer, but Connor's stubborn streak refused to broach the subject. "Tis done now."

Not happy with this reply, Jo raised herself on her elbow and looked down at him. He sighed, knowing she would be unlikely to let it go until she recieved the truth.

"There is nothing *done* that can't be *undone*," she stated. "I really can't decide who is more stubborn, you or your sister!"

"She is," came the quick reply, making Jo laugh.

"Yeah, right. You need to take a good look in a mirror sometime soon, Laird MacKay."

Connor grabbed Jo in a bear hug, rolled over, and pinned her beneath him.

"The mirror shows me things I would prefer ta ignore." He began kissing Jo's neck, nuzzling his scratchy five o'clock shadow against her soft skin.

"Oh no you don't! You're not going to divert my attention that way."

Connor sighed again and pulled his head back to look at her. "It's nae worth the conversation. It's in the past."

"No, it's not. She's right here in your castle.

Right under your nose. She will never be in your past, no matter how stubborn you are."

"Weel, it's her fault. She chose ta be a Sinclair."

Jo studied Connor's face; his jaw clenched, the muscles twitching. She noticed he did this when angry, or holding his emotions in check. "You don't choose who you fall in love with, Connor. It just happens."

Her words had the desired impact for he understood the two of them were a prime example. He knew so little about her, due to her memory loss, but it made no difference. He fell for Jo, and there was nothing he could have done about it. Oh, he tried. Tried to ignore her, tried to be sharp or curt with her. But it was wasted effort in the end.

"Ye think she feels for him, as I feel for ye?" Connor asked. It was the first time he came close to verbalising his feelings for her.

"Yes, you fool. Haven't you noticed the way they look at each other? Alick's eyes follow her wherever she goes. He dotes on her." Jo laughed. "And it drives Meg nuts."

Connor lay quietly with his thoughts, his weight an intimate comfort.

Men! she thought. *They truly are from Mars!*

"I nae ever considered..." Connor stumbled on his words. "Until, you. I didn't know."

Jo looked into his eyes; her hands cradled his face, seeming small and pale against his stubbled, dark features.

"I've only known you for a breath in time, Connor. But I know I couldn't live without you. I know every time you leave the castle, I will worry for your safe return. I *feel* your presence when you walk into a room. Without even looking I know you're there. Sometimes I want the world to go away, and leave us be. I don't want to share you with anyone. When you touch me...I know I'm home."

Connors eyes were closed, absorbing her words deep into his soul. "I'm in love with you Connor. I feel for you what Meg feels for Alick."

His eyes opened, revealing the black pools within. She could feel the hardness of his desire against her thigh. He verbalised nothing, but spoke with his body. The sweet passion with which he captured her lips brought sudden tears to her eyes. She'd been kissed by Connor hundreds of times over the last several days, but none like this.

He took the weight of his body on his elbows as he cradled her face between his calloused hands, his thumb brushing her cheek. When he drew his lips away, her body felt like it was floating, her arms unable to move, her legs still entangled with his.

This man loved her. This amazing man, this mighty laird, loved her. She doubted she would ever hear the words from his lips, but she knew truth when it was laid at her feet.

"Ye will wed me when I return."

A tingle raced through her body. She and Andrew discussed getting married like a business partnership, but Connor's way would do her nicely.

This *command* to marry suited her perfectly.

Unable to keep the smile from her lips, she gave him her best military salute. "Yes, sir."

A slight frown marred Connor's features and he kissed her brow. "Ye have funny ways aboot ye."

Her hands began to play with the curly hairs on his chest. "I'm not so funny where I come from. In fact, I think I was quite ordinary."

"Ye, ordinary? Weel, the women of yer home must all be angels sent from heaven then."

Taking the compliment, she kissed him back, her hands running down his powerful back, cupped his bottom as her hips began to have a will of their own.

"Connor..." A gasp escaped.

"Aye lass, I feel it too."

****

Connor was one of the last to the stables. He was annoyed he hadn't the restraint to walk away from his betrothed. She already claimed some power over him. Most of the war party had already put their saddlebags on and were mounted. Alick and Dougal were contemplating going to fetch him when he approached.

"Nice of ye ta join us." Dougal frowned, then was heard muttering to himself about damn bloody women.

Connor, his face like thunder, threw his saddlebags on Thief and mounted his war horse.

With a wicked gleam in his eye, Alick said, "Cheer up, man. There are worse reasons fer being late." He laughed and rode off.

The sky hung heavy and dull grey, signifying snow later in the day as the sounds and smells of men and horses permeated the morning air.

On the main rampart, Jo arrived just in time. "Good morning," said Maeve, her voice laced with mock concern. "We wondered if we were going ta have ta come and rescue ye."

"Thought ye may be impaled ta the feather mattress." Meg joined in with laughter.

"All right, all right. Cut it out, you two."

The women laughed, and then fell into a companionable silence. Their faces showed the heartache and fear they truly felt as their men began to ride out of the bailey.

Jo wondered how anybody could compare the soldiers below with the men of her own time. The most violent thing she ever saw was a pub brawl. She hadn't liked it. The violence of this century was worse. But here she was, waving goodbye to a man she loved, watching him go without argument, to fight to the death with some mad mercenaries.

Sometimes she wished all this was a dream.

As the last of the men disappeared over the horizon, she marvelled at the beauty of the place. From here you could see the huge lake, dull and grey with the reflected clouds and the rugged hills behind, stark and untamed. She would have loved to explore the lake and the surrounding hills, but was forbidden to leave the confines of the castle. All three of them were. At first, for her, it was because they didn't trust her. But now it was for fear of the mercenaries their men were hunting.

"Weel ladies, that be that...again," Maeve said, resigned to survival in the Highlands. "Come, Meg. We shall help ye pack. Yer guards will nae wish ta tarry. They shall be restless if we dinna get ye moved on."

"Aye. I suppose so. There is nae more we can achieve by standing in the cold," replied Meg. "I hate goodbyes, but—"

"Just think how happy you'll be to be in your own home again." Jo offered, sure Meg would be having mixed feelings leaving Shreave.

It took but an hour to have all Meg's belongings packed. She sat astride a sturdy bay mare, her eyes shimmering with unshed tears.

"Now, ye take it easy with her," Maeve addressed the whole troop of fifty soldiers. "Ye go slow and no pushing on, if the snow begins. Ye find an inn and get shelter for yer lady."

Meg chuckled. "I shall be fine, my friend. I think fifty soldiers are enough to keep an eye on me. But, ye know Alick."

"Aye, weel then," said Maeve

Jo moved forward and clasped Meg's hand. "You take care. We want to hear as soon as the baby comes."

With a final squeeze of her hand, Meg's horse moved off, following the soldiers leading the way through the main gates.

Jo and Meave were left standing there. Castle Sheave would not be the same without her.

Chapter Twenty

The party of MacKay and Sinclair warriors followed fresh pony tracks for three days. Connor estimated a band of twenty to twenty-five riders travelled this way a mere hour ago. But it was an hour too late for the crofters in the small settlement of Preece, just over the border on Clan Sinclair land.

Connor squatted beside the ashes of a still warm fire. Once a small crofter's cottage, it was now nothing but charred timber and dried crumbling mud. The smell of burnt flesh hung in the air, bringing with it memories of Drumfold.

The villagers hadn't stood a chance. The raiders burned the six small cottages to the ground, some of the tenants incinerated within them. A few villagers ran for the cover of the forest surrounding the outpost but they stood little chance and were cut down as they ran.

Alick stood by a body on the ground. It was a young girl, not more than thirteen years of age. He bent and pulled her skirts down over her exposed bloodied legs. "Sons of bitches." Alick turned to him with murderous intent on his face. "We'll bury the dead. The living will nae last long with winter upon us. We must send them on ta Wick with five soldiers ta help with the wounded." Alick scanned the carnage, the muscles working in his jaw. "When we find them, we gut them." The hardness in his eyes was chilling.

"Aye," replied Connor, with equal intent. "There willna be questions, there willna be mercy." The two men looked at each other and a simple nod finished their conversation.

They turned to see Dougal coming out of the forest, the body of a child no bigger than young Davie, draped in his arms. He walked through the remains of the village and placed the baby on the ground along with the other dead.

Not a word was said, but each man's face said there was killing to be done.

****

One week after Lady Mehgan left Shreave Castle, Maeve counted supplies in the kitchens with Mrs. McBain and discussed meals for the coming week. At this time of the year, when the snow made hunting poor and the storerooms held only crop produce, careful planning was essential to ensure food supplies lasted through the freezing winter months.

As Maeve and Eva pored over the inventory sheets, they heard rapid footfalls approaching down the corridor. The sound held a sense of urgency and their heads rose together.

Young Colin almost fell into the kitchen in his haste. "Lady, Lady," he puffed. "An urgent message has arrived from Wick."

Maeve rose giving instructions over her shoulder as she headed to the hall. "Eva, prepare something for the man and bring it out. He shall likely be exhausted."

As she strode down the long corridor to the hall, a dozen different things forced their way into her mind. Someone in the hunting party was injured, or another incident with the raiders. She sent up a silent prayer. Her worst thought was Dougal being injured—but no, she would have sensed that. Almost sickened by her thinking, tying her stomach into knots, Maeve shook herself back to order.

The messenger stood at one of the side hearths in the great hall. His clothes were frosted around the edges, his nose red, and lips shaded with blue. As he shivered Maeve could see he was uneasy. "Weel man, what is it?" she asked.

"The Lady Megahn, Lady. The baby. It is her time. She be in trouble and asks for yer presence."

"It is nae her time," Maeve said. "What is this aboot? She was in fine health not days ago. I checked her maself."

The young man, not more than twenty years of age, shifted on his feet and his brow held a fine sheen of sweat. "I nae know, Lady. I was but told ta come and deliver the message. I canna say what is the matter. They say she asked fer ye, and a Lady Jo?" His eyebrows frowned, as if the name were unfamiliar to him.

"Colin," Maeve addressed the young boy standing behind her. "Go and find the Lady Jo. Tell her it is urgent. I think she will be in the nursery."

Several minutes later she appeared, concern written on her face, Colin had obviously given her the news.

"When did her labour start?" she asked anxiously. "She isn't full term."

The two women looked at the messenger. He appeared to back up a step, almost ready to take flight. "I nae know, ladies." His Adam's apple bobbed in his throat. He gulped.

"This is nae good." Maeve began to pace back and forth, weighing up the options, concern masked with confusion written across her brow. "It just makes nae sense. The Wick healing woman is far more skilled than I. Friends at a time like this are of little use."

Jo understood Maeve's words and the practical, if not ruthless way of assessing the situation. At this time of the year any travel was a great risk. The consequences of a blizzard could be tragic. And the raiders...

Maeve kept prodding the messenger for information, "What does the Wick healer have ta say? Did *she* send ye?"

"Nae, Lady. I was told the word came from Lady Sinclair." Maeve continued pacing. The messenger faltered before saying, "I did hear, but canna say if it be true, the Wick healer was taken ill several weeks ago."

This was the information that convinced Maeve to act. With no healer at Wick and Megahn in labour, there was no other choice. Meg would need help and a healer.

Jo and Maeve were soon mounted and ready to ride. They intended to ride swiftly, carrying only Maeve's medicine chest. They would borrow clean clothes once there. Ten mounted soldiers—a cursory protection, rode with them. They both agreed they would be unlikely to encounter trouble on the main roads with the combined forces of the MacKay and Sinclair warriors chasing the mercenaries.

As they rode out of the bailey and through the village, both women held back their fear. They would be devastated if anything should happen to Megahn. Jo wished Megahn into the twenty-first century with a neo-natal unit on stand-by, or a gynaecologist fussing over her. *Oh God, please let her be okay*.

As they galloped down the road, the freezing climate almost robbed their lungs of air. Jo could just make out the road under the thin layer of snow. Both were swaddled in thick layers of wool, but still the icy chill permeated their clothing.

Concerned her riding ability would be inadequate for the journey, Jo remembered Dougal's words from what seemed like a year ago. He was right. Maeve didn't sit a horse any better than she did and Maeve risked more than her. A wet nurse was found for young Davie, but if circumstances held them too long at Wick, her milk would dry up.

From the back of the fast moving group, the young messenger galloped along, smiling.

Two hours later, around a bend in the road, the party ran into the ambush. In a few short moments, ten MacKay soldiers lay slaughtered on the road.

Chapter Twenty-One

Jo woke with a start, aware of a pounding headache that throbbed all the way into her teeth. As she tried to move, sharp pain flashed through her scalp like knives entering her brain. Trying hard to get coherent thought into her mind, she raised her hands to massage her temples but found herself restricted by coarse ropes binding her chafed wrists.

She raised her head from the frozen dirt floor of what looked like a cave and observed her surroundings. From her position she could see at least twenty men milling around small fires within the cave. They looked rough, unshaven; the stench of their body odour made her gag. Drawing attention to herself was a bad idea so she lowered her throbbing head back to the dirt.

She could remember their hasty ride through the freezing countryside and feeling saddle sore after only a short while—but it didn't matter. Reaching Meg was more important than any comfort considerations. She and Maeve were joking about their discomfort and poor riding skills, more to relieve concern for their pregnant friend. Maeve laughed and... *Maeve. Maeve!* her mind screamed.

Panic consumed her as the haze in her mind cleared. Where was Maeve? *Oh God, please let her be okay.*

Trying not to be obvious, she angled her head so she could see above her head then beyond her feet. Maeve could be trussed somewhere behind her, and impossible to locate without great movement. Just as she was about to open her eyes for another peek, a rasping voice was heard.

"Check the bitches. They should be awake by now. I told ye not ta punch them sae hard. Ma cock can only wait sae long." There was crude laughter and bantering concerning turn-taking.

She froze, and her eyes remained closed. It took all her willpower to relax and not shake with dread. Bile rose in her throat, but survival was paramount and she couldn't help Maeve or herself if she was dragged off, raped, and beaten.

As someone approached, his footfalls thudding on the hard packed dirt, she tried to take her mind to another place, away from the fear. Her legs were viciously kicked and pain shot through her freezing limbs, she somehow managed to stifle a groan and remain still.

"Wake up!" the raspy voice commanded. He grabbed her bodice and shook her. She remained relaxed like a rag doll and was thrown back to the dirt, her head thunking as it hit the ground.

"Christ man, ye've probably brained them."

"What does it matter? It nae be their brains we be interested in." There was more laughter.

Oh God, oh God, oh God. Her mind screamed with panic, pain, and terror.

****

In a deep ravine a mere five miles away, Connor, Alick, and their men made camp for the night. There was more snow coming, and within a few days it would be pointless to seek the raiders. Snow would cover any tracks and the severe cold of the mountains would affect the men and their mounts. It was too risky.

As campfires were lit, dwindling food supplies were combined to prepare a humble meal. These men were warriors, used to living on meagre supplies for months on end. As Connor squatted beside a fire, his horse dried off and blanketed, the old frustration returned. How were the raiders eluding them?

It seemed at every turn they were always a step ahead. He was keeping a close eye on his cousin, still not wishing to believe he threatened Jo in any way, but he knew her well enough now to trust her. He would continue to watch the man, but he needed help. "Dougal," he called to his friend. Dougal finished blanketing his own horse and ambled over to warm himself by the fire.

"Aye?"

"I need yer help." Connor looked into the fire, considering his words before speaking in a hushed tone. He knew Dougal's hot temper and his already fierce dislike for Brian. "We should have found them by now. This isna right."

"Ye nae be telling me what I dinna already know. What of it then?" came Dougal's gruff question.

Connor's jaw clenched. Just the idea of what he was about to suggest left a sour taste in his mouth. "The traitor is one of ours."

Dougal went to rise in fury, his head already looking from side to side as if the suspect wore the word 'traitor' branded across his forehead. Connor grabbed Dougal's arm and held him in his squatting position by the fire. "Quiet my friend. When the time is right…"

Dougal looked a little sheepish realising his error. "Aye, man. It is just…"

"I know. We have been searching too long already. But now I know how ta bring an end ta this." Both men fell quiet for a moment, both knowing but unable to admit they longed to be back at Shreave, in a warm bed, with a warm woman—their own women.

"Who?" Dougal's voice was laced with ice.

"I will tell ye, man, if ye do naught ta raise

suspicion." Connor was fully aware of his friend's deadly loyalty to himself and Clan MacKay. And his short temper. "This will only work if we pretend ta be unaware of the deceit."

"Aye. *Who?*"

"Brian."

Dougal's eyes locked on Connor. "He will have ta be killed...when the time comes."

"Aye. But it will be by my hand, nae yours."

"I thought it would be easi—"

"Nae." Connor cut Dougal off. No more was said. They understood without explanation. Brian was cousin to Connor and if the treachery was Brian's, it was the laird's responsibility.

With a curt nod, Dougal acknowledged the right-of-kill. "Who would he be giving the information ta and why?"

"That my friend, we will find out. But for now patience is our best weapon."

"Do ye want ta tell Alick?" Dougal rushed on as if expecting disagreement. "I think it would be appropriate. Preece was his own. He has a right ta know."

"Aye," Connor said, noticing the look of surprise on his friend's face. Dougal would have expected him to spit fire at such a suggestion. "I think there is some connection here we have missed. I nae think it is coincidence our two clans have been targeted. I think Alick better think hard on his own rank and file. I think both clans have a traitor."

Dougal rose from his squatting position by the fire. "It is time ye talked. I think Alick and ye have much ta discuss."

"Aye," Connor replied.

But Connor *knew* what he and his friend were really talking about. Whatever was going on, the trouble with the raiders, the problems of trapping them, any motive for treachery, was somehow connected to Alick Sinclair. And there was only one thing the two men had in common that caused problems: Kira.

Chapter Twenty-Two

"What do ye intend ta do with them?" asked the short, wiry man. The question was directed to a man with deep, yellow shadows on his face from injuries incurred some time ago. His arm hung limp at his side, another result of the battering, and the cause of the man's constant pain. The severe cold and continuous pounding whilst in the saddle, topped with a poor diet and lack of sleep, left him a shadow of the man he thought he was.

His ideas of manhood were stilted and held no true form of the word. He was a bully whose manner of generosity was to kill a whole family rather than one, 'ta save the others from grieving' he would mordantly joke.

Looking up at the man who asked the question, he couldn't help dwell on the past. Never was there anyone to whom he felt an emotional connection. Except one. It was a tumultuous relationship with an explosive physical attraction.

He first saw her across the bailey, during one of the warriors' regular training sessions. Her promiscuous eyes spoke to him. They finally met in person on a warm spring day in one of the villages, and being the laird's only daughter, her bold advance surprised him. He'd valued his position within the castle guards, lowly as it was; it put food in his belly and gave him opportunities to steal from within the castle.

But, she was given to another, betrothed to a neighbouring clan. They still met in secret but the jealous resentment drove him wild. His anger festered and he hungered for revenge.

"What will we do with them, ye ask?" replied the bruised man. He contemplated the question. He looked across the cave at the two bodies thrown on the ground; his cold stare bored into their dormant forms. He'd thought about this moment for two long years and found it hard to contain his elation.

The bait needed to lure his prey straight into his hands lay before him. "I have plans fer them," he said.

"The men will nae like ta be kept from them."

"They took their fill at Preece and will do as I say."

"Ye hold control of them by but a thread."

The bruised man's hand moved like lightning to crush the other's throat. "I give the orders. Ye tell them *I* give the orders. If they want the spoils, I am the only one who can deliver them." He shoved the man, coughing and rubbing his throat, across the cave floor.

He hated to admit the other man was right. The men needed some sport to compensate for the lack of promised spoils or he was going to be in serious trouble. "Get bladders of ice water from the creek." He yelled, "It be time ta wake the bitches."

He scowled. The men would have their entertainment.

****

Alick's head was bowed in contemplation. Connor told him of his suspicions and Alick was absorbing the ramifications. Well after midnight, most of the warriors lay wrapped in their plaids and curled under temporary lean-tos by the fires for the night. Guards were stationed around the perimeter in case of attack, or so they were told. In the morning the guards would also be asked if anyone *left* the camp.

Dougal took first watch over Brian. He earlier

wondered aloud what motivated humans to turn on one another. Connor watched his anger and contempt for the man seething below the surface. Connor knew Dougal's thoughts mirrored his own. How could anyone willingly cause so much heartache and destruction?

As Dougal rolled over under his lean-to and pulled his plaid across his shoulders, he continued the masquerade. He appeared to sleep soundly, leaving Connor and the others to take their turn as camp watch. But although he closed his eyes and his breathing stayed deep and even, it was all a ruse.

Dougal was on watch. He was watching the enemy.

Brian remained unaware, wrapped and secure in his warm plaid five feet away from Dougal. If able to read minds, he would feel anything but safe. He would know a fear to surpass going into battle— because, in truth, Brian Dubois was being hunted.

"I find it hard ta swallow." Although Alick spoke softly, the lines on his face were tight.

"Aye. So do I. But here we are. I willna lose any more MacKay lives than necessary. If this has something ta do with us, or Kira...then it is time." Connor expected these words to be hard, but he was surprised how easily they came. Over the past weeks a fragile respect developed between the two lairds, or maybe the ghosts of the past were chased away by a sword-weilding water nymph. Either way, for Connor it felt right to be discussing Kira with her brother.

"What is it ye wish me ta say? I only know what Kira told me in her letters. As a young child, Kira was spoilt, and then in her teen years she chose diversions causing no end of concern within the Castle. She learnt ta manipulate those around her, blame others for her own mistakes. Kira was troublesome from a young age."

Connor understood it was hard for Alick to speak his sister's name. He well understood Alick's love. Megahn would always possess a piece of his own heart. He asked, "What did she write ye?"

Alick looked uncomfortable. "She was unhappy. She nae liked ye. She just wanted ta come home."

"Aye. I thought as much. We didna suit well. I tried ta make her happy but her anger and resentment...seemed impossible ta overcome. What did she say in her letters? Why did she hate it at Shreave sae much?"

Alick ran a hand wearily through his hair. "I think Kira was troubled. I think maybe her upbringing fostered her demeanour. She liked ta have her own way."

Connor appreciated the honest answer, but Alick still hadn't answered his question. "What did she say in her letters?" he repeated.

Alick sighed. "She said ye beat her."

"What! She said what?" Connor rose from the fireside and paced beside it. He needed to get a hold on his anger—anger not directed towards Alick. "She told ye I beat her?" Connor lowered his voice, conscious this conversation needed to remain private." I wouldna ever...ever."

"Aye, man. I know...I *know*," emphasised Alick.

The two held each other's gaze for a moment and understanding passed between them. Alick shook his head ruefully and continued, "Kira was spoilt and selfish. Before yer betrothal she became unbearable; cursing and nae bending ta anyone's wants or wishes. My father was concerned where she would end up, if she kept going the way she was."

"And what way was that?" Connor's suspicions mounted. "Why did your father suggest the betrothal ta ma father?"

Alick rose from the fire and faced Connor. "There was a man."

Connor's jaw clenched at the memories of Kira, the tumultuous times and her ability to reserve her malice for Connor alone. The castle went about the betrothal celebrations with great excitement having no idea what Connor dealt with to save Kira's honour, whether she deserved the consideration or not.

Alick continued, "He was being trained as a warrior and showed great potential. But once he met Kira, his obsessiveness, and hers, became a thorn in ma father's side. He threatened ta send her away from Wick, and her man. But she cried and promised it was over. Ma father was a good man...but I dinna believe he handled Kira well."

The two men gazed into the flames for a moment, each caught up in their own memories. A light dusting of snow fell but neither seemed aware of it. "When ma father suggested a marriage for Kira, he hoped a new life would eliminate the dilemma. Ma guess..." Alick looked Connor in the eye. "Was it was nae ta be."

Connor almost laughed at the understatement. For months he tried to reason with his betrothed and help her settle into Shreave, but for all his kindness and patience, she fell pregnant. He almost felt sorry for Alick...almost. Connor spent a year of his life dealing with Kira Sinclair. Castle Wick endured her much longer. Connor appreciated his counterpart's honesty and it was now time for some of his. "The child...it wasna mine."

Alick took a deep breath and expelled the air causing a plume of condensation to billow in the light but frigid breeze. "Nae?"

"The child wasna mine," Connor repeated. To ensure Alick was left in no doubt, he said, "We never shared the same bed. We never shared the same room."

Alick looked bewildered and confused. "But ye

were betrothed for three months before she fell in. Yer telling me…" His doubt visibly vaporised as a thought crossed his face. "Damn the man. Damn the whoreson. He followed her. He bloody weel followed her like a dog after a bitch in heat." Alick looked ready to kill. "Son of a bitch," he ranted.

Alick now paced like a caged animal and Connor waited, allowing his friend to calm down. His friend! When did that thought creep into his mind?

"I think we have both been deceived." Connor said. "Now we must figure out the rest."

"Aye." Both men squatted by the fire again.

"What is his name, Alick? I would know it before I kill him."

Alick looked as if he wanted to object but realised Connor claimed more right to his anger. "The deceit of the man went further than I imagined. He became a high-ranking warrior within our army but probably planned the downfall of our clans for some time. His name is Daniel MacKinnis. I beg forgiveness from ye, Connor MacKay. Had I known his and my sister's relationship was nae over, I would have asked ma father ta send him away. We were deceived. I thought sending her to Shreave solved the problem. But it caused ye troubles that should nae have been your concern. For that I am sorry."

It was rare in the Highlands to hear a powerful laird make an apology. Connor heard the sincerity in Alick's tone, and knew the man would have his own regrets to live with. For one, his sister died.

"I was betrayed too. I nae knew she was with him," Connor agreed. "Until she told me she was with child. Then I knew." Connor was tired. They both were. Such revelations were hard to take but were also cleansing. Much was learnt this night. But not all. "So what has MacKinnis got ta do with ma cousin Brian?"

"That I canna answer. But we will find out, you and I."

"Aye. We shall."

Alick leaned his arm across the fire. Connor did not hesitate to reciprocate. They clasped each other's forearms in a show of solidarity and both knew it meant more than that.

Alick's face held a resigned smirk. "Unfortunately, there is worse ta come fer me." At Connor's blank look, Alick explained. "Yer sister! Meg said I should have rid us of MacKinnis. I disagreed. There will be hell ta pay when she finds oot!" Both men chuckled, knowing what it was like to get a tongue lashing from Megahn MacKay-Sinclair.

"I'll just be happy ta finish it." Connor spoke almost to himself.

"Weel man, ye've already started it. Daniel MacKinnis is the man ye beat senseless at Shreave—the one who assaulted yer woman."

Connor rose from the ground. His whole demeanour changed as if a challenge was issued. "Ye will nae touch him. He will be mine."

Alick gave a nod.

Dougal approached and asked, "Have ye two finished warming yer arses?" His jest was easy with the tension usually surrounding the two men absent. His voice remained casual as he shared his information. "Oh, I thought ye might be interested ta know our prey has absconded."

Dougal had watched Brian slip out of camp and sent Neill to trail him. The MacKay and Sinclair warriors were woken and readied themselves without a sound. The word spread quickly, one of their own was the quarry. Never did a bunch of men look more dangerous.

Traitors did not live long in the Highlands.

Chapter Twenty-Three

Deerskin bladders of iced water splashed over the two women. Jo had faked unconsciousness with perfection, but was no match for the icy dousing. It felt like shards of glass piercing her skin, snatching her breath away. A sense of dread overwhelmed her as she tried to sit and catch her breath. Upright for the first time in hours, she heard groaning and turned to see Maeve trying to rise. But they were given no time to right or rouse themselves.

Someone grabbed Jo by the front of her dress and hauled to her feet, her legs buckling under her as pain shot through them. Pain from the kicks received earlier, from riding, and finally from lying still on a cold floor for hours. She was half dragged to the centre of the cave and thrown like a piece of rubbish back to the ground.

Before she'd time to get her senses in working order, she heard Maeve scream as she too was dragged across the ground by her hair, feet thrashing as total confusion consumed her mind after being unconscious for several hours.

"Leave her alone, you bastards. Don't touch her," she screamed, trying to rise and defend her friend, but stumbled clumsily over her own skirts. Before she could utter another word, the man dumped Maeve beside her and backhanded Jo across her face. The impact was great enough to swing her around a full turn before she fell flat on her face again, gasping for breath and fighting consciousness.

"Keep yer fists ta yerself, ye stupid bastard. We want them awake."

She turned to where the voice came from as the group parted and a man stepped forward. Comprehension washed over her, but instead of terror she felt the inevitability of Murphy's Law. "I see you have a bigger pack of mangy dogs surrounding you this time." She spat blood from her mouth without even realising. Shaking but determined, she rose to her feet. "I like the new look Laird MacKay gave you. Do you think you'll ever be able to use that useless arm again?" She recklessly taunted the man who assaulted her at Shreave, as he jerked his battered body and limp arm across the cave towards her.

Daniel MacKinnis laughed and lurched forward, his eyes roamed up and down her body, repulsing her. She held her face straight, showing no fear. It was the only thing she could do. If she drew the men's attention to herself it may buy her time—for what she didn't know, but attention needed to be directed away from Maeve, who was still semi-conscious on the ground.

"Yer full of feist for one who has nae chance of escape...nae chance ta run...naebody near ta hear ye scream. You be either brave or stupid." MacKinnis limped nearer with each gibe, but came no closer than five feet.

Jo noted his hesitation, sure he remembered her own fighting skills. "You're a coward." She spoke with disgust, but bile rising in her throat almost spoilt the charade. "I can't believe these men follow you. If you're their best choice as leader, then the rest must be more gullible than children." She was unsure if the mercenaries realised she insulted them, but she needed to cause some disorder to buy time.

It seemed to have worked. Many of them frowned, looking to their leader. "Why do you follow him anyway? Has he promised you riches or 'spoils' I think you call it?" She spat out more blood again. Less, she absently noticed this time. Platelets working properly! *This is crazy.* She ordered her thoughts. "Are you expecting to be wealthy after this?" she taunted. "You're fools! All you'll get from this man are lies and cold arses."

The men murmured to each other, doubt travelling through the group like a rolling sea wave. The stench emanating from them was disgusting, but she'd little time to think of it or what may come later.

Raising his voice to be heard, MacKinnis barked, "This bitch knows nothing." He rounded back on her. "Ye think this is about ye, do ye not? Ye think ye are the important one here." He laughed. "Ye are just the bait, ye useless bitch. It be the lairds we want. We shall use ye ta get them. Then we shall take off their heads and leave them fer the dogs. We shall tie ye up next ta them sae ye can watch…them…rot."

His deliberate emphasis of the lairds' fate left Jo frozen in terror as the men began to nod their heads, their mood once again swayed in favour of MacKinnis. If these men succeeded in getting Connor and Alick it would be her fault—hers and Maeve's. They were the leverage needed to get close to the lairds. They were fooled into leaving the safety of the castle and would now lead their men right into a trap. Her face betrayed her feelings.

"Ooh, now the slut realises." Bolstered by the men at his back, MacKinnis took two limping steps towards her. His battered face inches from hers, his fetid breath made her gag. Her courage and optimism evaporated in the face of their predicament. "But before we kill MacKay and Sinclair, they shall know what it feels like ta have someone else rut with their woman. They shall know what it is like ta have their woman split by another man, or in your case...*men.*" Her blood turned to ice at the words. *Oh, God help us.*

"So, Kira's child was yers?" It took everyone by surprise to hear another female voice. With the attention on Jo, Maeve was almost forgotten.

No, Maeve. No.

But it was too late. Maeve drew the focus to herself already. She lay half-raised on her side, unable to conjure the strength to lift herself fully. "Ye were the one she pined after. I canna say I agree with her taste in men."

Daniel MacKinnis glared at Maeve, his eyes full of contempt. "Shut yer mouth, bitch. Dinna speak her name ta me. She was better than ye and all the other women in Shreave. She knew how ta please a man, not like ye frigid sluts."

Frigid slut? How does one become a frigid slut? Jo asked herself while unable to believe, how in such circumstances her frantic mind could have picked up the contradiction.

"She should have been mine, but yer lairds planned against me. I was nae good enough. Well, who be laughing now, bitch?"

For the first time, Maeve glanced at Jo. Her eyes pleaded for Maeve to cease drawing their attention, while Maeve's assured her friend she knew what she was doing.

"Aye then," Maeve continued, pain shelved whilst she tried to raise a hornet's nest within the mercenary group. "So what ye are saying is ye have all these men here ta help ye avenge a lost *love*? I wonder if they know this. I wonder if *yer men* realise this is why they've been freezing their arses off. And how were ye going ta pay them?"

"Shut up!" MacKinnis lunged for Maeve, but was brought down by Jo as he moved past her. She took out his knee and sent him crumbling to the earth. Someone grabbed her from behind in a painful hold which she extracted herself from with an elbow to the midriff, followed by one to the nose. As scuffles broke out, screams and curses rang through the cave as she managed to reach Maeve on the floor. They held onto each other.

"Enough!" The hollered command came from the cave entrance and was so loud it left ears ringing. Standing in the shadows was a tall form dressed in MacKay plaid and none present reacted with defence or alarm. The man surveyed the scene. MacKinnis sprawled out on the ground; his hands held his knee and his face showed pain and fury. The rest looked confused, wondering if they'd been deceived. If so, there would be a bloodbath.

A red-headed man with a dirty beard stepped forward to address the new arrival, "Where is our coin? Ye better have it in yer saddle bags or ye are dead."

His face calm, betraying nothing, Brian Dubois stepped into the light. "We will have it soon. Now we have the wom—"

"The whores will compensate us for but a few minutes. We want what we are owed. Now!" There were murmurs of agreement through the group and they closed in around Brian.

From their position on the floor, the women knew brief relief as the attention passed to Brian. They held onto each other. If either let go they would fall to peices, doing neither any good; holding on at least lessened the trembling.

"Nay, wait." Brian took a step forward. "I have something." He reached into his sporran and pulled out a sack of coins. He threw them at the mercenary spokesman, who caught and tested the weight. He then took out a coin and bit it with his teeth. "This be nae enough. Where is the rest of the gold?" the man demanded.

"It's sitting on the floor," Brian calmly

proclaimed. He took another step towards the women and was pleased to see most of the men back up. "They are worth ten times that amount in ransom." He stared at them coldly. "*Ladies*. So glad ye could join us."

"Ye bastard." Maeve looked shocked and saddened one of Clan MacKay's own was responsible for this treachery and, Connor's cousin no less. Connor had given Brian a solid position within Clan MacKay, ensuring a prosperous and good life. But now the man betrayed his own blood; blood by the mother, but blood nonetheless. "Why?" Maeve's struggle for answers, for reason, showed in her eyes.

"Ye think I would be content ta run and do Connor's bidding fer the rest of ma life? Ye think he deserved ta be laird more than I?"

Brian crouched before them, his calm manner more terrifying than violence. "He will die—and as the only family left, I shall be laird."

"What? Ye think they would elect ye after all this. Are ye mad?"

"I am nae mad, Maeve. I am nae even a mercenary. I am cousin Brian."

Maeve's blood ran cold as ice, "Ye are going ta kill them. The lairds, the warriors...and us?"

"Oh, now she understands. Clever girl. After a ransom is paid, of course. Oh, I shall be *injured* in the skirmish. But I shall survive the battle, and as a hero I will succeed Connor MacKay."

"Ye are insane," Maeve breathed.

Angered, Brain lurched forward and seized Maeve's hair, dragging her to a standing position. He wrenched her face to within an inch of his leering smile.

Jo tried to retaliate but was dragged away from her friend. She screamed, but to no avail. A small dirk was placed across her throat, immobilising her. She felt the blade's edge pierce her skin with a sharp sting and could do nothing but remain still and watch.

"I always wondered what Dougal saw in a tavern whore. We shall just have ta find out."

The men cheered and Jo saw one rub his groin, an erection already visible under his woollen trews. Bile rose in her throat once again.

How are we ever going to survive this? "Leave her alone you sons of bitches. Leave her alone." She screamed in rage but it was no use. A droplet of blood trickled down her neck, restricting her movement again. She tried to fortify herself for what was to come.

The mercenaries were now temporarily compensated with the gold coins and a promise of a hefty ransom to come.

They had run out of time. Jo knew it, and she felt certain Maeve knew it.

They were alone. Connor, Meg, Alick, Dougal—none knew they were missing. They didn't know they were no longer within the safety of Castle Shreave. Jo wondered how one prepared oneself for the terror and degradation to come. At this moment the best she could do was to endure it.

****

The MacKay and Sinclair warriors followed Brian and Neill's tracks for about three-and-a-half miles, stopping at a crag with a well-worn trail. They could not risk ascending in single file until Neill came back with more information. Neither could they risk a trap or encountering their quarry descending the pathway.

They silently awaited Neill's return, hopeful Brian's careless belief no one suspected him would lead them straight to the mercenary's hideout.

Neill signalled his arrival with two soft whistles on the icy breeze. He came across Alick first, crouched low behind a copse, his dirk readied and his other hand on his sheathed sword. "Where are Connor and Dougal?" Neill asked in hushed tones.

Alick gave one sharp, soft whistle. Within seconds Connor appeared from the shadows with Dougal behind him.

Neill, known by Connor and Dougal most of their lives, was considered trustworthy and unflappable, so the look of trepidation on his face made Connor's stomach clench with anxiety. Something was wrong.

Connor knew Dougal was uneasy. His friend told him earlier, since they began trailing the tracks in the snow, a restlessness he'd never felt before plagued him.

"What man? What is it?" asked Dougal, almost afraid of the answer.

Not realising his own breathing ceased, Connor's eyes bored into Neill.

"They have two hostages."

Chapter Twenty-four

A sense of calm infiltrated the warrior party. Blades digging into the freezing ground for the softer dirt beneath made the only sounds. Life seemed to have slid into slow motion, even though only a matter of minutes passed.

Consumed with their own thoughts, Connor, Dougal, and Alick tended themselves, becoming unrecognisable with dirt and melted snow mixed to camouflage their pale skin. Only the whites of their eyes were visible, and the intensity of their manner was as chilling as their blackened faces. Each man prepared for battle; prepared to die if need be.

****

Daniel MacKinnis sat on the cold floor leaning against the cave wall; sweat covered his brow and a trickle ran down the side of his face. His knee was dislocated and the intense pain caused him to vomit. No one within the cave cared about him and he wondered what life held for a cripple. If, when the time came to leave, he could not mount his own horse, he would be left behind. It was hard enough keeping up with the mercenaries after the beating he received from The MacKay.

Travelling to Shreave with The Sinclair proved most convenient. It gave him the opportunity to pass information to Brian and to gather information for himself on the movements and travel plans of those within the castle.

He grimaced. His one mistake was to harass the tall bitch. Ousted from the Sinclair army and now injured, he stood little chance on his own.

But he would see this through. He would ensure a ransom note was sent to Shreave. Oh, how he wished, more than anything, he could see the face of Connor MacKay when the news arrived. If not for a chance meeting with Brian Dubois in a tavern, he may never have gained such a sweet opportunity for revenge.

A scream rent the fetid air within the cave followed by the sound of ripping material.

Fun for the men began.

****

It took five minutes of violent argument to decide who would go first, and which woman they would prefer. But they truly didn't care, as long as they got their fill. Cousin Brian was afforded first turn on Jo. After paying the mercenaries their gold, and with a promise of more to come, he was considered first in command. She was his by right. First to violate Maeve would be the young man who lured the two women from Castle Shreave. It elevated his status within the group.

MacKinnis, all but discarded, was not even considered.

But, having heard of Jo's ability to defend herself, the men displayed caution. Whispers of witchcraft rippled through the throng. How else could a mere woman defend herself against a man? Even with her arms pinned to the ground above her head and ropes further rubbing her bleeding wrists, she used her legs so viciously that Brian was still buckled over grasping his crotch. Her terror was so great, she hadn't even realised her aim hit true.

The thing which did register in her frantic mind was Maeve's screaming sobs. Jo tried to catch a glimpse of her friend amongst the legs of the cheering men, absorbed in their horrendous sport. She could see the mercenary who'd tricked them into leaving the safety of Shreave. He was undoing his breeches, a crazed gleam in his eye as he stared at Maeve. Two men held her friend's arms above her.

Without even realising she was doing it, a yell of rage tore from Jo's throat, but a slap resounded so hard across her face her vision blurred and she vomited on the hard packed dirt.

"It be yer turn now," the voice taunted. She opened her eyes to see Brian take full advantage of her as she lowered her guard to be ill. He held both her ankles in a vice-like grip and launched himself on top of her. His weight compressed the air from her lungs and crushed her ribs.

She took no time to concern herself with this as she was mere seconds from being violated. His hard erection poked through her skirts, demanding entrance. His free hand ripped the front of her bodice down the middle, exposing her bare breasts for all to see. A loud cheer went up.

Everything happened in slow motion, as if she was an observer in a freakish nightmare. She screamed and cursed; the taste of blood strong in her mouth from the last hit. Her mind ceasing to acknowledge, refusing to accept, what was happening to her. Seconds later another scream echoed off the cave walls, so deafening she did not realise the voice was her own.

Then she heard a roar. A bellow of pure rage. It was so loud she was overwhelmed by the unseen terror.

Brian was gone; men were running and yelling and more cries were heard. She tried to surface from the hazy confusion, one thing became more apparent then anything else—Brian was no longer on top of her—and all the other men waiting to take their turn were running, some tripping or stepping on her in their haste to...what?

Screams, more screams. As another man's foot came into contact with her body as he rushed past, she realised she would be trampled to death if she did not seek shelter. Bewildered and scared, oblivious to the fact her breasts were still exposed, she began to crawl to the edge of the cave. Fear drove her—fear Brian would return, or anyone else wishing to finish what was started.

Before crawling two paces, she was lifted into the air, carried by the back of her dress like a large, floppy handbag. Her shoulders popped out of the garment, its torn bodice unable to support her weight. Someone unseen hurled her against the cave wall, the air knocked from her lungs as she landed on something soft.

Through tears of fear and panting like she'd run a hundred miles, she looked up to see who threw her so. A shadow came out of nowhere and slammed her head back down onto the softness beneath. "Stay there!" The words were spoken with such force she did as told, and when she realised who gave the order, understanding swamped her.

Recognition and gratitude invaded her brain as Neill moved back into the ferocious battle. Warriors wielded broadswords, carnage littered the floor of the grotto, and a rivulet of blood ran past her as the dirt floor turned red.

The fierce power exuded by the warriors was grotesque but fascinating as she watched weapons slash, sever, and behead without mercy.

As a vague form of sanity returned to her and the paralysing fear abated, she realised Connor must be nearby. Instead of this thought comforting her, it brought forth a new kind of panic for his safety. *Please don't let him be hurt.*

Before she'd a chance to seek him, a soft groan from beneath drew her focus. *Maeve!*

In the horror of battle, niceties and consideration were obliterated and she hadn't realised she'd been thrown to safety right on top of

Maeve. That Neill was sent to protect them meant Connor and Dougal were not far away.

She tried to untangle her dress; it gaped to her waist and twisted round her legs. At the same time her eyes checked Maeve's condition. She seemed to be unconscious, flat on her back, her dress torn down the front similar to her own. Her face was bruised and swollen and fury filled Jo as she saw the bite marks on Maeve's neck and breasts. The intensity of the anger momentarily paralysed her.

Only her ability to defend herself delayed the violence long enough to save her from penetration. Brian's disgusting molestation would haunt her, but it was nothing compared to the degredation suffered by her friend. As she reached out her hand to touch Maeve's face, a tear of anger and grief slid down her cheek. Her own indecencies were pushed aside as her disgust and loathing took over. Under these horrific circumstances, one was grateful for small mercies. But mercy was not on her mind as she eyed the bloody throng of warriors, seeking the man who did this to Maeve.

Calm invaded her mind. Though never one to seek retribution, now *she* wanted revenge. This was no office tiff, nor a management power struggle. It was a raw, no rules applied, struggle for survival. Kill or be killed.

And she wanted to kill.

She was about to rise and seek out her prey, if he was not already one of the bloodied corpses littering the cave floor, when Maeve's soft brogue pulled her back. She whimpered, "Dougal?" Then again. "Dougal?"

"Maeve. It's okay. It's Jo. I'm here, I'm here."

As Maeve's eyes sought the familiar voice, a pinging noise sounded above their heads amidst the battle screams. It was so resonant it sounded like a smithy's hammer hitting the anvil and her split second response was to duck, throwing herself protectively over her friend, afraid one of the mercenaries came to annihilate them. When no killing blow sliced into her back, she raised her head to see what made the sound.

Jo did not believe in God, or God's will, or even divine intervention, but what she saw lying in the bloodied dirt beside her made her question her beliefs. Her *sword*, her *own* tailor-made, light-weight sword lay within her grasp.

She hadn't given her weapon a second thought, barely remembering she owned one, since their violent capture. But now realisation struck her. One of the mercenaries must have procured it as part of his booty. But now it was returned.

And she knew what to do with it.

****

The MacKay and Sinclair warriors devised their ruthless attack with precision, overcoming the problem of how to formulate a surprise attack when only able to climb the crag in single file. They were unsure if a sentry was posted at the cave entrance. When Neill did his reconnaissance, no mercenary manned the post. But this may have changed. Nothing could be taken for granted.

Due to the terrain and confined space within the grotto, surprise was paramount. If the alarm were raised before the men could position themselves on the narrow ledge outside, the warriors at the front of the charge would have no chance and be cut down before they could breach the interior. But all worked better than planned. No sentry, and within the cave every mercenary, their minds on other matters, faced away from the entrance.

As the first dark foreboding shadow gained entrance to the hideout, a death knell sounded.

Laird Connor MacKay's demon eyes surveyed the scene and he became the great warrior he was renowned for; chilling, brutal, precise, and merciless—as one with his sword.

At his shoulders stood two more hellish apparitions: Dougal and Alick's faces were also blackened out, the whites of their eyes bright in the darkness as their souls demanded revenge.

Bellowing war cries echoed off the walls in the initial assault, deafening in their ferocity. It caused such shock and confusion, Connor dispatched three men before the echoes bounced off the walls. With Dougal and Alick at his back, they quickly split a path through the middle of the mercenaries, weakening their defences by dividing them. By the time this manoeuvre was complete, fifteen more warriors entered behind, broadswords raised and swinging, blade edges glinting in the firelight.

The enemy was so taken by surprise some were unarmed having discarded their weapons in anticipation of a different kind of sport. Fools.

****

Maeve mumbled when she saw Jo grab the hilt of her sword, "Where do ye think yer going with that?" Maeve's abused face would take weeks to heal, her spirit longer.

Jo knelt next to her friend, finding it difficult to contain her cold rage. "I have a good sword, Maeve. I can't lie here and do nothing. Besides...it happened to us—*to us*. Those sons of bitches deserve it."

Maeve could not answer before Jo shrugged her shoulders as best she could back into the remains of her dress and crawled away along the edges of the cave her eyes intent—seeking, searching.

It didn't matter which one she saw first. Brian or Maeve's rapist, either would do. If someone told her three months ago she would be prepared to kill someone with her own hands, that she felt a rage so intense, an injustice so profound, she was prepared to kill another human, she would have said they were insane.

But this was no dream. The feelings rioting within her mind were honed and true. Senses focused, she would watch and wait for her chance, and when it came she would take it. And she didn't have to wait long.

In all the terror and confusion since their capture she failed to notice a tunnel, disappearing into the rear of the cavern. She moved towards it, sword at the ready, seeing one of her targets.

The young mercenary backed away from the foray, skulking towards the rear exit.

****

Connor and Dougal were at the forefront of the grisly battle. With over half of their enemy already dispatched to eternity, they could now pick and choose their next victims. Their own soldiers would stand aside, should they desire to take on an enemy already under their sword.

But Connor and Dougal were searching, too. As the first to enter the cavern they saw everything, all be it for a few seconds, before their chilling battle cry rent the air and they unleashed their unrelenting anger. Now the clash was waning; they took time to think on those images.

As they stood back-to-back with their swords raised, circling, searching, Dougal's massive form tensed and Connor sensed the change.

They both swivelled at once and saw the filthy youth who defiled Maeve, raising his sword for a crushing blow that would slice Jo in two.

****

She'd delayed his escape. His blade waved menacingly before her face as blood lust rose in his eyes.

"Do ye think ta touch me with that pathetic blade, stupid slut? Come on then," he taunted, as his finger curled towards himself, calling her to advance. "I'll split ye with ma sword rather than ma cock."

His disgusting banter and the stench of his sweat made her more determined in her assault. As his broadsword wheeled in an arc around his head, all her training in the ancient art came to the fore as she sidestepped the downward blow with smooth grace, off-balancing the youth, who expected his sword to strike flesh and slow the descending swing. But the heavy blade's momentum swung through, giving her ample time to take the advantage and bring down the face of her blade on the back of his exposed neck.

Disbelief registered on his face and wasting no time, she kicked him hard in the arm driving him to his knees before her.

Blood ran from a cut on his shoulder, not lethal, but effective enough for sweat to bead on his brow. His face betrayed the pain that must be running down his sword arm. She edged her blade against his neck, ready to slice open his throat. But she held back, pushing firmly enough on her blade to nick his skin.

So he knew he was at her mercy.

"Go on then," he snarled with false bravado, his head held frozen, hoping the blade would slice no further. "Finish it, if ye have the balls." Sweat mixed with his blood ran down her sword. "Useless woman! Good fer naught else but ruttin'..."

It was a mistake to taunt her. She gripped the sword hilt and pulled it towards herself—just a little. The movement had the desired affect on her prey as he screamed, feeling his skin sliced by her blade. "You bitch, you bitch." His body trembled.

Jo, confident of the advantage, firmed her grip on the sword and bent over her victim to whisper, her lips close to his ear. "What's your name?"

His eyes darted around in bewilderment while

his head remained still. The slightest movement could drive the blade further into his neck.

"Are ye mad? Just finish it." Spittle covered his lips. "Why do ye care what ma name is?"

"What. Is. Your. Name?" Her fierce whisper caressed his ear as the sword's pressure increased to emphasise her point.

"Donald. Donald Fergusson."

"Well, Donald Fergusson." Her eyes flashed with venom. "How does it feel to be helpless? Are you scared Donald?" Her soft breath steamed, warm against his lobe.

As Donald Fergusson prepared to die with her blade millimetres from his main artery, neither realised the battle around them ended. The air crackled with emotional tension, blinding them to the silent audience gathered around them. The MacKay and Sinclair warriors, blackened, bloodied, and almost unrecognisable, stood mesmerised by the courageous woman before them. The woman prepared to defend her friend, defend their clan— with a small sword.

Donald's head fell forward and his shoulders began to shake as tears of fear and resignation ran down his cheeks. He was broken...by a mere woman.

She firmed her grip intending to kill him when a long arm reached over her shoulder to clamp a bloodied hand over hers.

"I'll nae have his blood on yer hands, lass. But I would be honoured ta use yer sword ta take ma kill." Dougal's voice broke the silence, low and vicious.

Jo relinquished her sword. Dougal had every right to seek revenge for Maeve.

As she stepped back she bumped into a soft wall. A hand snaked around her middle holding her steady against his strength. He smelt of man, sweat, and blood. He reached under her legs and swung her up, cradling her against his chest as he moved to exit the cave. The warriors parted to allow them passage. Some touched their swords to their brows in a rare salute—to honour Jo.

Chapter Twenty-Five

Baby Davie sucked his thumb; his eyes fighting sleep but losing the battle. Jo ran her hand over his downy scalp in soothing movements. She spent much time in the nursery over the past two weeks. It comforted her to be with the children. Their innocence helped restore her faith in human kindness. *"Go to sleep my baby, close your little eyes,"* she sang softly.

Unnoticed by her, Connor stood in the doorway. The scene before him sent unfamiliar feelings through his heart. He wondered how it would feel to see her hold a child of their own. But as soon as the thought came, the familiar, unwanted shadow passed over him and darkness shaded all that should be good. Even though they tried to go about their lives as if all was normal—they could not.

And they were not the only ones wrestling with demons. Since their return from the abduction and horrific battle, Maeve withdrew into herself. Jo tried to draw her out, but to no avail. Maeve would say, "I am fine. Go aboot yer business." But they knew Maeve was far from well.

Jo knew Maeve's monthly cycle was past due. Dougal held his wife close after her rape, but no end of comfort seemed to penetrate her stupor. Maeve shut him out. She built a wall around herself and would let no one in, as if she were punishing herself. She and Dougal had layed together before he left to hunt the raiders, so if she were pregnant, the new babe she carried was likely Dougal's. But the doubt ate at her soul.

Jo observed Dougal walking around the castle surrounded by an unapproachable cloud of anger and guilt. He thought they should have attacked sooner. He should have never left her alone. He should have sensed she was in danger—all useless, ridiculous remonstrations. When she tried to approach him, Dougal glared ferociously, his eyes speaking volumes. *Back off.*

So an invisible haze of tension hung over Castle Shreave and its inhabitants. Everyone knew what happened, although some of the tales were embellished. One Sinclair soldier lost his life when the raiders were surprised and dispatched. One mercenary was unaccounted for. All other injuries, whether by blade or bruised emotions, would heal in time.

Servants and alike tiptoed around the edges, unsure of themselves. Maeve was always there for advice and direction but suddenly she was not. Meals were brought to the tables, late and maybe a few cheese wheels short, but life continued on as normal as possible.

Connor advanced into the room; his eyes watching his betrothed's soft lips as she sang her lullaby. She'd been open and honest with him since her rescue. She experienced nightmares each night, and woke within the warm cocoon of his protective arms and soothing words.

He made no sexual advances towards her in the last two weeks, offering comfort and understanding. Even though Brian hadn't raped her, the violation was so traumatic, so personal; she would carry the emotional scars for years to come. The nightmares were grisly and blood filled. In her dreams she was the one who took the head of Donald Fergusson, and his blood spurted over her face.

Connor's warmth chased away the terror. "I think if ye coddle the lad any more he shall have nae hair left on his head." At his light-hearted tone, her head rose from the baby, her eyes locking with his.

His dark eyes covered her and caused the fine hairs on her arms to stand up. She took in every detail of him, his wide shoulders; his dark, braided hair; the way his eyes spoke more than his words; all within a face that could grace the pages of *Vogue* magazine. God, she loved him. But it was his strong, silent manner that aroused her more. He sought no homage; never made others do what he would not do himself. And he contained his anger and lust for revenge well, so she thought.

After the gruesome body count, no trace of Brian Dubois was found. His partner in crime was found broken and battered, his throat slit by his own hand. But Brian was gone.

Connor chuckled, Jo realised she stared at him overly long. She grinned, embarrassed for having exposed her feelings. She lowered her head to hide the blush, Connor reached down and tilted her chin back up to face him. "Never be ashamed ta show me yer feelings, Jo-Anne. I feel the same."

Tears stung her eyes and she ceased her ministrations on Davie's soft head to take hold of Connor's calloused hand. "How honest would you like me to be about those feelings?" she asked, as her chin began to quiver.

"As honest as the earth, Lady."

"Then listen well, my laird." She kissed the palm of his hand. "I love you with all my heart. More than anything, I want to feel your child move within me. I want to grow old with you. When I reminisce about things I've done, I want to share those memories with you."

Connor knelt in front of her chair, his eyes never leaving her face as she continued. "When our children grow, they will learn from us all about kindness and loyalty. They will be given responsibility so they become trustworthy, we will be tolerant so they learn patience, and we will encourage them so they grow to be confident. But most of all they will be unconditionally loved, so they learn to have faith."

Connor raised his other hand to touch her face, but she forestalled it, catching and holding it to her heart. There was more to say.

"You weren't there the day they found me...in the woods." Connor nodded acknowledgment. "I need to tell you how I got there and where I'm from. I owe you the truth. And then you can decide..."

Connor swallowed a bothersome lump clogging his throat, his eyes drinking in her face, red nose, red eyes, and quivering lips. He slid his arms under Davie's tiny body and disappeared with him into the side room. When he returned, the baby tucked safe in his crib, he reached for her hands pulling her to stand before him. "There is naught fer me ta decide. Ye are mine. Nae other will ever take ye from me again."

"No. You don't understand."

"What more is there ta know? I dinna care if ye were running from some wrong or mistake. I dinna care if ye were lost and cannot remember where ye came from. Now is all that..."

"Connor! I know where I came from. I know who I am. I have always known." Connor pulled back a little; his eyes waited for her to continue. "I need to tell you about my home."

****

As time ticked by and the embers in the grate burned low, she told Connor MacKay all about her past—about her time.

"So ye say this c-a-r can go faster than a war pony?" Connor shook his head in bewilderment. "I should be thinking ye are mad...but I know ye too well."

They strolled into the laird's chamber, the nursery having come alive with waking babies and a fussing Mrs. Moray to afford them any further privacy. She was conscious of how difficult it would be for him to take all this information in. But it was important to her he knew where she came from. *Really* knew.

She was relieved when he hadn't discounted it outright. He listened to her talk of her work, Melbourne, politics, and how it made for such a safe society; and dozens of other unreal but important pieces of news. She talked herself hoarse.

"Well, my laird," she said, tentative, encouraged he'd continued to listen, but hesitant he was overwhelmed. At least she refrained from telling him man walked on the moon. "What do you make of all that? Can you still love the crazy girl who says she's from the future?"

Connor pulled her into his arms and held her close, his head resting on the top of hers as she nestled into the protective shield. "I already told ye Jo-Anne. It nae matters about yer past."

"But, do you believe me, Connor?" She pulled her head back to look up at his face.

"Aye. I do."

Tears spilled down her face as relief and gratitude overcame her. "Thank you." She raised her lips to his. "Kiss me, Connor. Please."

He needed no more urging. Connor had held himself back since the assault, vowing he would not touch her until she was ready. There were times when he wanted to ravish her and wipe away all traces of Brian Dubois. His self-control snapped on several occasions over the weeks, but he would walk away and find something hard to hit. His fists sported many graze marks.

Their lips met in a kiss that spoke of love and tenderness. Soon it was not enough. Their tongues duelled and desire coiled around them. She unfastened Connor's belt and he stood motionless and let her take the lead. His belt hit the timber floor, and his plaid and under-shirt quickly followed. She stood back to admire him. "You are beautiful, Connor MacKay."

"What? Even with ma boots still on?"

They laughed and loved and took pleasure in undressing each other. When she stood naked before him, Jo looked down, shyness creeping over her features. "Connor," she asked, "do I still look the same?" The moisture in his eyes made hers widen in surprise when their gaze met.

"Ye are more beautiful now than ye have ever been," he answered.

Jo led him to their bed. They made love. It was timeless, passion filled, and precious.

Later, when they lay in each others arms, Connor asked, "Ye didna tell me how ye think the time travel happened."

She sighed, her breath tickling his chest. "I'm not sure," she mumbled. "But I think it may have something to do with a gift I was given."

"Aye. What gift?"

"It was beautiful. But I think I lost it when I arrived in the forest." Jo sat up beside Connor and draped one leg across his groin. She wore a sweet smile on her lips as she remembered June's gift. "It was an antique Celtic necklace." She described the rubies and the pattern surrounding them. She broke from her musings and looked at him. "Connor, your face is pale. Are you okay?"

He resumed his shuttered look. The look he gave when he was concealing something, or some emotion. "It is naught... I was just...thinking," he stammered, trying to ignore the knot of fear tightening his chest. He plunged his face into her breasts and flipped her to her back. She squealed with delight, the unusual incident forgotten, just as he intended.

After blowing raspberries on her breasts, causing her to giggle, he rose over her, pinning her to the bed "Ye are mine, Jo-Anne Dunstan. Ye will never leave me. I will never let ye go. Nothing will ever take ye from me." It was said with such passion and conviction as if saying it aloud would make it so, "Ye were sent here fer me. Of that I am sure."

"I'm not planning on going anywhere."

But he saw the brief taint of fear in her eyes. He knew she wondered as he did—could she fall asleep one night and wake up back in the twenty-first century? It would be impossible without the necklace, she felt sure.

As Connor held her tighter, his last thought before slumber overtook him was to go and speak with Maeve. She may be the only one who could help him. Dougal's wife had the Sight. She may have some idea.

He could face up to a cave full of thugs and go to war wielding his sword to defend his home, but the thought of losing Jo from his life gutted him to the core.

Fear gripped him.

If the necklace could bring her to him, then could it also take her away?

He was very, very familiar with the precious jewelled necklace she described.

Chapter Twenty-Six

The next few weeks passed in a blur for Jo. She took over many of the chatelaine duties within Shreave. Even though their wedding wasn't until spring, as the laird's betrothed it was expected of her, and she began her new role with pride and enthusiasm.

Everybody within Shreave already knew her, so her change of duties was much easier. Being new to the castle was a challenge in itself without the responsibility of being its mistress. Often, clans were united by marriage and young teenagers, as the betrothed, would find themselves with the enormous responsibility of running a huge keep. She was appreciative of her own maturity.

Adolescents from the twenty-first century would be studying, playing sports, going to the beach with friends, or any other of a hundred recreational activities. She couldn't decide if she was grateful for her own teenage years or embarrassed for the frivolous pass-times of her youth.

She was also thankful for the friendships developed over the past months and the loyalty shown to her by Connor's men-at-arms. Following the cave battle, the warriors now looked at her in a different way to what they may have viewed women in the past.

At first it made her uncomfortable to be saluted or given respectful nods as she walked past the barracks or armoury, but now she found it comforting. Connor's presence made her feel safe, but he wasn't always there, such were his duties.

She only needed to squeak, and any of the soldiers would jump to her defence, protecting her with their lives.

It was humbling.

The weather confined everyone indoors and this meant increased activity within the hall. Highland winters limited outdoor occupations, and she found it hard to breathe the frigid air into her lungs. Her clothes kept her warm enough and her new sheepskin boots were her saviour, but the icy air made her admire the Highlanders even more. They went about their business unaffected by the freezing cold and deep snow.

On a crowded day in the great hall, Dougal approached her. A conversation between the laird's betrothed and his second-in-command was not to be remarked upon, but Jo was surprised. No, shocked.

It was the first time Dougal Haig approached her. It seemed he ignored her. He never initiated conversation, never acknowledged her, and if he did need to consult on a matter it was always done by proxy—via Neill, Maeve, or Tannan—anyone but himself.

She was not used to being viewed with suspicion. But she realised Dougal believed unless you were born in the Highlands, you would *always* be an outsider. He was the most stubborn man in a kilt.

Instead of Dougal looking at her with reservation, she saw something else in his eyes. Without thought, she reached for his arm and led him away to the linen alcove at the side of the hall. She suspected Dougal never let anyone drag him anywhere in his whole life. But he wore the look of a man searching for answers. He looked defeated.

"Dougal, what is it?" She took a step back to give him some space, yet still he filled the room. He reminded her of Connor. The two men were so different, yet so alike, commanding attention wherever they went, whether they wanted it or not. At Dougal's lack of response, she tried again. "Dougal. What's wrong? Is Maeve okay?"

Dougal's shoulders slumped, his weariness evident as he sat on a wooden chest. He wore the look of a man on the edge—only just holding on to his manhood and fighting for composure.

"Ah dinna ken what ta do. I've tried everything. She distances herself from me more and more every day. I canna get through ta her." His shoulders began to shake.

Jo found it easy to offer comfort, but this time felt at a loss. She sat quietly and watched, as Dougal let loose his emotions. He was a proud man, stubborn and obnoxious, but there was one thing undeniable—he loved his wife. He adored her, and he felt the distance Maeve placed between them. It tore him apart.

"I think..." She chose her words with care. Not even she was able to discuss with Maeve the violence within the cave those weeks ago. "I think Maeve feels guilty."

Dougal stood, his face a cloud of outrage. She held his arm so he couldn't leave.

"What has she ta be guilty aboot?" he yelled, frustration pouring off him in waves. "She has done naught wrong. She was the victim. Why would she feel guilt?"

"I only know how *I* feel, Dougal." At her honest words Dougal paused and held eye contact with her as she continued. "I always thought I was pretty smart. I thought I could read people well, but I misjudged. When Maeve decided to go to Wick, I agreed. The messenger..." She faltered. This had been hard enough to discuss with Connor. To be repeating it again was no less difficult, but she felt it would help Dougal to understand Maeve's position.

"The messenger was young. He seemed nice. We were fooled. Donald Fergusson was a liar and a creep. He found our weakness. But we should have been smarter. We knew when Meg was due. Looking back it all seems so obvious. But…"

"Nae lass. It was nae yer fault. It were mine."

"How do you figure that?"

"We knew they were devious. We played cat and mouse with them for weeks. We should have seen it coming."

"Rubbish!"

"Nae. We should have taken more care, left more men ta defend ye."

"What difference would that have made, Dougal? Do you think it would have stopped us from going to Wick?"

Dougal gave a reluctant chuckle. "Ye two are much alike, but different as weel."

"That's funny. I was just thinking the same about you and Connor."

They sat in silence for a few moments; Dougal regained his composure and the bridge of distrust, so long between them, was crossed. After a while Dougal, his voice hoarse with emotion asked, "What do I do?"

"Be honest with her. Tell her you love her. Tell her you understand. Tell her if she keeps holding onto this grief, her children will suffer too. Maeve thinks she has let you down somehow. Let her know she hasn't. Let her know you are proud of her. She must also know, the child she carries will be loved, no matter what—because it comes from her body."

There was silence. Dougal's head was bowed. "I'm nae going ta pretend it will be easy," he mumbled. "But I wouldna let this babe come between us. Truly, I think it be the luckiest babe ever. He shall have ma Maeve as a mother."

It was the most gracious statement she'd ever

heard. It was the moment Jo truly realised, that despite all his grumblings and suspicious nature, he was a man of deep loyalty and honour.

"That's the most honourable thing I've ever heard any man utter." She looked at him when she spoke and her own voice choked. She reached out and grasped his hand. "You're a good man, Dougal Haig."

He squeezed her hand back and looked to be struggling with his next words. "I nae...I nae ever thanked ye."

"For what?"

"Fer Maeve. Fer defending her."

"Pretty stupid, hey? Lucky I didn't get myself killed. I've never...I've never felt so much hate before. When I saw...I just."

"Thank ye."

Jo looked at the man next to her. His battle-worn façade hid a heart of gold. "You're welcome."

"Am I interrupting something...or would ye two like some more time alone?" Connor stood in the alcove entry, his arms folded, leaning against the stone archway, one eyebrow raised in mock question.

"Oh, damn it, Dougal," she quipped. "Caught out at last. Do you want to tell him or should I?"

The twinkle in her eye gave the game away, but Dougal played along. A chance to rib his friend back for a change enticed him to retort, "Ye tell him, lass. After three rounds in the linen room, I nae have the energy."

****

Forty miles away at Castle Wick, a scream, accompanied by a string of vile curses and colourful oaths rent the air. Silence followed and the servants of Wick let go the collective breath they were holding. But none of them believed it was over. They wanted it to be, but first babies always took the longest.

****

Tannan finished running the mares behind the stables in the turn-out yard. It was an exercise area used in the winter months. Ponies grew restless, fat, and lazy cooped up in their stalls during the harsh winter. Years of experience working with his father taught him that a highland pony was very much like a Highlander—free spirits who would not be held still for long. Regular exercise, even in the bitter weather, was important to keep the stock healthy and happy.

As he stabled the last mare he heard Millie's familiar prattle as she skipped into the stable. Maeve followed, brushing at her hems to release the powdered snow stuck to them. A fresh coating of white had fallen overnight, covering the discoloured slush trodden over with the coming and goings within the bailey.

"Morning ta ye, Lady Maeve. Is that my little angel coming ta visit me?" Millie strutted up the centre aisle of the stables. Tannan always spoilt the child, filling her with self-importance.

"Aye, Tannan," replied Maeve. "Though it be too cold fer riding, she still insists on coming fer her regular hour."

Both adults laughed as the child hoisted herself onto the top rail of the stall containing a foal and its mother. Tannan noticed Maeve's smile didn't quite reach her eyes.

"When can I ride him, Tannan?" inquired Millie, looking with longing at the young colt. "Can I ride him soon?"

"Nae, lass. He belongs ta the laird. He will be trained as a war pony, but I am sure yer Uncle Connor will take ye for a wee ride on his back at some time."

At Millie's crestfallen look Tannan added, "The grey mare in the end stall is ready ta foal any day.

Could ye go and check her fer me? See what ye think?" Given such an important mission, the child, full of superiority again, raced off to do Tannan's bidding.

"Ye are wonderful with her, Tannan. It is time we found ye a wife so ye can raise yer own bairns," Maeve said, her eyes followed her child.

"I nae think I could ever be as lucky as Dougal. What think ye?"

Maeve's head dropped. The usual brusque and efficient body language was absent. Tannan had a knack for reading people well. However, one need not be very astute to see all was not well in the house of Haig. "Nae so lucky, I think," she said, almost to herself. She went to walk away, but Tannan stalled her.

"I was wondering if ye could do something fer me? I know yer probably busy..."

Her face brightened at his request. "Aye, Tannan. What is it?"

"The smithy finished a job fer Connor. He left it here, to save his old legs the walk through the snow. Asked me ta pass it on. Could ye take it back with ye?"

"Of course," Maeve replied. She didn't notice the look of purpose on the younger man's face.

Tannan held a hessian sack. As he unfolded the material Maeve saw the small beautiful sword within. It was Jo's sword. The sword used to kill Donald Fergusson.

Maeve's face paled as her eyes locked onto the blade. Tannan pulled the weapon from the scabbard and felt the weight of steel in his hand. His eyes assessed the steel as he would a fine horse. "I nae be a warrior like Connor, or Dougal...but I say this is a fine piece. Aye, small but fine. What do ye think?"

"I...I didna notice it was missing...I mean, Jo hasna worn it, and..." Maeve said continuing to stare at the weapon. Tears welled in her eyes, the weapon releasing a barrage of memories, but Tannan ignored her emotion.

"Ye see here?" He pointed to the hilt. Maeve's eyes followed his gesture. He saw her take a slight breath when she noticed two beautiful emeralds embedded within the hilt. A sword was often left unadorned until an honourable deed was performed with it. Tannan continued to study the weapon, holding it before him, dull sunlight crept between the boarded stable walls glinting off its razor sharp edges. "It is a sword of honour now. It has paid a tribute of the highest worth. A man brought honour to its blade by protecting two women. One he protected from bloodletting, and the other, well...she will nae ever need ta look over her shoulder again."

Maeve stood staring at the sword. A tear escaped her lashes and ran down her cheek. She opened her mouth to speak, but nothing came out.

"This sword will be spoken aboot for many decades ta come." Tannan slid the blade back into the scabbard and handed it to Maeve. She reached out and took it; her eyes met Tannan's. "Ye should tell yer children aboot it, Maeve." He continued, "So they can tell theirs about a love sae strong and loyal and honest...a marriage that could withstand anything."

"Tannan, Tannan," the shrill cry of a child broke the moment as Millie ran back down the stables. "Tannan, Tannan, I can see a nose coming oot. Come see, come see."

"It seems Doctor Millie has more talent than we thought!" quipped Tannan.

"Aye, it does." replied Maeve as she wiped her face with her shawl. She hugged the sword to her breast and looked at Tannan. "But I think she has a way ta go before she is as smart and wise as the young stable master."

****

Maeve found Connor inspecting weapons in the armoury. After a long campaign, weapons could become neglected and it was important they were all ready to use at a moment's notice. But his soldiers and servants were well trained and the scrutiny unnecessary. The swords were as sharp as razors, shields oiled and shone like glass, and arrowheads and quivers were clean and all accounted for.

Pride filled him as he made his way among the rows. Clan prosperity was based on its ability to feed and defend itself. Clan Mackay was prosperous with a hundred and fifty men at arms and another few hundred foot soldiers from the villages to call upon.

Shreave was a formidable force, but it was not always so. Connor's grandfather was embroiled in clan wars for fifty of his seventy-five years before his death. The financial cost was a constant burden which saw the decline of affluence and the crumbling of the castle. It was the old laird who saw to much of Shreave's repairs in easier times when the clans were not at each others throats. Connor took over with the same passion and ability to design and construct dwellings. The blueprints sat in his chamber and were for a new wing. During winter, the castle would all but burst at the seams with people. Adding an additional twenty rooms would make it possible to walk across the hall at night without stepping on someone.

"It's nice ta see them all hanging on the walls and nae in use," Maeve commented. Connor showed no surprise at the voice. Nobody could ever sneak up on him.

"Aye. It bodes well fer Shreave."

"We have ye ta thank fer that." Sensing his silent query, she continued, "I was on ma way back so Tannan asked me ta deliver this ta ye." She handed over the wrapped sword.

When Connor realised what it was, his face changed. Maeve thought she saw excitement on the laird's face. This stony-faced giant rarely showed any form of emotion, other than anger. But maybe she was too harsh. Surely there was more to this man than she thought if he could win the heart of such a woman as Jo.

"It is beautiful, the sword, what ye have done ta it. Tannan showed me. I hope ye dinna mind?" Maeve asked.

Connor inspected the two emeralds embedded within the hilt. "Nae. I dinna mind. They are the colour of her eyes."

"I...I would love ta see her face when ye give it ta her."

"Then I shall present it ta her this eve in the hall."

"Oh, nay...I mean..." The sword represented too many raw edges and Maeve was uncomfortable with the idea. She felt a private presentation would be more suitable and she explained this to Connor hoping he would understand.

"So ye think I should give it ta her when we are alone?"

Maeve was grateful Connor valued her opinion. The blade now carried a kill and she wasn't sure how Jo would react to seeing it again. "Could I, I mean, what if I ask her ta come ta the nursery, and we can, well, Dougal and me...and ye could..."

Realisation registered on Connor's face and she could see he understood the small, jewelled sword perhaps symbolised more than a woman's heroism. Maybe this sword could help to heal wounds unseen by the eye. Maybe this gift could bring together those torn apart by grief, guilt, and treachery.

"I think, Maeve, it would be most fitting for ye and Dougal ta be present. This sword symbolises friendship...and more. I would be honoured if ye were there."

Maeve was lost for words. When did this laird become so wise and eloquent?

"Thank ye, Connor."

"Fer what?"

"Fer...understanding."

"Thank Jo-Anne." Maeve nodded but as she turned to leave Connor spoke again. "I have been meaning ta speak with ye." It seemed to be a day for surprises. She waited for Connor to continue. He paused, obviously choosing his words with care. "Do ye know where Jo-Anne comes from? I mean...really know?"

Maeve did not want to betray her friend's trust, so was unsure how to answer. "Tell me what *ye* know."

Connor ran a hand through his tangled hair. "What I know?" He pondered that a moment. "I used ta think I was a rational minded man. I thought I could control most things within ma life. That is until recently."

"Control is just an illusion, Connor. It makes us feel secure, even if we are nae."

"Aye. So it would seem. Sound advice for both of us I would think."

Maeve laughed. "Aye. Dougal was right. He always said we were too much alike."

They both smiled.

"Jo comes...from a long way away," Maeve hedged.

"Aboot four hundred years away?"

Maeve was surprised, but pleased. "She told ye?"

"Aye."

"I'm glad. Ye needed ta know. And she needed ye ta know, ye understand?"

"Aye. What does it mean, Maeve? Why?"

"I canna say Connor. But, I think the two of ye are linked by a bond in time. I'm nae even going ta pretend I understand it, but I think she came here for *ye.*"

Connor levelled his gaze at Maeve. "Can she be taken from me?"

"Ah dinna ken."

"What about the necklace?"

"What necklace?"

Realising Jo had just begun to suspect the antique necklace was the cause of her travels Connor relayed the information.

Maeve paled and he knew she was also very familiar with the jewel he described. Though she'd never seen it, stories about the priceless piece were handed down through generations of MacKays.

"Where is it?" Maeve croaked.

"Locked away," Connor stated. Maeve's obvious concern tripled his own.

"Good."

Maeve's legs wobbled and she sat on a wooden crate used for hanging arms on the upper racks. The MacKay necklace was legendary. It was given to the laird's wife upon the delivery of their firstborn son. "Does she know aboot the legacy?"

"Nay."

"Good. Leave it be. She will worry."

"What does it mean?"

He hoped Maeve had an answer, but she told him no, though did offer some theories. "Maybe the past and the present are linked and it is simply a part of the life cycle. Nobody really gets older; it is an illusion. We just go round and round."

"But, can she be taken from me?" There was desperation in Connor's tone.

"Oh, Connor. Ah dinna ken...ah dinna ken."

Chapter Twenty-Seven

Heavy snow fell before dusk, sending all creatures great and small for cover into Castle Shreave. The great hall teemed with bodies and Connor looked forward to the planned extensions being complete.

The small informal ceremony was held in the nursery after the evening supper. Just the four of them attended; friends with more in common than they cared to admit.

Connor presented the sword to Jo. At first she was shocked to see the blade again but she understood the sword was a badge of honour. The weapon represented courage, fealty, and friendship. It spoke of endurance and fortitude. Any abhorrence she may have felt holding the blade in her hand again was banished by remembering the evil life it exterminated.

"It's beautiful," was all she could manage as the emeralds glinted in the fire-light.

"So are ye," Connor replied, his gaze never leaving her face.

The informal ceremony over, Dougal and Maeve began to feel like they were intruding. Their friends needed time alone, and so did they.

****

"You didn't tell me you had my sword. I thought you must have hidden it or something," she said after Dougal and Maeve left the nursery.

"Nae. Nae hidden."

"I can see that. Thank you. It's beautiful."

"Ye are welcome. It was the just thing ta do. The

sword has honour. So does its mistress."

She chuckled to cover her embarrassment. "You sound so seventeenth-century!"

Connors brow furrowed. At times he found it hard to understand her sense of humour. He was getting better at it, but was still coming to terms with the idea of her past—or future.

"I'm sorry, I don't mean to sound flippant. It's just, things you take for granted feel more like fairy tales to me."

Connor ran his knuckles over her cheek; the fire in the nursery hearth fanned warmth across her skin. "I willna lie and say it is easy fer me either. But, if this is a fairy tale, then I am glad ta be a part of it."

She stepped into his arms, sighed, and said, "I get scared sometimes." Connor looked down at her, an unspoken question in his eyes. "Not of bad men or raiders," she added. "I'm scared about us. I wonder if this is all a dream, and...and I'll wake up one day. Alone."

Tight fear gripped Connor's chest and his arm around her tensed. "Ye shall never be alone, Jo-Anne. I shall nae ever leave ye."

"But what if...?"

"Shhh. Ye canna spend yer time worrying aboot what may be. Ye have ta live and love for the present. Ye ken?"

"You're a good man, Connor MacKay," she mumbled into his broad chest.

Connor's hand slid down her back and cupped her bottom. He squeezed, pulling her pelvis against his awakened groin. "I canna hold ye without wanting ye. Ye are like an addiction with me."

She chuckled again. "I'm more than happy to oblige you, *my laird.*"

Connor bent his head and claimed her lips, tasting of warm honey, sweet and delicious. His tongue delved into the soft corners of her mouth, seeking and coaxing hers in return. She answered alike, beginning a duel of racing passion. She felt absorbed by his skin, her body having no will of its own as she melted around the edges and clung to him.

His hands rucked up the edges of her dress as he slowly sank to his knees, taking her with him. With her legs straddled either side of his thighs, she could feel the air invading the warm heat of her centre, arousing her even more. God, she couldn't get enough of this man. His mouth plundered hers and his hands ran up her thighs and she let out a low moan. "Please." She wasn't sure if she said it or he did, but she pushed his kilt to the side and wrapped her hand around his arousal. She was certain this time. He was the one who groaned.

They touched and caressed each other, but the unanticipated sound of a baby crying instantly doused their foreplay. Both breathing heavily like they'd just run up a flight of stairs, Connor began to laugh. It was infectious, and she joined in, hurriedly righting her dress and moving Connor's plaid back into place. They only just stood up, when Mrs. Moray came bustling in from across the hall.

Her hands flew to her cheek in belated surprise to see the laird and his lady standing before the low burning fire. "Ooh," she exclaimed. "I'm sorry, ma laird, I didna see ye." Then, with a more critical eye she assessed the rosy-cheeked girl and the tousle-haired man, quickly surmising what they were up to. "I need ta check the bairns. I wasna disturbing ye, was I?" she said, with a hint of mischief in her voice.

Jo blushed, annoyed Connor felt no embarrassment about being caught with his pants down; or rather, his kilt up. "Hello, Mrs. Moray," she choked out. "We were just, err..."

"Stoking the fire," Connor chipped in.

"Aye. I can see," the nanny replied, a twinkle in her eye.

"We'll leave you to it then, Mrs. Moray," said Jo. "Goodni—" It was too late. Connor grabbed Jo's hand and dragged her to the door without another word. She ran to keep up.

The laird had unfinished business to attend to.

"Aye, then. Goodnight." Mrs. Moray laughed. "Perhaps there be some stoking in yer own chamber ta do?"

Hearing the older woman chuckling, she was mortified they almost got caught in such an intimate position. Angry with Connor for arousing her so easily, she tugged on his arm to stop him. "Connor, we could have been caught. We should have waited. I'm so embarrassed."

Connor stopped, pulling Jo back into his arms and kissing her thoroughly yet again. She mumbled a protest into his mouth, then laughed at his determination. Finally he said, "That old biddy willna care none. We are even at last."

"Even?" she asked, puzzled.

"Aye. When I was a lad of fifteen, I caught her and her husband in the hay loft." Connor shuddered. "It left a permanent scar, I can tell ye!"

Like two mischievous school children, the laird and lady entered their chamber. The laird stripped his unresisting betrothed down to her bare skin. He threw her onto the bed, tossing off his kilt and boots. He was ramrod hard and made no apologies for entering her with haste. Their sex was fast, and so, so good.

Lying on their sides facing each other, she kissed her warrior on the lips. "I love you."

He gathered her close, tucking her head beneath his chin, and uttered a silent prayer. *Please God, let her stay with me forever.*

****

She was a little late for breakfast the next day. Not a good example set by the chatelaine and lady-to-be. But nobody seemed to look twice at her. Connor left their chamber ten minutes earlier and she supposed the castle folk assumed she'd been doing the laird's bidding. His bidding involved a morning bath in the pool, amongst other things. In the bitter cold and snow, the days began later than in the warmer seasons. Even at eight o'clock it was still almost dark, and the daylight hours seemed so brief.

The tables in the great hall were already cleared and the floors were in the process of being swept. The smell of fresh rushes, ready to spread about the hall, filled the room. Fiona came through the hall door with another pile in her arms. Her nose was red and her cheeks high in colour; the sparkle in her eyes animated her features. Normally timid, she seemed to glide around the room with a newborn confidence and Jo wondered at the cause of it.

Jo's mind was distracted when her stomach rumbled. She veered off into the walkway leading to the kitchens before anyone could catch her with the first problems of the day. Normally such things didn't bother her, but she always got tetchy when hungry. "Good morning, all," she said as she entered the kitchens. She was surprised to see Maeve and Eva sitting at the wooden table. They were having a conversation seeming to require privacy. Staff had retreated tactfully, leaving the two women alone, making her feel intrusive. "Oh, I'm sorry. I didn't mean to disturb you. I'll come back later."

"Nae, lass, nae," offered Mrs. MacBain. "We were just beating the hog," she said as she rose from the table.

Maybe that's where the saying 'chewing the fat' came from. "Are you sure? I didn't want to inter—"

"Jo, fer heavens sake, friend, take a seat."

Maeve's eyes sparkled.

"And how are you today, Maeve?" Jo asked, her raised eyebrow indicated she suspected more than she would say.

"Do ye really need ta ask that?"

"I have a feeling I don't. You look like I feel; like you've been loved to delirium and happily had nowhere near enough sleep. Am I close?"

Maeve couldn't suppress her grin. "Aye. I have tried ta be less obvious, but..."

"Why try?" Jo smiled, but then her face became a little more serious. "I'm really, really happy to hear it Maeve. Truly."

"Aye. Thank ye. I have come ta understand some things just happen. Ye can either run from them, or deal with them. Running made me unhappy. It solved nothing. So..."

Jo brimmed with happiness for her friend. "You're a brave woman. You do realise that, don't you?"

Maeve looked at her with solemn understanding. "Thank ye."

Jo slid her hand across the table and Maeve took hold of it. They squeezed. No more was said on the matter.

Mrs. MacBain, correctly sensing she could now approach, walked over and put a fresh bannock on the table between the women, followed by a bowl of honey and some fresh butter.

"So, fill me in on the latest within the walls," Maeve said. "I feel I have missed oot on a great deal. Foolish, aye?"

"Maeve don't start with me. Stop berating yourself or I'll kick you."

Both women laughed.

"Yer a good woman, Jo. And a good friend." There was a silent pause Maeve broke with a change of subject. "Have ye heard anything from Wick yet?"

"No. But it's not surprising. The snow is too thick to risk a messenger with good news. Mind, if a war was brewing, I'm sure we'd hear!"

"Aye well, our anxiety doesna count in the grand scheme of things. I'm sure everything went well."

"A girl or boy do you think?"

"A girl would be bonnie fer Meg, a lad for the Sinclair. But ten fingers and ten toes was always good enough for me and Dougal."

There was another pause, Jo wanting to broach the delicate subject of Maeve's condition, but not wishing to intrude. Instead she filled her mouth with honeyed bread and chewed, leaving the subject untouched.

"I dinna expect ta hear from Wick for another two months at least. Hopefully the snow will have cleared by then."

"It's hard to get used to," Jo said in muffled tones, the fresh bannock sticking to the roof of her mouth. "All this snow. It's beautiful, but it makes life very difficult for a while."

"Aye. But wait till ye see the spring. It makes it all the more special." Maeve broke off another piece of bread and smothered it with butter.

Jo couldn't help but admire the simple pleasures these folk appreciated. It was an uncomplicated and good life, providing there were no wars.

"Christmas will be a fine affair this year, aye? It will be grand ta see the laird with a lady ta oversee the occasion. Ye have nae seen the feast before. It's grand. Eva outdoes herself, aye, Eva?"

Mrs. MacBain waddled over with a jug of warmed milk and filled a cup each for her ladies. "Oh, nae sae much. It be nothing." But the head cook blushed with the praise.

With their hunger assuaged, Maeve asked Jo to come with her to her chamber. "I have something for ye. It has been ready for a long while, but, well, I should have given it ta ye sooner."

"What is it?" she asked.

"Ye shall see. Ye shall see."

By the time they mounted the last step on the third floor, they both wore a healthy glow on their cheeks. Once inside Maeve and Dougal's chamber, she realised she'd never been inside it before. It was very similar to the laird's, only a little smaller, with no study area.

Maeve was on her knees delving into a large wooden trunk. She came back to her feet holding a parcel in her arms, wrapped with plain linen.

"Come. Sit with me." Maeve led them to the bed and they both sat on the edge. "I had this made for ye. I realise ye have nae mother, not here or back...home...so I took the liberty of organising this for ye. I hope ye dinna think it was presumptuous of me, but..." Maeve handed her the parcel. "It was an honour fer me ta do this fer ye."

She knew this was Maeve's way of saying thank you for their friendship. It was a gift of love as well as gratitude.

Taking the parcel from Maeve's hands, she laid it on her lap. The linen covering was a big square of material, turned over at the corners to form a kind of pouch. The edges of the linen were lined with golden embroidery; a yellow ribbon tied around the middle held the envelope closed.

She undid the ribbon with excitement and anticipation bubbling inside her. As the edges fell away, she couldn't withhold a gasp of pleasure. Folded inside was an ivory dress, made of soft, fine wool, with delicate embroidery around the modestly cut neckline. The bodice held the same embroidered pattern but the sheer amount of it must have taken someone months to accomplish. It gave the gown an incredibly rich look. She couldn't help think the wedding dress too beautiful to wear.

"Ye like it aye?"

"I love it," she breathed in awe.

"Unfold it. Hold it up."

She lifted the dress from the wrapping and let it unfold to the floor, and gave another gasp as the full effect of the dress was appreciated. The sleeves from shoulder to wrist were done in an intricate handmade lace. Jo had no idea what sort of talent was required to toil on such a garment but she knew it was immense, and would have been costly.

"Oh, Maeve. It's beautiful. Thank you." She hugged Maeve but Maeve was too excited for pleasantries.

"Come on, try it on. Try it on. I've been waiting forever ta see ye in it." Maeve almost pushed her off the bed in her eagerness to get her into the bridal gown.

When Jo looked in the mirror, she saw a stranger. The stunning woman looking back at her was tall and elegant. She hadn't felt like this since the day she stood in her bathroom with June's priceless rubies around her neck. It seemed like such a long time ago.

"Aye. I knew it would become ye. Connor shall nae be able ta keep his hands off ye," Maeve said in reverent tones. "Ye are a beautiful woman," she added with honesty.

"I don't know what to say."

"Say naught. I know what it means ta ye. That is thanks enough."

Maeve took her plaid off and threw it over Jo's shoulder. "Ye see. This is why the lace is only on the sleeves. It would be too scratchy all over. The wool plaid is warm, but terrible against the skin if ye are nae used ta it. With those lace-covered arms poking oot, no one will ever mistake ye for anything but the laird's wife."

"I hadn't thought about a plaid. It never

occurred to me I would have to wear one."

"Oh, aye! Ye shall be presented with yer own plaid at the wedding. Connor will place it on ye. It is part of the ceremony and signifies ye honouring the laird, and Clan MacKay. Ye shall be expected ta wear one from then on."

"Well, Maeve, you better give me lessons on how to do them up. I think I'll need a bit of practice getting the folds tucked in around the belt."

"Ye have two months ta get it right. We'll work at it, aye?"

Chapter Twenty-Eight

Christmas at Shreave passed with much ceremony and feasting. It was a joyous time. With no real family for most of her life—apart from the Newburys—Jo threw herself into the festivities with enthusiasm. Clan members came to Shreave bundled in plaids and blankets to catch up with family and friends who lived and worked within the walls.

From the outside looking in, the castle gave the appearance of organised chaos. There was much eating, drinking, celebrating, children running wild, dogs eating scraps, dancing, musicians playing, and more eating. It continued this way until the New Year arrived.

Although she enjoyed herself, it was quite a relief when everyone left and things returned to normal. She saw little of Connor during the week. His attentions were required everywhere. They would both collapse into bed in the early hours of each morning, exhausted but content. Their intimacy was swift, intense, and very satisfying. She longed to spend more time alone with Connor, but his duties continued to pull him in the opposite direction. She would often wake in the morning with his side of the bed long cold. She made a comment to Maeve about her desire to spend more time with her betrothed before their wedding, only six weeks away.

"Aye. It can be like that sometimes. The responsibilities of a laird are time consuming. Ma mother used ta say 'things will be well, as long as ye lay yer head on the same pillow when the moon is up.' She was a very practical woman."

"Laying the head? Well, err, that isn't a problem." A blush crept up her neck and Maeve laughed.

"Oh, is that nae bonnie. After all this time ye still can blush."

"All right, all right. Cut it out."

Maeve laughed louder so Jo changed the subject. "I wonder if we'll get a message soon from Meg. I hope everything went well."

Maeve noted the abrupt topic change and said, "It is another month or so before we shall hear anything, I expect. Snow is still too deep fer travellers far away. But that is nae the problem, is it? We need ta connive some time for ye and Connor ta do whatever ye would like ta do...alone." Maeve's eyebrows wiggled up and down in mischief.

"To talk, go for walks, have an hour together, uninterrupted."

"Weel then. I have an idea. Leave it ta me." She brushed her hands together as if it was a done deal.

Maeve convinced Connor to take Jo on a tour of MacKay lands two weeks before their wedding. She insisted if Jo was to fully understand the people of Clan MacKay, she should become familiar with the villages and the lay of the land before the wedding.

With one eyebrow raised, Connor gave Maeve a cynical look. He intended to introduce Jo to the surrounding districts, but there never seemed to be time, so Maeve's push was what he needed. Also, good fortune sent unseasonably warm weather for the first month of spring with new grass pushing its way through the patchy snow, making the ground suitable for travelling.

They set off on two horses, a packhorse carrying enough warm blankets, clothing, and food to last them four days. She hoped for a longer escape, but as long as they were alone, she was grateful for any amount of time.

They followed the main road for two hours when Connor explained the village of Drumfold was only another mile down the road. She remembered the people of Drumfold; how could she ever forget? The person who stood out most in her memory was sixteen-year-old Christine who was so viciously raped. She often wondered if Robbie MacBride married her. It would be an even greater injustice if he did not.

Maybe she would see Christine as they rode through the village. As this thought occurred to her, Connor veered his horse off the main road and onto a narrower sidetrack. The patchy snow trampled by horse hoofs indicated the path was recently used.

"I thought we were to travel through Drumfold?" she inquired as she looked over her shoulder, the main road disappearing through the trees behind her.

"I said we were near Drumfold. I didna say we were going there." Connor's face was as unreadable as ever.

"Okay, then. Where are we going, mystery man?"

"Ta Sithig Shack," was all Connor said.

"Y-e-s. Oh, come on. I need more details than that. What's Sithig Shack?"

"A hunting shack, or it was. It hasna been used for several years."

"So you're taking me for a romantic few days to a dilapidated, unused hunting shack?"

Connor frowned at her comment. "Sarcasm doesna become ye. And who said anything aboot romance?"

She stared at him with an incredulous look upon her face. "Well, if romance is incomprehensible to you, at least you could pretend you're going to enjoy spending time alone with me." Connor said nothing, but from her position behind him she could see his shoulders shaking as he chuckled.

"You're teasing me."

"Nay, woman. Well, perhaps a tad."

They rode in companionable silence for another hour. Evidence of recent use dotted the trail and she didn't pay much attention to the tracks, but Connor did. To her eyes it looked like mushed up snow mixed with mud and leaves, but she soon noticed Connor scrutinizing the tracks. He dismounted and squatted down for a closer look.

"What is it?" she asked, a faint shadow of unease making her voice sound deeper than normal.

Connor focused on his task, moving small leaves out of a hoof imprint so he could better see the indentation.

"One pony only," he commented, more to himself than to her.

"What's the problem? Surely just someone from Drumfold has been this way hunting now the weather has cleared." The day shone bright, clear and sunny, with not a cloud in the sky. The air was chilled, but after the long winter, it almost felt like a summer's day and she was pleased with her deduction.

"Aye, it could be," Connor said as he rose from his squat and hoisted himself back onto Thief. "But the villagers dinna ride shod ponies."

"Who does?" she asked.

"Higher ranking nobles or trained warriors."

"So what if a more prosperous person has been this way? Why is that a problem here?"

Connor was deep in thought and she tried to banish her sudden fear as she realised the isolation of their location, and fears of raiders, and violators, forced there way into her memory. She hoped never to feel fear again, not at that intense level. Perhaps easier to do in her own time, but not, it seemed, in this one.

She knew Connor well enough now. If he demonstrated only mild concern, then there may be something more serious going on.

Connor noticed her unease and manoeuvred Thief closer. "Dinna worry, lass. Tis nothing." He reached out a hand and cupped her cheek. She turned her face into it, closed her eyes and kissed his gloved palm. Connor clasped her jaw and turned her head to claim her lips in a tender kiss. His face was cold against hers but the inside of his mouth was warm and welcoming, as she tasted it with her tongue.

"Be careful, ma lady." Connor pulled away. "Or ye shall have me throwing up yer skirts here in the snow."

She gave him a radiant smile, her eyes full of love and mischief. "Be careful, my laird, or I may throw up your plaid and join you on your horse!"

Connor gave a groan. "Come on, woman," he said as he took hold of her reins and began to lead her horse along the narrow path. "Or yer tempting will nae get us ta Sithig any time soon."

It was another hour before the quaint but dilapidated Sithig Shack, nestled at the end of a small valley, came into view. A brook of melting snow trickled close by and as they drew nearer she was pleasantly surprised. She saw a sturdy, well-built log shack with a shingled roof. Although it looked old, it held romantic appeal. She hoped the inside was in reasonable condition and it would only take a short time to make cosy so they could spend their four days in comfort.

Connor dismounted and draped Thief's reins over a hitching post in front of the house. She envied the way his powerful body dismounted the horse. Her muscles, although more used to being in the saddle, softened up over the long winter.

She lifted herself up in the stirrups and slowly swung her right leg back over the horse's rump. She knew from experience the hard part was maintaining balance with the right leg on the ground whilst the left was still in the stirrup.

But she need not have worried about her lack of horsemanship. A strong pair of arms wrapped around her waist and lowered her to the ground.

"Thank you, kind sir," she said. Then, with resignation, added, "Your future wife has many talents...though riding, it seems, will never be one of them."

Connor's arms tightened even more around her waist, holding her close against his body, as he murmured into her ear. "Aye. But she swims like a water nymph and she fights like a warrior. Come. We have some work ta do before Sithig be fit for habitation." With a firm squeeze of Jo's backside, he strode away and opened the door of the shack.

Neither of them felt the eyes upon them, hidden in the trees.

Watching and waiting.

****

The first message arrived from the outside world four hours after the laird and his lady departed Shreave. The messenger was cold, but happy to be the bearer of good news. Laird and Lady Sinclair delivered a healthy baby boy before Christmas. All were well, and weather permitting, would attend the wedding of Laird MacKay.

The castle buzzed with excitement. Megahn was still a much-loved part of the MacKay clan and the news delighted all who knew her. Mrs. Moray and Eva MacBain started knitting as soon as they learnt Meg was with child. They both remembered with fondness the daring tomboy who ran wild with Connor and Dougal. They also admired her free spirit and taste for adventure.

Maeve was also delighted with the good news, although she felt more relief than anything. She also fought doubts within her mind as her body showed the signs of pregnancy. Dougal was adamant any child she bore would be a child of his, regardless of the biological father.

Maeve was also very busy with wedding preparations. She assured Jo she could manage without her for a few days. She knew Jo felt a little guilty going away so close to the wedding, but her desire to be alone with Connor outweighed her conscience. Now with the good news arriving from Wick, Maeve was even more excited. It would be a double celebration.

But as the spring weather and the good news lifted the winter shadows from the walls of Shreave, news arrived from the village of Drumfold. Robbie MacBride, his face intense, had ridden hard via a shortcut. He strode into the hall and with an air of urgency made straight for Maeve. "Where is the laird, Lady Maeve?"

"Aye, there. Tis Robbie MacBride, is it?"

"Yes, ma'am. Do ye know where Laird MacKay is?"

"What is it, lad? Is all well at Drumfold?"

"I need ta speak with the laird," he persisted.

Realising the news would not be given to her Maeve told him Dougal, in command during the laird's absence, could be located in the stables with Tannan.

As Robbie reached the stables, Dougal was leaving with Colin. Since Connor's departure Colin became Dougal's shadow and was driving his mentor crazy. Dougal recognised Robbie and frowned. "What brings ye here, lad?" he asked.

"I need ta speak with ye, Dougal."

"Then speak, man."

Ten minutes later there was much commotion

within the bailey. Ponies were readied, swords checked and shcathed, and women hastily stuffed warmer clothes into saddle-bags belonging to their loved ones. Within twenty minutes, thirty riders galloped out of Castle Shreave, Robbie MacBride amongst them.

He may be just a farmer, but Drumfold and Christine needed avenging.

****

Jo cleaned for an hour and a half. Their temporary home was tidy but grubby. Connor could tell the shack was recently used and whoever it was their housekeeping skills must have been below Jo's standard. "Who do you think was here?" she asked Connor when he came inside with a load of fire wood.

He chose his words carfully. "Sithig is one of many hunting shacks dotted across our land. When Shreave runs low on meat, Sithig and other shacks are for shelter and a meeting point for the hunters. Sometimes a hunt will last a week or more and each shack is situated so the surrounding forest is not over-hunted within any given year."

He watched Jo accept his answer. What he failed to mention was Sithig hadn't been used for a few years. As the town of Drumfold grew more prosperous, the population increased, and new boundaries were drawn so as not to deprive the people within the village of fresh meat. Somebody was here using the dwelling and it would not be a tenant from Drumfold. Nobody in Drumfold rode a shod pony.

"There now. That looks heaps better." She stood back and nodded in admiration of her handiwork.

Connor made a fire in the hearth then came in with two huge cooking cauldrons filled with icy water from the brook. He hung them on the hooks mortared into the large stone fireplace.

"Nae enough for your ladyship's bath, but, once it is heated we shall find a way ta clean each other up."

At his suggestive tone, she couldn't wait to finish dinner.

During their meal Connor seemed a little distracted. The horses were blanketed under a substantial lean-to against the back of the shack and twice already he went out to check them. She was also very aware he hadn't removed his sword from his belt. When he made another excuse to go outside she resented being treated like a fool.

"Right, that's it. What's going on?" She stood before the fire, hands on hips, eyes blazing. Connor's expression was as unreadable as usual. She scowled. "I'm no fool, Connor."

Connor sighed. "Nae. Ye are not."

She sat down again, satisfied with Connor's reply. "So, tell me. What is it? The tracks?"

"Aye."

"And what else aren't you telling me?"

"Ha. I was told as a lad, when choosing a wife ta make sure she is biddable and uneducated. Less trouble."

"Lucked out there, didn't you?"

Connor reached out with his hand and palmed her cheek. "Aye. But I dinna think I should like ye any other way."

"Good answer, Laird MacKay. So what's the problem?"

Connor let out a deep breath, relieved to be sharing the information he held. "We are nae alone."

For some reason she was not surprised yet didn't know why; maybe she was aware of Connor's alertness for hours without acknowledging it, or maybe she sensed a presence herself. Then a thought occurred to her. "But the horses haven't been unsettled. Wouldn't they tell you if there was a stranger lurking about?"

"Aye. They would."

"So, it must be someone we know then?"

"Aye."

It was the way he made the short statement and the look in his eye that turned Jo's blood cold, and as a sneaking suspicion rolled over her skin, she felt nauseous, a combination of fear and loathing. It consumed her and made her want to retreat and hide. But she rallied, stubborn and brave, refusing to submit. "It's Brian, isn't it?"

"Aye."

****

"If he does anything ta hurt our girl..."

"Now, now, lovie. Dinna do this ta yerself."

Eva and Maeve were sitting at the big table in the kitchens. Maeve was a mess. As soon as Dougal and the war party left, she went to the kitchens and collapsed in a crying heap. Eva let her continue until she cried herself out. "Better oot than in," she said. Eva MacBain had a practical way of dealing with problems often prompting castle inhabitants to bring her their troubles.

"We should have known he would nae have fled. He is so sick in the mind he still must think he can kill whoever he likes ta get what he wants." Another hiccupping sob wrenched itself from Maeve's throat. "If he hurts her, I..." Maeve couldn't finish her sentence.

"Now, dinna be silly, lass. Do ye have such little faith in Connor that he can nae defend her?"

"But they dinna ken he is there. They think they are alone." Maeve was just too frantic with worry to hear sense from anyone. Eva poured a healthy dram of whisky in a large cup.

"Drink this." It was needed to calm Maeve down. "That baby of yers will come oot pickled, but..." Both women laughed, then paused. Neither knew how to comment or talk about the baby. Maeve hadn't, so far, discussed this pregnancy, unlike the joyous discussions about all her others. *I wonder if it will be a boy or girl? Will it have dark hair like Dougal? Do ye think Millie is a bonnie name?*

Eva's instincts told her the time was right. "What cycle were ye in when it happened?"

Maeve didn't hesitate to answer. "He, I...in the cave I was in ma third week of cycle."

"Arrh, so yer fertile days may have passed?"

"Aye. But ye know as weel as I, Eva, it nae counts fer much."

"Did ye and Dougal...during yer fertile days?"

"I canna really remember," Maeve said with a sigh. Then with a smile on her face. "But, knowing us!"

Eva chuckled. "If I was a betting woman, I would guess Dougal. Bloody, lustful beastie he is."

Both women laughed again.

"Thank ye Eva."

"Ye be welcome, lovie."

****

"He must know we're alone. Why hasn't he made a move?"

"Ah dinna ken. But I am sure he nae thinks we know he is here. And that is ta our advantage." Connor stoked the fire and threw on another log. It was dark outside now, which made her feel even more vulnerable. Connor seemed unaffected by the situation but what she couldn't possibly know was the seething anger and yearning for revenge filling his mind.

Connor's rage began the second Neill informed him the raiders held two hostages. It ate at his insides and consumed his mind from dawn till dusk. Over the long winter, Connor wanted to ride out into the snow and hunt his cousin down. He longed to see his sword slice the man in two.

He imagined she would be shocked if able to read his cold-blooded thoughts.

But his warrior instincts taught him to be patient and he knew within his heart such an opportunity would soon present itself. He wished she was back in Shreave, but he could not change that now. Still, he would not leave her alone in the shack. Connor learned many years ago to never underestimate an adversary. If he was alone, he would pursue Brian through the snow, toying with him, stalking him. He wanted Brain to feel real fear, just like she had.

"What shall we do?"

"We wait."

"Wait! While we know he's out there? Surely we should be doing something?"

"We are. Waiting."

"Connor!"

He felt contrite for his seeming lack of concern. Other Highland warriors would not be too concerned at this stage either. But she was no warrior, even though she demonstrated more courage than he'd ever seen in any other woman. Jo-Anne did not even come from the Highlands, but from a time, where according to her, people were much safer and rules were strict. Even if someone did something bad to you, a representative of what she called the legal system would rule over the incident and prescribe punishment. It was unnecessary to defend your home or seek retribution yourself. It all sounded very unsatisfying to Connor.

Where was the justice if a man was unable to seek it himself?

"Brian will do naught until he finds ample opportunity. Whilst we are in here, we are safe."

"What makes you think that?"

"Sithig is a small hut. Ye canna swing a sword in here."

She looked perplexed at how he thought this was reason enough to relax.

"Oh, and have a nice weekend!" she huffed under her breath. "But he could throw a knife. Just open the door and throw it."

"The door is bolted."

"Er...he could set the cabin alight, then. Burn it down."

"That is a woman's way."

"A what?"

"A woman's... Jo-Anne, ye are safe fer now," Connor emphasised. "And I have known Brian Dubois nearly all ma life. He visited us often when I was a bairn. When an alliance was formed with ma mother's family and Clan MacKay, he came ta train with us. With Dougal and I. We have run together, fought together, and wenched together since we were thirteen years old. I know this man."

She looked thoughtful for a moment then said, "But do you really know this man? Did you know him well enough to realise he was plotting to kill you? Did you ever think he would try to get to you by abusing and holding Maeve and I hostage?" She faltered. "I'm sorry Connor. It's just, I don't see this situation as black and white as you do. I think he's unpredictable and desperate. He's been homeless for the winter. Maybe only just surviving on what he could hunt. He could even be ill after the long winter, and he knows this forest as well as you do."

He absorbed her words before commenting. "He is as strong as I. And I could live and hunt this forest, in all seasons, fer the rest of ma life if I had ta. He could go without food fer days and still be strong. He is a warrior, like me. But, I have heard what ye have said. I nae think it is so. But I will nae forget yer words. Will ye rest easier now?"

She laughed. "Oh yeah, sure!" she replied.

"We really must work on yer sarcasm. The

laird's wife should be delicate and amiable," Connor teased.

"What can I say? I'm a twenty-first century Aussie!"

Connor took her hand and raised her from her stool by the fire, taking her face between his rough, battle-worn hands. "I would nae change ye for all the gold in Scotland." His warm breath danced across her face as he said the words and the intimacy kindled a familiar fire within him. "Aussie or nae, if I say we are safe, then we are safe." He tipped his head forward and kissed her lips.

She pulled her head back. "Do you know what happens when two people fall in love?" At Connor's inquisitive frown, she continued. "They learn to read each other's emotions; they gather information about each other and subconsciously store it in their minds. The slightest frown, twitch of an eyebrow, clench of a fist, sigh or blink of an eye, can enlighten a lover with a canvas of truth. In other words, Connor MacKay, you're a liar!"

Connor's jaw dropped, but he should have expected her to speak her mind. Why did he even bother to keep things from her? He knew she was intelligent and admired her ability to analyse and add meaningful suggestions to any argument or banter. Was she blunt or rude at times—oh, yes!

He struggled to keep a grin from his face. "Am I sae obvious?"

"Only to me. Stop trying to protect me. I don't want to be kept in the dark. Always be honest with me no matter what. Okay?"

He leaned his head forward onto her brow, resting it there, and sighed before he spoke. A lock of his dark hair fell rakishly across his eyes as they drank in the sight of her. "I am sorry. I nae mean ta deceive ye. I just..." He was glad she could not read his mind. His true feelings towards Brian were pure violence. She asked for honesty, so he said, "I would like nothing more than ta leave Sithig and hunt him down." His eyes closed as he tried to tether his anger. "I would track and stalk him for days if necessary. I shall find and kill him. For the raids, for Drumfold, for Preece, but most of all..."

Placing her fingers over his lips she whispered, "I know...I know." She stared into his eyes. "I never considered myself a person of violence and it's hard for me to accept that I also want Brian dead. But I fear for you. If we were living in my time, so many of the fears I feel would be non-existent."

Connor sensed her turmoil. "I'm a warrior. It is how we survive in *my* time."

She sighed. "I know. I just wish it could be different."

He slid his arms around her, pulling her hard against his body. "Ye have nothing ta fear."

"Oh, don't start again." She looked tired and scared and began to cry. "Is it always like this?"

"Like what?"

"Do you always have to be looking over your shoulder?"

"I am the laird. It is ma job ta look over everyone's shoulder." He understood this was no comfort.

"I understand. But I don't have to like it."

Connor kissed her. The tears aroused him beyond comprehension; he needed to erase them and possessing her was the only way he knew how. Her tears also angered him. He saw them as a mark of his own failure to protect her. Knowing he was unable to shield her from abuse by Highland outlaws chewed at his insides. He'd never failed anybody before.

Why did it happen to the one person who meant the most to him?

Connor was relentless in his passion. The more

he plundered her mouth, the more he longed to taste her. It occurred to him it was some time since they kissed in this manner. Was he so busy since the New Year he couldn't remember kissing his own woman? No wonder she wanted to spend some time alone with him.

Their desire steamed like the water in the cauldrons heating above the fire. But bathing was forgotten as Connor cupped her bottom and pulled her against his rampant arousal. Romance and foreplay were unnecessary.

His hands roughly stripped her clothing. Naked, she felt erotic and sensual as her sensitised skin rubbed against his plaid. His hands touched, probed, and cupped while his mouth devoured her soul. His fingers found her most sensitive spot and gently massaged. Her legs gave way beneath her. Tension and pressure drew like a bowstring within her, a soft groan built deep within her throat. She relinquished control and let the craze overcome her, throwing back her head she called out his name. Her spasms were long and took her to a place where time and reality disappeared.

He supported her entire weight within his arms and as her feet touched the cold dirt floor of the shack and her eyes refocused, she became aware of a fierce pounding throughout her body. Desire returned, hot and unfulfilled, needing to be consummated. Lifting her eyes to his, a tight spasm of lust overcame her.

The glow of the fire reflected within his dark eyes and the intensity of his stare took her breath.

His lips quirked with pride and she knew the pleasure it gave him to bring her to sexual fulfilment so easily. She felt no embarrassment for losing control with open honesty. Her genitals tingled as she looped her arms around his neck and rubbed herself against his plaid. The need to feel him inside her was overwhelming.

She kissed him and he responded with equal ardour. Her hips writhed and pulsed against his body. When the fervour became too much for both of them, Connor pulled away and tore his plaid and shirt off.

No ceremony, precursors, or hesitation necessary. Both knew exactly what the other wanted, as Connor lifted her onto the edge of the rough, hard-planked table. She wrapped her legs around his hips.

He entered her body swiftly; his need to claim and possess her as desparate as her own. His eyes were closed in ecstasy as a deep groan, unbidden, vibrated his vocal cords. She was wet and ready for him.

As Connor withdrew and thrust again, she arched her back and lay across the table, opening herself to him, holding nothing back. Her head fell over the far edge exposing her neck and throat as her pulse beat in time with his. She felt totally incapable of thought as their mating intensified. When Connor was at his peak, she raised her head, opening her eyes so she could look into his face when he came.

It was perhaps the one time she considered him vulnerable. It was the one glimpse she ever got of the man within. The one time he held no control. As Connor's body became rigid and his seed spurted into her warmth, she felt complete.

He collapsed across her on the table, but she didn't feel the roughness of the timber beneath her skin. All she noticed was his comforting weight as his sweat-swathed skin blanketed her. When Connor's breathing returned to normal he pulled away from her, the rush of cold air chilled her flesh. He carried her to the small cot and covered her with furs.

He built up the fire so it would last the night and moved the cauldrons to the side, where they would stay warm until morning. All she wanted to do was lie close and be held by him.

Watching him tend the fire, she noted how he collected their weapons and placed them by the cot. A small dagger also rested beneath the furs by Connor's head, evidence of the unfinished business plaguing them.

She nestled into his warmth, her sated body relaxed. As drowsiness consumed her, she was aware of a stinging sensation on her bottom. Connor would have to remove the splinters in the morning.

****

Two miles away, a plan was formulated and put into action. Unbeknownst to Connor and Jo, Shreave men formed a circle and slowly, silently, moved inward through the cold and darkness. Soft whistles indicated the position of each individual. Their form of communication needed to be altered. Brian was one of them, and knew all their tactics.

They halted within five hundred yards of the shack, surrounding it on all sides. Though they encountered no sign of Brian, Dougal was sure they all moved with sufficient stealth and skill to not alert the hunted. Dougal longed for the opportunity to kill Brian even though the right was Connor's.

He'd hoped to find him before reaching Sithig, but it was not to be, which most likely meant only one thing; Brian Dubois was close to the shack and would strike soon.

Chapter Twenty-Nine

As the morning sun rose to stain the horizon, Connor put more wood on the fire. Jo was fast asleep on the cot and to his relief, had been all night. He feigned sleep until she, sated by their ardent lovemaking, drifted into slumber.

He'd tucked the furs around her so she would not miss his warmth. Then he dressed and sat, silent, sword strapped to his side, knowing Brian was close.

Thief whinnied softly and he wondered if Brian would steal the horse, but that was not his way. Since they were children running wild on MacKay land Brian was aggressive. He relished confrontation; running from it would be his last thought.

Dougal was a good judge of character, and since the kidnapping Connor berated himself for not taking note of his friend's opinion. But, having no male siblings of his own, Brian was the closest thing Connor had to a real brother. How foolish. Connor realised he never acknowledged Dougal's accurate perception of Brian's character. Or the fact Dougal was more his brother than anyone else. He would, as soon as possible, amend that. His thoughts wandered to his sister, Megahn. She acted more like a brother than a sister and he could not decide if she was born that way or steered in that direction with his encouragement.

He couldn't help but smile at the thought of his hellion sibling. As the hours of the cold night were ushered away by the dawn he thought about Meg.

She should have delivered her child by now. He sent up a silent prayer all was well.

Connor had prepared himself for combat but first he must wake Jo-Anne and tell her his plans. He would not insult her again by assuming she was too feminine to contribute meaningful comment or comprehend his tactics. He felt a sense of quiet pride he could share these things with her.

He leaned over the cot and shook her awake. "Jo-Anne, wake up lass," he whispered. She sighed and rolled over towards his voice.

"Why are you whispering?"

"We have company."

Her eyes shot open, as conscious thought chased away her slumber. "What? Where?"

"Shh." Connor placed a finger over her lips. With his other hand he pointed towards the back of the shack.

Looking over her shoulder at the log wall, comprehension dawned. Brian was lurking outside. Fear in her eyes, she asked, "What are you going to do?"

"Rest easy, woman," he said. "Do ye have so little faith in me?" Connor walked to the table and slid his dagger into his boot and seeing her look of unease, he added, "Just a precaution."

Flinging the furs off the cot she scrambled to find her dress, crumpled on the floor where it landed in the heat of passion the night before.

Her nipples hardened in the cold light of dawn and as her head popped through the neckline she caught Connor staring at her breasts. "For God's sake, Connor," she whispered, "keep your mind on the job."

He allowed her irritation, understanding it would help chase away her fear. "My job nae starts till I unlock the door, woman. Ye have nothing ta fear now...or later."

"I'm sorry, it's just..." she said no more, and rushed into his arms. "Tell me what you plan to do."

"Yer ta stay inside and bolt the door. I will go and check the horses," he continued in hushed tones. "That is what I would normally do first thing in the morning. It willna raise suspicion. Once ye hear our swords, ye are ta mount Thief. He is obnoxious, but verra fast. Ye'll follow the path back ta the main road and ride inta Drumfold. Wait for me there."

"I beg your pardon? That's your plan?" she asked, dumbfounded. Her voice rose and Connor once again placed his finger over her lips.

"Aye. Ye'll ride inta Drumfold..."

"No, no, no. You misunderstand me. I asked what *your* plans were."

Connor looked perplexed. He would never become accustomed to women who did not do as they were told.

"I *plan* ta keep ye safe, woman."

"I have a sword too, you know. I won't be packed off to Drumfold whilst you're out here fighting to the death, thinking it's some kind of game."

Connor frowned; she was missing the point. "It is a game." Connor held no fear of Brian Dubois; he longed for the battle and revenge.

"It is not a game."

"Jo-Anne!" Connor raised his voice a little. "I know ye nae understand this and find it hard ta accept, but this is the way of the Highlands. This is *my* way. I use ma sword ta protect the clan, ta dispense justice, ta defend the weak. And I use it ta protect those I love." Connor sighed and cupped her face in his hands. "Ye told me of yer time. Here, I am the judge, the jury, and executioner."

"Brian abused *me*, and was responsible for Maeve's rape, Connor. Don't I have the right to see justice carried out, too?"

Connor considered this and realised she

deserved, even more than he, the right to justice.

He released her and retrieved her small, but deadly, sword. "Keep this by yer side at all times. Never be apart from it, aye?" At her nod he continued, "When I leave, ye shall lock the door. Nae let anyone in." Connor took her hand and clasped her fingers around the hilt of her sword. "Ye will do as I have asked?" She nodded again.

Without a backwards glance Connor unbolted the door and exited Sithig shack. It was a few seconds before her senses returned to her such was Connor's efficient departure. She stepped to the door and slid the bolt, Connor's shadow dimming the light through the door slats, waiting for her to complete his instructions. As the metal shot through the ring, he disappeared, leaving her to ponder if she won the argument or not.

By the time Connor took three steps from the door, his worries evaporated. It was an understatement to utter, 'we have company.'

Connor smiled to himself, realising they were surrounded.

****

Brian Dubois squatted in the lean-to containing the horses for the better part of an hour. His muscles were tightening; he already worked a cramp out of one calf. He expected Connor to check the horses at first light, but it seemed the comfort of a willing woman slowed the laird's pace. But then, Connor MacKay always was weak.

When they were young, Connor was the one to save the horses and never run them to the ground when chasing game. Horses were but a tool. If they couldn't keep up then what use were they? Connor always advocated a clean kill when hunting. He never understood the thrill of seeing an animal writhe in pain.

It always riled Brian that Connor could best him

in a duel. From the earlier days of their childhood, Connor out-thrust, outmanoeuvred, and outwitted him. But never once did Connor leave his mark on the defeated. If the tables were turned, Brian would have jumped at the chance to leave a scar on the skin of Laird MacKay.

And now the man was even more vulnerable, because he'd a woman. Women were good for one thing, and Brian had unfinished business with the laird's betrothed. The banging of the shack door interrupted his thoughts.

****

She stood frozen by the door.

Resisting the urge to run after him, to make him stop, make him safe. But if there was one thing she learned in her months in the Highlands it was men fought and women waited. As unfair as it was, a woman's help was unwanted.

She held her breath and listened for the first clash of swords.

Her blood ran cold at the sound of a gunshot.

She stood still for a few seconds, frozen, shocked, then without conscious thought, slid back the bolt. Clutching the hilt of her sword, she ran from the shack.

This was it. The man she loved was facing death.

Courage came, masked in rage as she raced out into the early morning chill.

She rounded Sithig Shack in a sprint, with no idea what she would find or how she would intervene. But if Connor was dead, dying, or injured, she would not leave him to die alone, or sit in the shack waiting for Brian to come to her. She would not give him the satisfaction.

Panting, from the run and her anxiety, she stopped beyond the lean-to and surveyed the scene, feet apart, sword clenched in both hands, poised, and ready to attack.

Men encircled the clearing behind the shack—MacKay clad men. She recognised Neill across the way, but almost jumped out of her skin as a voice, inches from her ear spoke. "And what do ye expect ta be doin' with that, lass? Take us all on with yer bonnie sword?"

She was in no mood for Dougal's patronizing banter. She wasn't laughing. Brushing him aside, all her focus was drawn to the centre of the circle.

Within it, two men faced each other. It was a great relief to see Connor, not dead on the ground with a gaping bullet wound but up on his feet, though the reprieve was fleeting as Brian raised his sword and brought it crashing down over Connor's head. Connor raised his own to block the blow.

"Relax your battle stance lass, he is just playing. Naught ta worry over," Dougal explained as he placed his hands over hers and pushed the sword down. "Relax yer hands. He nae needs yer help."

"How, what...I heard a gunshot?" she murmured, her eyes never leaving the battle unfolding within the ring of Highland warriors.

"The swine pulled this on him." Dougal pulled a single shot pistol from his belt. "Brian is better with a sword than a gun."

Jo looked at the gun, an old fashioned relic, but a modern weapon of the current time; she blessed its unreliability and lack of precision. Technology be cursed.

A loud grunt from within the circle brought her head back to watch the fight. It was Connor. Brian swung his sword at Connor's left side causing him to bend at an odd angle to counter swing. It was then she saw the dark blood soaking through Connor's plaid on that side. Her heart jumped into her throat. "He's bleeding, Dougal. Stop the fight. He's bleeding," she uttered in a shocked, low voice, her palms sweaty with fear. "Dougal?"

"Nae, nae, lass, tis nothing but a scratch. Dinna fash yerself."

"How do you know that? He could bleed to death, he...he could..."

"For the love of Christ woman, stop fretting so, ye are causing me ta miss the action."

She turned and stared at Dougal. "This isn't a game, you bastard!" Her fear and frustration reached boiling point. "They could kill each other."

"Weel then, that would be the point, would it nae?"

Without thinking, she grabbed the front of Dougal's plaid and pulled his nose down to hers, her eyes blazed into his. "If he gets one more scratch on him..." Her knuckles were white from the forceful grip. "Or he dies...you son of a bitch...I'll kill you!"

She spoke the words with such vehemence, all the one hundred and twenty kilogram Dougal could do was stare at the fearless women who threatened his life. Nobody...*nobody*, openly threatened Dougal Haig.

If any man shirt-fronted and threatened him this way, they would have been gutted and left lying on the ground to bleed to death. But the Highland warrior gave her a solemn nod of agreement.

She pushed with her hands to shove Dougal back and focused on the fight, her back to Dougal, her dismissal of him blatant. Her shoving effort hadn't physically moved Dougal an inch, but the laird's betrothed, in the eyes of the silent observers, yet again demonstrated her courage. Connor chose well.

Watching every thrust and parry, she was too absorbed in the fight to notice the looks on the faces of those around her. There wasn't a man within the MacKay circle who didn't admire her, quietly wish she were his, or appreciate the example set by

Dougal—how to acknowledge courage when it was deserved. His lack of reprisal spoke volumes.

For the next ten minutes, every time Brian raised his sword above his head, she stopped breathing. But soon she recognised Dougal was right. Connor toyed with his cousin *and* was enjoying himself.

Sweat poured off the two men as they exerted themselves again and again, dodging blows and wielding the heavy broadswords high over their heads. They made it look as if the swords were as light as rapiers.

For a brief moment, she surveyed the warriors lining the circle, and was shocked at how calm and reverent they looked. One lad in particular gripped the hilt of his sword as hard as she did her own. The MacKay warrior next to the lad placed a hand on his shoulder and muttered something to him. It had the desired affect, and he sheathed his sword.

Robbie MacBride would have to be satisfied to let the laird seek revenge today.

She realised a man was about to die by the hand of her fiancé. She wondered when she became accustomed to this kind of violence. Maybe it was her fear for Connor overriding everything else. Or maybe horrific memories of cruelty and physical abuse she thought buried were not so deep after all.

Upon reflection, she understood there was much anger within her soul screaming for justice. She thought of Maeve and her unborn child, Christine and the village of Drumfold, and the innocent children of Preece. This man, and the mercenaries he lead, were vile scum, with no place in society, and no deserving place on this earth—no matter what century.

The more she looked upon Brian Dubois, the more loathing she felt. He made her skin crawl. He looked filthy and unwashed. Every now and again she would get a familiar whiff of his odour. It made her gag.

The returning memories called her to arms and Dougal's hand reached across to rest on her own again, pushing her weapon back down.

"I told ye lass, Connor nae needs yer help."

"I want to kill him, Dougal. I want him dead."

"Aye. No more than I."

The tone of his voice told her he needed retribution as much as she.

Connor and Brian did not speak a word during the fight. Their hatred was evident on both faces; there were no regrets and no mercy would be shown. Two men, bonded by blood and upbringing who could have been brothers for life, would fight to the death.

The MacKay warriors stood like silent sentinels, watching their laird mete out Highland justice—raw, crude, but honest.

Laird Connor MacKay ended the duel by plunging his sword into his cousin; the manoeuvre so powerful his sword tore through Brian's body and protruded, coated in blood, through the man's back. Connor's blade held Brian on his feet and his eyes began to glaze as death crawled over his body.

"Ye will die this day, Cousin," Connor said in hushed tones, his chest heaved as he caught his breath. Brian was alive enough to comprehend the words and fear them as the blood oozed down his kilt from the gaping stomach wound. "Ye have dishonoured yer clan and yer family." Connor clenched his hands tighter on the sword hilt and jerked the blade upwards. Brian's eyes bulged outward as the intense pain rammed throughout his body causing it to spasm as his life bled out. Connor continued to hold him upright on the gored blade. "And ye dishonoured *me,* when ye dared ta touch Jo-Anne and the wife of ma kinsman." Connor jerked the sword again. Brian began to choke on his own blood, a trickle spilling from the corner of his mouth.

With one sudden backward heave, Connor withdrew his sword from Brian's body and watched as the man fell at his feet, waiting until the body was still.

A MacKay war cry rent the air, as thirty MacKay warriors honoured their leader.

****

She could not stop shaking. She'd never before witnessed such intentional violence. The clash with the raiders was hideous and necessary to win, but Connor toyed with Brian like a cat with a mouse.

She was repulsed.

She was relieved.

Guilt assailed her, overshadowed by a sense of unreality, as if she were in someone else's dream. Like the day she arrived in the Highlands in an unfamiliar forest surrounded by warriors.

Her emotions contradicted each other with every fleeting thought. She wanted to run to Connor and tend his wound, but in the same instance she wanted to run *away* from him in fear—from this bloodied scene that was almost incomprehensible.

She'd witnessed a side to Connor she'd never seen before; the judge and the jury. It was breathtaking, grotesque, horrific, inspiring, and brutal, all at the same time. She wasn't sure how to process her emotions and come to terms with it.

The weight of a heavy plaid thrown about her shoulders jolted her from her trance.

"It seems, lass, I have need ta bring ye a plaid again," Neill said. "Come. Tis warmer in Sithig, by the fire."

Led away in a zombie-like state, her cheeks ashen, Neill sat her on the low stool by the fire. She became aware of her teeth chattering and her damp dress, results of the morning air. Neill went to leave the shack, but her faint voice asked, "Where is he?"

Halfway out the door, Neill stopped and turned to face her. He looked troubled, unsure how to handle the simple question. The laird now had a wife, well almost, who now commanded honesty as much as The MacKay.

"He's gone, Lady."

"Gone? Where?"

Neill stepped back within the warmth of Sithig and pulled the door closed to keep in the heat. "I canna say. He willna go far. He just needs ta...ta come ta terms with things. Ye ken?"

Neill looked concerned at her lack of response. "He is an honourable man, the laird, that is. He willna fight unless necessary, or deserved. Ta see him today, for many of us, was a privilege."

At her sudden look of horror, Neill began to open the shack door again, obviously wishing nothing more than to make his escape. But he would not turn his back on his lady, who already drew breath to speak.

"Privilege? Privilege?" she said, aghast. "You must explain to me one day, Neill, how watching a man butchered, any man, no matter the crime, can be so appealing to all of you." She turned towards the fire and stared into the flames, dismissing Neill, who exited without dawdling.

Chapter Thirty

Jo looked up as Maeve brought the heated blankets into the laird's chamber and laid them across her legs. Behind her, Fiona carried a tray of warmed spiced mead and hot fresh bannocks with butter, honey, and a wedge of cheese. As Fiona bent to set the food down, she noticed a large love-bite on the young woman's neck.

"Thank ye, lass," acknowledged Maeve, who'd also noticed the love bite and earlier wondered the identity of the randy male canoodling with the girl.

Fiona nodded, gave a small curtsy and slipped from the room. Maeve poured a drink for herself and Jo, then sat opposite her friend before the fire. "Weel then. Ye'll nae be goin' far until ye rid yerself of this red nose."

With perfect timing, Jo sneezed and blew her nose in a most unladylike manner before bringing the warm drink to her lips to soothe her parched, sore throat. She felt ill since the incident at Sithig earlier that morning, but blamed her emotional state rather than the physical. Soon after Neill departed, Dougal announced they would be returning to Shreave within the hour. She hadn't warmed up since her heroic dash out of the shack clad only in her dress. She had shivered constantly, before and during the long ride home.

It was a silent journey for her. None attempted to draw her into conversation, but they conversed amongst themselves as the ponies moved forward unsteered by their riders. They knew their way home.

By the time they topped the hill overlooking Shreave, she'd drawn some conclusions. The first was she was unwell! The second crept into her consciousness as her horse plodded along, its hoofs muffled by the melting snow—she loved Connor with all her heart.

But, more than this, although the brutality didn't sit well with her, she understood without it the land would be utterly lawless. Aggression had its place here in the seventeenth century, but she didn't have to like it.

"It's the first cold I've caught in years. That'll teach me for running around outside without my cape," she told Maeve.

"Aye, weel, from what I hear ye ran out like an avenging angle, come ta defend God himself." Dougal had told Maeve how moved he was at Jo's courage and knew, without a doubt his brother, not of the blood but of the soul, would rest easy with this woman by his side for the rest of his life. Jo laughed. "I didn't think. I heard the gunshot and..." The memories of that moment made her shudder. "I thought..." She couldn't continue.

Maeve topped up her goblet of mead, put some food on a plate, and handed it to her. "Here, eat. Ye need ta keep up yer strength ta fight a cold."

She did as she was asked, but the food was tasteless on her tongue. Her appetite deserted her and she couldn't decide if it was because of her cold or her anxiety over not knowing where Connor was. They returned to Shreave hours before; all except the laird.

"And worrying willna make it all better."

"How do you do that?"

"What?"

"Read my mind."

Maeve guffawed. "Lord, woman. It is written on yer face for everyone ta see. Do ye think we are all blind?"

Jo's eyes fell to her lap as she lifted the plate of food and shoved it back onto the table. She sighed. "Oh, Maeve. Where is he?"

"He'll nae be far away. Connor is a big boy. He can take care of himself."

"No. It's not that. It's just...I turned away from him. I was so shocked at what I saw. I was afraid and confused." She ran a hand wearily over her face as if trying to wipe away the doubt and worry. "I should have stayed and, and supported him, or something."

Maeve reached over to the table and put the plate of food back onto her lap, raising her eyebrows, glaring at her friend. Jo got the message and bit into her bannock.

"Now ye listen ta me. I'll nae have ye worryin'. I have spoken with Dougal, and he knows Connor better than any, and he is sure Connor just needs some time ta himself. Brian Dubois got what he deserved, but it doesna mean it sits weel with Connor ta kill one of his own. They grew up together. I nae think the kill will bother Connor, but the betrayal will. Loyalty is foremost with The MacKay. I've seen him suffer bigots and drunks, but he will nae take kindly ta traitors."

Jo observed her friend with admiration. "And you think Dougal knows him better than you? I reckon your observations within this castle beat all, Maeve."

"Aye, weel, maybe so, but ye'd do weel ta listen ta Dougal, too. Connor will be back."

Jo rested her head against the back of the chair, her cold and the ride had exhausted her. Maeve sat quietly, watching and waiting for her to unload the worry from her heart.

"What if he saw me? What if he saw the look on my face after...after Brian died? I should have stayed close by. I should have shown him my support. But what did I do? I walked off in disgust. Maybe I've shamed him in the eyes of his men? Maybe he's furious with me for my behaviour? Maybe he's angry with me for *my* lack of loyalty. Oh, Maeve! I feel like the biggest idiot."

She began to cry, releasing the worry, frustration, and horror of the preceding twenty-four hours in a choking blubber of tears. Her already running nose became a tidal surge, causing Maeve to leave the room to retrieve more hankies. By the time she returned Jo was in a calmer state, feeling much better for the release.

"Here." Maeve thrust the clean hankies at her friend. "Ye may need these before the night is oot."

Jo couldn't help but smile at her ever-practical friend. "The way I'm feeling at the moment, you'd better bring me all the castle towels!"

The women laughed and spent the next hour poring over possible scenarios. Their eventual resolution was to wait until Connor returned and all concerns could be addressed.

****

Connor MacKay sat upon Thief, surveying the land before him. There was no grander sight than looking across the pastures with Shreave dominating the horizon. This was his home. It always called to him.

As the rising sun sent long shadows across the meadows Connor had an irresistible urge to gallop the rest of the way, but his inner turmoil stopped him. He'd been alone with his thoughts for two days, but it took a mere two hours of it to come to terms with taking the life of his cousin.

He washed away the blood and guilt in a freezing creek, stitched the wound on his side, and promised himself never to let his mind think of Brian Dubois again.

However, he was unable to reconcile his guilt at allowing his betrothed to witness the violence at Sithig. He knew she was unused to displays of hostility and in her time, disputes were settled without aggression. There was not even a death penalty in her country; it was considered barbaric.

He blamed himself for the look of disgust and fear in her eyes after he pulled his sword from Brian. It was against his better judgment to leave her in Sithig shack whilst he sought his prey. He wanted her away from the bloodshed but she twisted his normal good judgement and tangled his thoughts. What would she think of him now? He was barbaric? Ruthless? Yes. He would own up to both of these, but only when it was justified. Would she ever look at him again with longing in her eyes? Or would she forever view him with aversion?

His transgression was to let her witness what women seldom saw. Men went to war, women stayed behind, never to witness the brutal battles. It was enough they sewed up the pieces when the injured returned.

Connor nudged Thief forwards. *Stop delaying*, he chastised himself. All the pondering in the world would not solve his dilemma. He must face her but the thought of this knotted his stomach. So this was love. Love was to expose one's heart and soul. Love was to risk rejection. One only felt pain if brave enough to love in the first place.

And brave he was.

He lived with the fear of losing her.

Every time he remembered the family heirloom of gold and rubies, his heart turned to stone. He tried hard not to think on it and though he did not show it, was relieved to wake each morning with his love still nestled beside him.

As he rode through the gates and into the bailey, he knew all was not well. Shreave had a feel to it, like a living, breathing entity. This morning he could tell a gloom settled over the castle. Something was amiss.

Colin raced out to take Thief's reins, the boy's eyes lowered to the dirt, unable to make contact with his laird.

"All's well, lad?"

Colin failed to answer the question. His adoring eyes resembled huge saucers, holding a combination of fear and sorrow.

"What's amiss, lad?" Connor felt an invisible shadow cover him. "Colin. Speak, lad."

"Connor," Dougal called. He exited the castle and came straight towards him. "It be good ta see ye, brother." Dougal's gaze was direct and honest.

"And ye, ma friend. What is amiss?"

****

Maeve mixed a fusion of herbs to help reduce Jo's hacking cough. It helped, but not much. Her main concern was to alleviate her temperature and stop her shivering, even though she was burning to the touch. "Here, take some more of this. Yer throat will be raw if we canna lessen the cough."

Raising her head from the pillow she allowed Maeve to pour some of the vile tasting liquid down her throat. She grimaced. "Oh, Maeve! It tastes disgusting," she uttered in a husky voice. "Who made the rules in this century that all medicine must taste foul?"

Maeve was most grateful her friend was still able to offer complaint, never seeing anyone this sick before and still conscious. It was remarkable. The village folk, if privy to the situation, would be accusing Maeve of witchcraft. Maeve thought it may be the vaccinations Jo told her of. This was the reason for her resistance to whatever 'germ' she picked up—if one could believe her stories about microscopic bugs!

Maeve could hear a rattle in Jo's lungs, but her body fought on. Jo joked she was too infused with preservatives to succumb to disease.

"I can't believe how weak I am," she croaked. "I feel like a newborn kitten. I've never been so sick in my life."

"Well, hold yer tongue then and rest," admonished Maeve. "Ye need ta sleep."

Jo could tell her friend's abruptness was born of fear for her patient's health.

Lying there she couldn't stop her eyelids from falling with exhaustion. An hour ago Maeve helped her to the chamber pot. By the time she returned to the bed, she felt like she'd run a marathon and wondered if she had pneumonia.

She began to mumble to herself. "Where are the antibiotics?" *There's Panadol in the bathroom cupboard. Why can't Maeve find them?*

She would ask for them after her nap.

Fifteen hours later she was still unconscious. Maeve hadn't left her side; her condition deteriorated rapidly.

****

News spread through the castle. There were far more people than usual milling around the great hall, their eyes turned to the staircase, hopeful of good news whenever someone descended. But it was not to be. As the hours wore on and darkness fell, people drifted away to their own beds, though some chose to stay the night, curling up on the rushes by the hall fires. As the sun rose and the castle awakened like a sleeping beast, the news came down, there was no change. Their lady was still unconscious.

A shout was heard, "The laird has returned!" The folk of Shreave stood and shook out their rumpled, rush-covered plaids. They longed for the laird's presence, to pay him homage for disposing of a known traitor. They all heard of the stunning battle between the two men. It would go down in MacKay history.

They also waited for his return so he could make things right upstairs. They hadn't any idea how it was to be done, but Connor MacKay was their leader and he would make things right.

But what they saw within the next seconds dampened their spirits, as Connor crashed through the hall doors, pushing the heavy timbers aside as if they were plywood. They watched him race up the stairs and disappear above the landing. Not one of them would ever forget the look upon his face.

****

The sound of a car driving past was most annoying. Don't they know I'm trying to sleep? Go away.

The noise was clear but elusive. There were clouds fogging her judgement and she was confused by her surroundings. It was like a mirage. She could see it, even smell it, but she couldn't touch it.

The bed under her back was so soft. She never wanted to sleep on a straw mattress again. Was this a dream?

As she lapsed into unconsciousness once more, she could hear a low rumble next to her ear, followed by a stubborn meow...

****

Maeve's head shot up as the chamber door crashed open. She held a cold compress to Jo's forehead and her arm dropped as she straightened up to stare at the man in the doorway.

Maeve was a practical woman and always good in a crisis. She'd nursed many over the years understanding and believing death was a part of life and just another journey. So when Connor walked to Jo's bedside—Maeve broke down and sobbed. The sobs went unnoticed by Connor. He only had eyes for his love, who looked paler than death.

"Ah dinna ken what ta do for them, Connor," Maeve gasped between hiccups. "I've done all I can, but I canna make her waken."

Connor said nothing, but lowered himself onto the bed beside Jo. He reached out his hand and cupped her face. It was hot, very hot, and damp at the same time. Her hair was wet around her face from the fever and cooling compresses Maeve used. He didn't even notice his own hands shaking.

"When did she lose consciousness?" whispered Connor, as numbness crept over his soul.

"Over fif...fifteen h...hours ago."

Both of them had seen this before. Many Highlanders succumbed after a long cold winter, not during, which to them made no sense. It took the old or already frail, but occasionally it would take the strong as well. To see her lying there surrendering to the ailment was heart-wrenching.

Connor leaned forward a placed a tender kiss upon her forehead. "I am sorry," he whispered, his head resting on hers, his lips inches from her mouth. "I should have been here. I should have come home sooner." He stared at her, one hand on her rattling chest, the other on her face. He willed her eyes to open. But they did not.

Maeve slumped into the chair, her legs unable to carry her from the room to allow a modicum of privacy for her laird to come to grips with the situation. Visibly fighting to control her grief, she jumped when a hand squeezed her shoulder. Dougal had caught up with Connor after he raced from the bailey. "Come, ma love. Leave them be fer a time. There is naught ye can do at the moment." As Dougal went to lift his heartbroken, exhausted wife from the chair, they were halted by Connor's voice.

"Stay," was all he said at first. Then, "Ye said ye dinna ken what ta do for them? What did ye mean by 'them'?"

Maeve's face crumpled and a hiccupping sob tore from her throat.. "Jo's with child. I...I dinna think she even knows it yet."

Neither man questioned how Maeve could know this.

The pressure in Connor's chest felt like a mortal sword wound. It cut into him, tearing through his soul.

Chapter Thirty-One

June Newbury sat in her armchair, a cup of cold, untouched tea beside her on the coffee table. The TV was on, but the channel nine newsreader's words went unheard and her fingers fiddled with a loose thread on her cardigan. She couldn't explain it, didn't understand it, but her instincts kept nudging her.

She stopped pacing about an hour ago. A stint in the garden dead-heading the roses didn't calm her. So she remained before the television, uninterested in the broadcast.

When she did reach for the remote control, she turned it off and rose from the chair. In her kitchen she pushed the button to start the kettle boiling again. Pointless. As she gazed out across her back lawn she sent up a silent prayer. *Please God, keep her safe. Protect her and bring her home.*

****

It was midnight and Connor refused to leave her side, though he sent Maeve away to her own bed, lest she become ill herself. He was home now and could worry enough for all of them. Racked with guilt, filled with 'if onlys' and a heart full of regret, Connor stubbornly blamed himself and no one else. If he took better care of her and never left her alone in Sithig—if only he insisted she mount his horse and ride to Drumfold.

It didn't matter how often Maeve assured him the sickness would have already been brewing in her body for a few days. She also emphasised it would not be a direct result of their trip to Sithig Shack.

But Connor would have none of it.

He was responsible for the safety of his woman.

He should have taken better care of her.

In the end, Maeve gave up and Dougal carried her off to their chamber where he held her close while she cried herself to sleep.

Jo's features were paler than the linen she rested upon. Dark circles marred the skin under her eyes, dry lips cracked, her brown hair lay dirty and lank from perspiration. He knew she would be appalled to see herself looking this way. She was not a vain woman, but she did take pride in her appearance.

Connor's thoughts were distracted by a soft knock on the chamber door. At first he did not answer, expecting it to be Maeve or Dougal, who were in and out constantly, but when no one entered he uttered a low, "Come."

Eva MacBain poked her head around the door, "Pardon me, ma laird. Maeve said ta bring ye up some sustenance around midnight. I hope ye dinna mind the intrusion?" Connor said nothing. Eva entered and placed some food and ale on the table by the fire.

If it was Fiona or one of the other young house servants they would have scampered off straight away, scared by the dark look on the man by the bed, but Eva was no new kitten. She'd been around long enough to have even changed a nappy or two on the laird himself.

She edged her way over to Connor, who either did not notice or feel obliged to acknowledge her presence. "There still be no improvement then?" No answer from Connor. "Maeve said I was ta make sure ye ate something. Ma laird?" Connor looked up at Eva. She was everyone's second mother, including his. Maeve knew he would do as asked by Eva MacBain.

"I suppose ye'll nae leave me unless I put something in ma mouth?" Connor said with a wry grin.

Eva stood hands on her hips in a 'don't argue with me' stance. "Aye. Ye know it, lad." It was a long time since anyone called him lad.

Ten minutes later, sitting at the small table next to the warmth of the fire, Connor ate his fill and drank half the ale in his goblet. Eva did not move from beside Jo the whole time. Connor leaned back in his chair, the emotion of the day seeming to press him back.

"She be a bonnie lassie, is she nae?" Eva commented, as she drew a damp cloth across Jo's forehead. "May I say Connor, ye chose well."

It was a sincere comment. Eva observed Jo since her mysterious appearance at Shreave, and learned to admire the young woman with the outspoken ways.

"Aye," Connor said.

"She be the same age as ma eldest, Shauna. But Shauna nae has the skin of a newborn babe, like yer lady. Beautiful." Eva finished wiping Jo's brow and put the cloth back into the bowl of cool water. Turning to Connor she said, "It is said the mineral water of the springs is medicinal. Ah dinna ken if it is true, but..."

Connor still did not reply.

"Weel then. I best be going. Ye call oot ta me if ye need anything. Anything, ye hear?" And she left the room leaving Connor dwelling on her last words.

The warm spring waters came from deep under the ground and it was said fairies bathed in it, leaving traces of their magic behind. Nonsense of course, but...

Connor rose from his chair, sure Jo could not get any worse. The waters were very warm, and it may do her good to be bathed and breathe in the steaming air. Connor placed his arms under her shoulders and knees and lifted her from the bed.

Within minutes he traversed the tunnel and entered the cave. She had been naked beneath the covers. Connor wasted no time removing his own clothes before entering the dark, swirling waters dressed in breeches and shirt. He was too worried the cold air in the tunnel would do more harm to her if he dallied. She felt weightless in his arms as the water lapped over her body, caressing her skin with its warmth. Connor felt peace descend upon him. His water nymph loved the pool so much.

After a while spent walking around, Connor sat on the steps with her nestled in his lap, her hair floating around her like an angel's halo. In contrast, her breathing was too laboured and he could tell there was fluid in the back of her throat that needed coughing up, but she was still unconscious and unable to do so.

He leaned his head on the top step. Her body submerged, lying on top of his own, her head tucked underneath his chin. He began to sing the Gaelic lullaby he often sung to Kaitlyn and Millie. Somehow it seemed appropriate.

But his song soon stopped.

He wept.

****

This is how Megahn Sinclair found her beloved brother, crying; his grief sent a stab of pain slicing through her. As she stood silent, unable to form words, Connor, aware of her presence, looked up.

From where she stood, Meg was unable to tell if Jo were alive or dead as her pale body floated above the darkness of her brother's; the sombre silence evidence of her plight. This was a fading visage of the woman Meg came to love and respect.

"Connor..." was all Meg managed before the sight of his grief triggered her own tears.

"Ah dinna ken what ta do, Meg. Ah dinna ken what ta do," he stated before a sob broke from his chest and he fell apart.

Meg went to his side, her slippers and the edges of her plaid dangled in the water as she sat next him, his head in her lap. "Ye are doing all ye can, man," she said as she stroked his brow and kissed his forehead, her tears mixed with his. "Ye are doing all ye can."

Relieved, she watched the rythmic rise and fall of Jo's chest.

****

In response to a message sent by Maeve, the Sinclairs had left Castle Wick with haste, their newborn son wrapped and slung against his mother's chest. Alick expressed concern it was too soon after the birth for his wife to be riding so far.

"Fer heaven's sake Alick. How long do ye expect me ta rest? I'll nae break, ye know," Meg said, and as usual she won the argument. The small family and their escort arrived at Shreave before midnight.

None complained at their late arrival; it seemed the whole castle was already awake and waiting for any news from the third floor. Meg and Alick could sense the sadness within the people. Each clan member was inexplicably tied to The MacKay. They grieved with him.

Dougal stood in the room as Maeve explained the heartbreaking situation to the new arrivals. Alick stood beside Meg whilst she breastfed the babe by the warmth of the fire.

Minutes before the arrival of Meg and Alick, Maeve came to check on Connor and Jo. When she found the room empty, the smell of sulphur in the air confirmed their whereabouts. Whether it was a good idea to take Jo into the waters at this point in time was questionable. But for some reason, Maeve felt at ease with it.

Meg, never one to mince words said, "So, what ye are telling us, Maeve, is ye think it miraculous she has survived this long?"

"Aye. I have nae seen the like of it before."

"It sounds like it will take all but magic ta heal her," Meg murmured, almost to herself.

Each caught in their thoughts, none spoke for a moment. Then Alick entered the conversation. "So is there nothing we can do ta help with what ails her? We have an excellent healing woman..."

"Alick," Meg spoke tersely, breaking from her thoughts. "Maeve needs advice from nobody." Then she sighed. "I am sorry, ma love." She reached out her hand, Alick stepped forward bringing it to his mouth to kiss.

"Nae apology needed, my heart," he said. "Has the babe finished?" Meg looked down at her breast. The baby was fast asleep and she hadn't realised. "Here, let me take him. You go and see yer brother. He needs ye more than anyone right now." Alick bent down and lifted his son into his arms, cradling the precious bundle against his massive chest. "Go now," he prompted. Meg longed to see her brother, but she was frightened by what she might find. Jo could have slipped away already.

"She is with us," Maeve said, "but her condition is grave." Meg nodded and took a step towards the study. "Wait! What was it ye said before?" Maeve asked with urgency.

Meg looked a little confused. "Er...I...what, that ye need nae help?"

"Nae, nae. About needing magic ta make her well? That's our answer."

The story Maeve told, made them at first think she was losing her mind. But as the tale unfolded, it became clear she was quite serious.

"I always wondered aboot the lass," commented Dougal. "She was just...never like the other women.

But…the twenty-first century?"

"Surely," Alick cut in, "ye canna believe this?" He looked at Dougal.

The conversation continued for some time, the four people offering comments and listening to theories offered by the others. In the end, it was the women who believed it possible, while the men reserved their judgment.

Meg summed it up. "So, what ye are saying, Maeve, is if we produce the necklace, Jo may return ta her own time?"

"Aye. It's a stretch, but ah dinna ken what else ta do."

"And ye are sure she would get this special medicine, 'anty-botics,' ta make her well again?" Dougal asked, showing his trust in her.

"Aye, ma love. That is what I hope. I canna say if it will work."

Each couple stood there, wondering if this insane theory could save a woman's life. The fact they were even contemplating the story being true was crazy.

"Where did Connor hide the necklace?" Alick asked.

"Ah dinna ken," replied Maeve.

Chapter Thirty-Two

Megahn Sinclair loved her brother with all her heart, but she needed him to put aside his grief while she explained their plan and then he could tell her where he hid the family heirloom.

Connor's tears were momentarily spent. Meg reached into the water and removed her ruined slippers. But she could not wait any longer. It was time to broach the subject.

"Connor," she said, "I know this is a difficult time for ye, for us too, but..."

"Hello, Meg."

Meg smiled with love as her brother acknowledged her. "Hello, brother. I shall nae ask how ye have been."

"Where is the babe?" Meg was amazed he would think of her son as his own world crumbled around him.

"Sleeping in his father's arms. He spoils him," she replied.

"It nae really matters though, I think." Connor's hand ran over Jo's stomach and Megahn did not miss the movement as she struggled not to be overwhelmed by the tragic events.

"Nae. Ye are right. It nae matters," she replied, leaning forward and brushing a lock of hair from her brother's face. Fortifying herself, Megahn broached the topic she and the others discussed at length. "Connor, Maeve told us about...Jo's home."

Connor stared at his sister, but made no reply.

"Maeve says the MacKay jewels may be the only way ta save her."

Connor still remained silent.

"We thought, that is, Alick, Dougal, Maeve, and I, thought...if we gave the jewels ta Jo, maybe, just maybe, she would be sent home. The 'anti-botics,' or whatever they are called, could maybe save her?"

Connor ran his hand up and down Jo's arm, feeling the tickle of soft hairs against his palm. At his sister's words, he ceased all movement; his face gave no indication of his thoughts concerning what she said but there was a spark in his eyes.

"We thought it may be worth a chance." She pushed their case." It may nae work, but..."

Taking Meg by surprise, he rose in one fluid movement, exiting the pool with Jo cradled against his chest. Megahn had trouble keeping up with him. As he entered the bedchamber the three adults within at first stood stunned to see the drenched laird carrying his dying, naked betrothed through the room.

Maeve reacted first. "Put her on the bed, Connor," she ordered. "Alick, get more furs from the brown chest. Dougal, get Connor some dry clothes."

The two warriors averted their eyes from Jo's nakedness whilst Maeve pulled the covers back enabling Connor to place her within. "Move!" she ordered when they still stood motionless. "Dinna stand there like dumb mutes!"

The two seasoned warriors almost ran into each other in their haste to accomplish their given tasks. Meg witnessed this as she entered the chamber, panting from her chase up the tunnel. She loved Maeve for her ability to reduce the two men, one a laird, to such a frantic state.

Within minutes, Jo was cocooned within heavy furs and Connor was dressed in dry clothes. Connor wasted no time initiating the discussion. "Maeve," he directed, "speak ta me."

Maeve explained her plan to Connor as she

dried Jo's face. Connor stood before the fire with his back to the group, arms outstretched, hands resting on the mantelpiece, and his head bowed, considering his choices. Jo would surely die in this room, or he could send her back to her own time, to heal with medicines unavailable in this time.

Either way, he would lose her.

Dougal and Alick stood like sentinels at the foot of Jo's bed. This was Alick's first sight of his sister-in-law-to-be. His expression indicated he believed Maeve was right and it was a miracle Jo still lived.

Dougal's eyes were on Connor's back and his clenched hands.

"Connor?" Meg stepped up behind her brother, her slippers squelching, and placed a hand on his back. He was trembling. "What is yer decision?"

****

June Newbury tossed and turned all night; she heard every car, cat fight, and every red-eye flight over the house. As she stood in her kitchen making another cup of tea, she wondered why she just didn't make it cold in the first place.

The sun rose over the neighbour's roof and Lewis already scratched at her back door. But she wasn't complaining. Both she and the cat missed Jo. They were good company for each other. She longed to pick up the phone and say, 'Hello dear, how are you?' But this was impossible; June knew wherever her dear friend was, there were no phones.

In fact, June knew Jo was nowhere in this century. She knew a thing or two about what Jo was going through. June's beloved husband Ronald had an interesting past—very interesting. Not everyone can say their husband knew Bonnie Prince Charlie *and* he approved of the marriage to the lass with the strange accent!

But there was something wrong with this courtship. June sensed it in every bone of her body.

It was a family trait—or curse. All of June's female ancestors were gifted with the Sight.

****

"I best be going. I may be missed," the girl said, reluctant to leave. "If Mrs. MacBain finds oot, I shall be in big trouble." The man's hand reached out and grabbed the young woman as she went to leave the bed. Pulling her back down beside him, he caressed her naked body. "Dinna go yet. Ye can stay a wee bit longer." She giggled and obliged.

They heard the stable doors crash open and a loud voice yell out, "Tannan! Tannan, man! Where the bloody heel are ye?"

Dougal Haig had a way about him that made people jump to attention, even when he was in a good mood, which by the sound of it he wasn't at the moment.

As rushed footsteps closed in on the horse trainer's abode at the rear of the stalls, Tannan already resigned himself to being caught with his pants down. When the door crashed open, Dougal's frame filled the doorway and when a shriek rent the air, he thought Tannan must have a piglet within his room, but then he saw the movement in the shadows.

Fiona stood there like a hunted rabbit. Staring, not knowing whether to run or hide, her bundled clothes held before her left little to the imagination.

But Dougal could not delay. He gave a slight flick of his head and Fiona scampered away without a backward glance, her white bottom jiggled as she raced past Dougal and out the door. Tannan looked unsure whether to laugh or be annoyed at Dougal's intrusion, but the strained expression on his face told him something was very wrong.

Tannan reached for his shirt and rose from the cot. "What is it, man?"

"Connor left something in yer care."

Tannan frowned with a hint of suspicion. "Aye."

"He needs it. And make haste?"

"But, he said I was ta hide it well and nae give it ta anyone but him?"

"*He* is the one who needs it."

When Tannan didn't move, Dougal became angry. "Do ye nae know me well enough, man? Connor needs..."

"Dougal!" Tannan raised his voice. "Nae ever question ma loyalty ta both of ye. Fer Christ's sake, man, let me get ma wits aboot me...and ma pants on!"

Dougal couldn't hold back a rueful grin. "Aye, er, I nae meant ta, ah, interrupt ye. I nae would have. But it is urgent."

"Aye. I am nae blind. How is the lady?"

"It is grave."

Tannan nodded. "I shall fetch it."

He disappeared into the tack room, which was attached to his own small chamber. Dougal could hear equipment jingling and planks being moved. Tannan returned with a chaff bag, rolled into a ball. "I believe this is what ye are wanting."

Dougal opened the sack. Inside was a dark velvet case.

"I nae asked Connor why it needed ta be hidden," Tannan hedged.

"It is a long story." Dougal nodded in acknowledgment, turned on his heel, and left.

****

The group waited for Dougal to return.

Connor sat on the bed beside Jo wishing to remember every freckle and line on the face of his beloved. He noticed her long eyelashes, swept closed with illness, and the shape of her brow and nose. All these characteristics he would commit to memory, never to forget. He inhaled through his nose, determined to remember her sweet, individual scent forever.

Megahn and Maeve wept quietly as the reality of what they were about to do settled upon them. These minutes might be their last with their friend—one way or another. None of them knew what to do, never knowing such unreal circumstances before. They wondered how one said farewell to a person who was going to travel through time, especially when you didn't truly believe it was possible.

Dougal returned, and Meg kissed Jo on the forehead and closed her eyes in silent prayer over her friend. "I will miss ye," was all she could say through her sorrow.

Maeve spoke no prayer but kissed Jo farewell and said, "Until we meet again, sister."

Unable to do anything else, the two couples left the chamber, leaving Connor alone with her.

****

Peace at last. It sounded like a conference was taking place within her room. And stay out! Can't a girl get some sleep around here?

It was so nice in the water. She'd felt like she was floating on air, the soft beating of her heart louder under the water—or was it someone else's? Yes, she was sure it was.

She should know whose heart it was. The fuzziness just wouldn't let up. She knew its owner was somehow important to her. There was some connection between them.

The clouds thinned. She felt happy. The sun tried to break through. But damn, these straw mattresses were uncomfortable.

****

Laird Connor MacKay stood next to his bed, staring down at the beautiful vision before him. She was every man's erotic fantasy. He chastised himself for such thoughts when she lay dying before his eyes.

The furs, dark against her naked skin, made her appear even paler. Her hair dried and fanned out across the pillow, small strands curling about her face. Connor lowered the furs to expose her chest. Her pink nipples peeped above the covers. She looked so peaceful and serene, like an angel from heaven.

But nothing drew the eye more than the piece of exquisite jewellery draped around her neck. It was remarkable. The antique gold chain carried a Celtic styled pendant with a large, blood-red ruby in the centre. Around the gem was a row of smaller rubies of equal beauty. It was old; very old. Connor knew nothing of its history; only that it was given to MacKay ladies upon the birth of the first son.

He just hoped whatever magical ability the jewels possessed would be enough to transport her back to her own time, and quickly.

Connor stripped off his clothes and climbed under the furs next to her. He rolled her onto her side to face him and held her close to his warmth. It felt strange to lie this way with no reciprocal contact. Her hands lay relaxed between their bodies, not caressing his face or running smoothly over his skin, arousing him. Her head, pillowed on his upper arm, was like a dead weight. But he still felt her warmth and her soft breath against his neck. It would have to do.

As time ticked by he spoke endlessly to her, determined not to fall asleep, terrified he would waken alone in his bed, frightened she may also die in his arms. As the hours passed, they remained alone. Connor felt no hunger, even though he couldn't remember his last meal. There was silence in the hallway and no noises could be heard rising up from the bailey. It was as if the castle lay with him, quietly mourning.

"Do ye remember the first time we met? Ye were the water nymph in ma pool. Ye were the most beautiful lass I had ever seen. Until ye broke ma nose!"

On and on he spoke, reliving the good times and the bad. She lay motionless, but it did not matter. Connor recalled the terror filled days of the raiders, the laughter when she was learning to ride, the stolen moments in the hayloft, and the long hours at night spent in each other's arms.

Connor poured out his grief and love, fighting the night and the need of his body to slumber. "I will never love another as I love ye," he said with a half-smile of sorrow. "Ye gave me reason ta move forward. Ye taught me how a man and woman are meant ta be. Ye brought laughter ta ma life. And I will love ye forever." Connor slid his hand between them, reaching for the pendant. It felt warm to the touch. "Ah dinna ken what yer life will be like when ye get home. But I wish ye love, and happiness. I hope ye have a life filled with laughter and family. I hope ye grow old with a man worthy enough ta call ye wife."

Connor could not speak for a moment. He bent his head to her breasts, held her even tighter and cried.

When his shoulders stilled and exhaustion dulled his grief, Connor whispered his farewell.

"I wanted ta see ye grow fat with ma bairns. I wished ta waken every morning with ye beside me. But I would rather give ye life. I would rather send ye home—ta *live*. I hope ye will remember me; for I shall never forget ye."

He kissed her gently on the forehead and lips, tucked her head beneath his chin, and let exhaustion and fate take its course.

Chapter Thirty-Three

The sunlight sliced into the room, as if determined to wake those who slumbered. A rooster crowed down in the bailey, and a sheep baaed from somewhere in the lower pasture. Morning dawned, still and peaceful at Shreave.

Connor felt warm and cosy within his bed, he felt no compulsion or inclination to open his eyes and rise.

As the persistent morning light beat at his eyelids and full consciousness crept upon him, the deep breath he was about to take stopped in his throat. Something was not right. His gut tightened as the events of the last twenty-four hours came crashing in on him.

He forced his eyes open, blinking as they adjusted to the morning light.

And there she lay.

In the same position as he layed her before sleep and sorrow overcame him.

She lay on her side facing him. He felt her face; it was warm. Her breathing was soft and steady.

She was alive.

She was still *here*.

As reality settled in and a wave of relief washed over his shattered nerves, something else became apparent to him.

Her hand was entwined with his.

It almost felt as if she were holding his, not him holding hers. At first he ignored it, putting it down to wishful thinking. She was still ill. But then he realised her leg was draped over his own. Did he place it there himself?

Connor lifted the covers, his eyes needing conformation. Yes, her soft pale leg was draped across his own dark hairy one. Her naked body looked like heaven on hearth to his hungry eyes. Could it possibly be?

As he examined every inch of his betrothed, a raspy, raw whisper drew his astonished attention. "Have you found what you're looking for down there?" Connor dropped the covers and reached for her face, his calloused fingers caressing her cheeks, his dark eyes staring into a startling pair of green.

"Jo-Anne. Jo-Anne," he breathed.

"Yes. That's my name. Why is my mouth so dry?"

****

June woke up in the early light of dawn, the sun peeping from behind the curtains. Two things were obvious. Lewis was in the bed with her. Damn cat. And she was aware she slept deeply. The trouble-free slumber of a person with no cares or worries.

Relief settled within her chest. All was well.

Jo would be home soon.

****

Within the next twenty minutes, the peace and solitude of privacy was shattered by the hustle and bustle of servants, family, and friends. It was like Burke Street in the chamber, the busiest street in Melbourne, with people racing this way and that.

As soon as Connor ran to the door and bellowed for Maeve, there wasn't a person within the whole castle who hadn't heard the news.

Maeve and Meg dressed her in a warm nightdress before tucking her under the covers again. Mrs. MacBain raced in with water, ale, and food. Dougal built the fire up, and Alick was issuing orders whilst minding his son, who was wailing in the hope of a generous breast.

As she surveyed all the commotion from the bed, she didn't understand what all the fuss was about. That was until Connor told her how long she'd been unconscious. And before she felt the *weight* around her neck.

She felt as weak as a kitten and though she was trying to fathom all that happened, she couldn't get her head around it, and already felt exhausted and in need of more sleep.

"Jo-Anne." The voice was soft and close to her face. Connor. "Drink a little more of this fer me, then ye can shut yer eyes."

She drank some more of Maeve's tonic. "Yuk," she rasped.

"Dinna complain, woman. It will make ye well again."

Maeve was standing close by watching her take the medicine. She couldn't believe how well she seemed, considering. As her eyes began to drift shut, Maeve began ushering people out of the room.

"Oot! Come now...oot! She needs her rest." When everyone left the room and silence descended, Maeve attempted to issue orders to Connor. "Nae too much ta drink at a time. Just sips whenever she wakens. Don't..."

"Maeve!" Connor said firmly, "I'm nae a fool. Now leave us be. She just needs ta rest." And then, with a sigh, he offered, "Maeve. I'm sorry. Thank ye."

"Yer welcome." Maeve made to leave, but then hovered by the bed, unsure. "I dinna understand what's going on, Connor," she whispered. "I didna expect her ta get better. And I didna expect her ta be here this morn!"

"Aye. Neither did I."

Maeve closed the door behind her, leaving them in peace. It was an eerie quiet compared to the chaos before. Thinking Jo was already sleeping, Connor went to sit by the fire. He was an emotional wreck.

He felt as if he was ripped apart and thrown back together again.

"Stay with me," came the raspy voice from the bed.

"I thought ye were sleeping," Connor said, turning back towards her.

"With that racket?"

Connor laughed. "Aye. Ye canna say no one cares fer ye."

She smiled. It was the most wonderful smile he ever saw.

He threw off his plaid, hastily donned before the invasion and pulled back the covers. "Nae my favourite night-dress," he teased as he surveyed Jo. "I prefer the skin-tone one!"

"My lusty Highlander. Stop complaining. Hold me, please."

Connor climbed into the bed and enfolded Jo gently within his arms. He said nothing for a long while. He couldn't find the words. They were choked behind the lump in the back of his throat. He couldn't help wonder what he did to deserve this gift from God.

Time drifted by. Neither knew nor cared how long they lay there. It was a closeness needing no words or comment. They were just happy to be. When she spoke, it startled Connor. He thought she was sleeping.

"Where did you find my necklace?" She moved her hand up between their cocooned bodies and clasped the jewel in her palm.

"Now there's a tale. A long story I shall keep until ye waken."

As Jo drifted off to sleep, she felt an unreal feeling of weightlessness.

She was drifting through the clouds.

Echoes of familiar voices sounded in her ears.

She felt safe, but was disappointed, no, sad.

She was sure she was leaving something very important behind.

Chapter Thirty-Four

Her body ached. As she rolled over in the bed it felt like her limbs ignored the commands of her brain. The simple task of twisting her torso was like trying to move a boulder with a walking stick—almost impossible.

Her head felt full of sawdust and her sinuses were clogged, resulting in a pounding headache. Her mouth felt filled with talcum powder. *God, I'm thirsty.*

She lay motionless, exhausted by the effort of rolling over. The pillow, soft against her cheek, cushioned her throbbing head.

I feel like shit! I'd pay a year's salary right now for one glass of water. As she tried to conjure some coherent thought, a distant noise caught her attention. Unwilling to open her eyes and let the daylight compound her headache, she tried to recollect what the sound was. It was familiar, but its origin eluded her. *If this headache would just go away*!

Deciding if she wanted a glass of water she was going to have to toughen up, get out of bed, and fetch it herself, she flung the bed covers back.

It was then she felt the sudden motion of the bed, as if someone just sat on it.

Meow. *A cat? Meow, purr, purr, purr.*

"Lewis...not now. Go away." Her sore throat protested the use of her vocal cords. "Unless you can get me some water?"

The cat demanded attention and head-butted her. The soft fur felt warm on her face as he nuzzled in close, the purring sound amplified in her ear and made her smile. It was a comforting feeling; a familiar situation.

"You are one lucky cat."

If she wanted a drink she would have to open her eyes, and she did, just a little, to test the brightness. *Oh no, no, no. Sunglasses. Need sunglasses!* Groaning, she swung her legs over the side of the bed and sat there a moment as a wave of dizziness overcame her.

The cat took advantage of the offered lap, extended his claws and purred as both front paws pricked her skin beneath the pyjamas.

Jo opened her eyes, felt the pain, and waited for them to adjust. It was then she realised what the familiar sound was. The cat flap. In the same instant she realised she was home. Her home!

Anxiety washed over her.

No no no.

She breathed erratically as panic besieged her mind. The sudden shock of her surroundings made her body shudder.

"Nooo," came her anguished cry. "Nooo," she panted.

She stood by the bed, but her illness and fear caused her to stumble. She staggered past the bedside table, knocking a lamp to the carpet. She didn't notice and lurched blindly on.

"Connor!" she screamed, her throat constricted with soreness and grief. "Connor! No...Nooo..."

Staggering down the hallway, Lewis watched her from the bedroom door, as she looked in every room she passed. Familiar wallpaper, ornaments, and furniture she recognised, but nobody there.

The silence was deafening, no clattering of horse hoofs from the bailey, no hustle and bustle, none of the musky smells of peat fires and fresh rushes.

"This can't be happening. Oh please, God," she

hiccupped.

When she reached the kitchen her legs gave away under her and she collapsed to the tiles in a heap. Her sorrow was palpable as the reality sank deep into her heart and bones. *I'm alone. I've lost everything.*

She lay on her side, consumed by indescribable heartache.

When coherent thought pried its way back into her consciousness, she slid her hand to her neck. The necklace was heavy and warm against her throat; she didn't try to rise but continued to lie on the kitchen floor. Silent tears ran unchecked whilst a numbness filled her soul.

"Connor, can you hear me? Do you know I'm here?" She pleaded as she raised her eyes to see rays of the morning sun shine through her kitchen window. "I'm here, Connor. I'm here." She closed her eyes to better see Connor's image; she saw him sitting proud and high upon Thief, him striding towards her across the expanse of the great hall, the desire within his eyes as he drew her naked body to his. The visions were so clear; his scent was a perfume within her nostrils.

I love you Connor MacKay. I shall never forget you...

****

June Newbury found her curled up on the kitchen floor. Racing through the house in a mad panic, her senses reeling for the last ten minutes, she knew Jo had returned. *Knew* it.

June was putting on the kettle in her own kitchen when an overwhelming sense of loss and grief overcame her. At first she ignored it, as the whole week was one of taunted emotions, like riding a roller coaster. Ever since Jo...went away, she'd been in tune with many of her friend's ups and downs. It was the Sight.

So when this feeling besieged her, she just cast it aside. It was not until Lewis tore out the house like a crazed banshee that she became anxious and raced after him.

Lewis left June for dead, jumping over the fence and not slowing even as he pushed through the cat flap on Jo's back door.

She was in such a fluster she arrived at Jo's front door without the key, and needed to return to her own house to get it.

Jo was gone for just over a week. But June knew she may have been elsewhere for much longer.

June bent down and knelt beside her friend. Jo's grief was obvious.

"Welcome home, my love. Come now. Come, come. Let's dry those tears and get you back to bed."

Jo hadn't heard June enter the room, but she recognised her friend's voice. *I'm not alone.* She opened her eyes and raised them to June's, a sharp sob caught in her throat as her sorrow poured out again all over June's welcoming lap. June reached for the tea towel hanging on the oven handle. She wiped Jo's face and nose and pushed the hair from her eyes.

"Come now, my love. What's all this blubbering? You'll have me mopping the floor soon," June said.

"I've lost him, June. I've lost him..." Almost unable to breathe, she sobbed into the tea towel. "What h...happened? Wh...why?"

"Now, now. Back to bed first. You are much sicker than I thought. What on earth did you get up to?" It took a few minutes to get the crumpled, defeated woman back beneath the covers. Once tucked in, June sat on the edge of the bed.

"Now, my dear. You are not to grieve so. This is not the end, it's just the beginning. Your journey has just begun." June's eyes held their familiar twinkle. Jo stared at her, her tears flowing freely. "My dear!"

Exasperated, June said, "Did you think I would have given you the gift, if you were to spend the rest of your life grieving for someone?"

A glint of hope sparked in Jo's swollen eyes. "But I've been there, and, and I was happy, and, I wanted to stay with him forever."

"And so you shall my dear, so you shall. But you are not going anywhere until you get better. I doubt they'd even let you on the plane in your condition. You just sit tight and I'll make a cup of tea and ring the doctor. I've known him for years. He'll do a house call and give you some antibiotics. We'll have you right in no time. I'll put honey in it..." June's voice trailed off down the hallway.

Her mind was reeling. What did June say? *'So you shall my dear, so you shall.' What's going on? And what plane?*

"June," she tried to yell, her raspy throat unable to project her voice much further than the doorway. "June!" A hacking cough followed the shout.

"Don't do that. You'll just hurt your throat," June's raised voice called out as she made her way back towards the bedroom. "You need to relax and rest, I'll..."

"June!"

"I'm right here dear. There's no need to shout. I need to make the tea. Lay back down." She rose from the bed and was sitting on the edge, her eyes intent on the older woman, her skin tingled with an impossible hope.

"June? Where...where is he?"

"Who? Oh! He? Well, I don't rightly know. But when I've got the tea made and poured and I've rung the doctor, I want to hear the whole story. Everything. Oh, my dear. What an adventure you've been on. I can hardly wait." June went to return to the kitchen.

"Wait. Where...is...he?" Jo emphasised each

word, her heart in her throat.

"In Scotland, of course, my dear. Waiting for *you*."

Chapter Thirty-Five

She stood before the large stone manor. It stood two stories high and creepers climbed the walls, nurturing its beautiful, historical appearance. At the tourism office in Inverness she was told the building dated back over two hundred years and used to be open to the public, but its new owner desired privacy and it was now closed to tourists.

Manicured gardens surrounded Sithig Manor, and Black Angus dotted the one hundred and fifty acres of rolling hills surrounding the house. However, the noise detracted from the serene atmosphere. The sound of sawing, hammering, and men's voices echoed from behind the manor. The front driveway overflowed with trucks and work vehicles. Major renovations were taking place and scaffolding extended beyond the roofline from the back of the building.

Her suede boots felt filled with concrete. It took minutes of pondering before she steered her rented Peugeot down the long winding driveway. Then she sat in her car even longer fighting a debilitating wave of apprehension.

After deciding she was acting like an imbecile, she got out of the car and slammed the door so hard she was sure someone would come to investigate. When nobody appeared, Jo let out a sigh of relief and stood by her car another few minutes, before starting to shiver.

It was a clear, cool morning; the last remaining patches of snow could be seen nestled beneath bushes, hidden from the sun. Retrieving her coat from the back seat, she walked up the entrance path to where she now stood, before a heavy timber door.

You're a coward, Joanne Dunstan. Just go in there and find him.

Her feet refused to move.

Spending two days at home waiting for the antibiotics to work, then another week for her to feel almost normal, her energy took longer to return than expected. During this time she'd asked June at least a thousand questions. Most, her friend was unable to answer.

"So what does the necklace have to do with it all?"

"My dear, I wish I knew."

"How can the same people live back then, but now be here in the present?"

"I don't really know, dear. Maybe it's an imaginary past, or maybe it's one and the same."

So here she stood, pondering the last three weeks of her life. Despite her request that June accompany her to Scotland, her old friend insisted it was a journey she needed to complete by herself.

All in all, she knew no more now than she did before, except for one thing. Destiny should not be ignored or written off as chance. Unexplainable things happen, a good friend once told her.

After painstaking searches via the Internet and enquiries via Ronald Newbury's relations who still resided in Scotland, she located the address of one Connor MacKay, Architect and Construction Engineer. A bit more research into a company called Laird International Constructions Pty. Ltd. told the story of a business partnership between two childhood friends that, after ten years hard work, eventuated in an international company with contracts all over Europe.

She had boarded the plane, her stomach in knots. Would he recognise her? June said it would be unlikely he'd know who she was, but assured her their attraction would be no different. What if he was already married? A few enquiries answered that question. No.

Oh God! Take a deep breath, woman! And don't be such a fool.

She walked forward and knocked on the door. There was no answer. She wasn't surprised as the noise surrounding the manor was quite loud. She reached for the handle on the front door and turned it. It was unlocked. Taking a deep breath, she opened the door and entered.

The interior of the manor was old but well kept. Heavy beams held up the second floor and the internal walls were stone, like the outside. Two large rooms led off the entrance hall and a long hallway disappeared towards the back of the house, the staircase rising beyond it. There were a number of doors leading off the hall, so she wandered along, peering into each room. All on the lower floor were empty but for building materials. The manor was undergoing a major makeover and extension.

She felt a little guilty roaming around uninvited but a good friend once told her, 'ta trust yer feelings.' So she did. She couldn't explain it, but although anxious, this somehow felt—right.

Halfway up the stairs a gruff voice startled her. "What are ye doing here, lass? This is private property now. It is no longer open ta the public."

It was Dougal.

She stared down at the man below her, and forced back tears by a quick succession of blinks. He was dressed in an old pair of jeans and a black T-shirt with an old flannel shirt over the top. Bits of plaster caught in his short-cropped hair and beard. He looked wonderful.

"Ye shouldna be wearing those fancy boots in here, tis too dangerous," he barked, then noticed the stranger was on the verge of tears. "Are ye okay, lass?" he inquired. "Are ye lost?"

It took a while to find her voice. "Er, I'm...no, I'm not lost."

Dougal frowned at her strange accent. "Ye are nae from around these parts."

"Er, no. Umm, I've come to see Connor MacKay."

Dougal's face turned suspicious and asked, "What business do ye have with Connor?"

Good question, she thought. "Err...I'm..." *Think quick, think quick.* "He made enquiries with my...company. Interior design!"

"Hmmph. Didna mention anything ta me. But, tis his property. Are ye here ta give an estimate?"

"An estimate? Yes."

"Well, ye've missed him. He'll nae be back for another hour yet. At least."

Her legs almost failed her. They trembled.

After failing to convince her to come back later, Dougal left her alone to view the building, but not before a suspicious stare and parting complaint, "Ye should have worn more suitable clothing. This is a building site, nae a fashion parade."

She felt deliriously happy. If Dougal was the same Dougal, then Connor should be the same Connor, just as June predicted.

She wandered the house, becoming familiar with the dwelling. It would be a magnificent creation when the renovations were complete.

Half an hour later she thought her heart would burst when Maeve entered the kitchen. She carried a cardboard box filled with fresh sandwiches and cakes, which she placed on an old table cluttered with documents and architectural drawings.

When she looked up she started at seeing Jo standing beside the window. "Oh, hello," she said. "I'm sorry, I didna realise there was someone else here...apart from all the dusty, smelly men ootside," she joked, screwing up her nose. "Do the boys know ye are here?"

She looked just the same, but different and fantastic, with very short hair gelled up in a sporty style. She wore beige corduroy jeans tucked into black leather boots and a brown cashmere jumper and scarf.

"Oh! Yes. Dougal said I should wait for Connor. He'll be back soon. I...I have an appointment with him." He heart was bursting.

A frown appeared on Maeve's brow. "Do I know ye?"

Jo hesitated, trying to hold onto her elation, not wanting Maeve to think she was mad, not wanting to scare her away. She replied, "I'm not sure. We may have met...a long time ago." She forced a lump back down her throat.

"I never forget a face. But, somehow ye be familiar but..." Maeve stepped forward and noticed a tear slide down Jo's cheek. "*Ye* know *me*, don't ye?" Maeve asked, her senses tingling.

"Yes," was all Jo managed as she tried to get her emotions under control. Maeve reached out her hand and captured Jo's. At the contact, Maeve took a sudden deep breath and a look of shock appeared on her face.

"Oh, my. My, my, my. This is so strong." Maeve squeezed her hand even harder backing away, pulling her with her to sit on old wooden chairs by the table. "Ye be pregnant. Nae, nae," she hedged, confused. "It be the want of a child is sae strong." Maeve looked abashed. "I get it wrong some times."

Jo smiled through her tears, then took a deep breath and said, "I've...I've got a story to tell you."

****

Connor MacKay returned to the manor later than expected. A white Peugeot blocked his usual spot so he parked his black Landrover on the grass and got out. He was hungry and he hoped Maeve brought the usual stash of food over for his and Dougal's lunch.

Since they stepped back from running the company, life was so much easier, especially for Maeve and the bairns. Connor and Dougal no longer spent months at a time overseas, supervising projects; others were paid to do that now. They worked hard for over a decade and the time came to enjoy the rewards while still young enough to do so. Sithig Manor turned out to be a hobby project for both men.

Connor's dream was always to buy and restore a home of his own. He lived in some of the best hotels in the world but he'd had enough. He planned to grow old at Sithig Manor.

Frowning as he walked past the Peugeot, Connor entered the manor.

****

The two women spoke at length; a quick and familiar camaraderie developed between them. Maeve hadn't ridiculed her words. She was rather excited and didn't want to leave Jo but she needed to pick up the children from a neighbour's property. Apparently, Mrs. Moray was a kindly woman, with a love of children!

There was still so much to discuss. Maeve insisted she call her on her mobile phone the minute she was finished with Connor.

Jo received a dinner invitation to the Haig's.

Dougal poked his head in the door and suggested Jo come back another day. "Thank you, but no. I can wait," she replied. Dougal frowned and returned to his work.

Left alone again, she wandered the manor. Her pretence of being an interior designer was an easy occupation to feign. She found herself imagining the wall colours and the type of furniture suitable for the rooms.

Her anxiety had lessened but she couldn't help wonder—how do you introduce yourself to the man you're going to marry? *Oh boy! This is crazy.*

Wandering through the rooms on the ground floor, she noticed a doorway that led to a cellar. Curious, she fetched a torch from the kitchen table, returned to the room, and descended a flight of curved stairs.

****

Connor walked down the hallway heading towards the kitchen—and food, he hoped, but was distracted by a noise. Retracing his steps he stuck his head into a room and noticed the cellar door open. It was usually kept closed as sometimes Maeve would drop in with the children and it was not a safe place for the bairns to play.

He stood before the cellar door and could see flashes of torchlight shadowing off the stairwell below. He called down, "Hello," and heard the startled gasp of a woman, the smash of glass, and then all was thrust into darkness. Concerned, he made his way down the stairs using the wall to his right as a guide.

"Hello!" Connor called again. "Where are ye? Are ye hurt?" No answer. He heard the soft sounds of a woman crying. "It's okay. Where are ye? I'll guide ye back up the stairs," he offered as he stepped off the last tread.

"I'm here," replied a voice, weak with emotion.

"Reach yer hand out and I'll find it," suggested Connor.

Unseen in the blackness, she lifted her arm and extended her hand towards the voice. A voice she feared she may never hear again. A voice so familiar, yearning filled her heart.

When his hand knocked hers, she grabbed hold and they both pulled, bringing their bodies up against each other. His was as familiar to her as the beat of her own heart.

The softness of the women in his arms took Connor by surprise. He didn't know who she was, but he felt protective of her along with an indescribable need to hold her. So he did.

They stood there in the darkness for a few moments, neither speaking.

He was first to step back and find his voice. "I'm sorry, lass. I didna mean ta hold ye, I…" He didn't get to finish his words. She reached up with her hands, placed her fingers on his lips and stepped towards him using her fingers to guide her.

The kiss was one sided, at first. She tasted his lips with her tongue, then seduced his mouth. She felt the hard strength of his body through the fabric of her clothing and the restrained passion in his stance.

He was bewildered.

Women often made moves on him and he knew when they were sincere, or just wanted his money. But this was beyond anything he ever experienced. Rather than push her away, his arms encircled her and his mouth responded. Within seconds there was a mutual passion heightened by some unseen connection.

Jo wanted to cry, but her passion mounted and all she could think of was making love with him. She *needed* to make love with him. She needed to feel this was all *real*.

He was unable to hide his arousal as it pushed into her stomach. She welcomed it. Connor pulled away and opened his eyes to look upon her, but there was only darkness, which disorientated him, causing slight dizziness.

They breathed heavily, standing in the blackness, neither knowing what to say, how to feel or respond.

Connor couldn't fathom the way his body reacted to her touch, how his chest constricted with a yearning so deep it unnerved him. But with certainty, ridiculous as it was, he knew this woman was his. He would let no other man possess or hurt her.

She was his.

Nothing ever felt so right.

"I love you, Connor MacKay. I have loved you for three hundred and eighty years."

Connor stood motionless before he asked, "Who are ye?"

Epilogue

Jonathon Dougal MacKay raced through the conservatory like a hurricane. He called for his father to come and see what he built in the gardening shed. In the last half an hour he'd designed and constructed what was apparently a toy car. Two mismatched pieces of wood were haphazardly nailed together; the lack of wheels would make it difficult for his parents to guess what it was but for a three-and-a-half-year-old, it was indeed quite a feat.

"Dadda, dadda, come see. I did it. I did it."

"I'm in the cellar!" a voice called out from deep within the manor. Jonathon reached the study and made for the doorway leading down to the wine cellar. "Be careful on the steps, lad. Ye come down slowly."

Not trusting his pint-sized rocket to do as asked, Connor met the boy halfway up the staircase; the boy leapt into his father's arms.

"Jonathon MacKay," came another voice, far sterner than his father. "What were you just told? You are not to run down those steps. You'll give us heart failure."

Although the reprimand was given, Jo could not hide her love and pride as her son told his father all about the car he made. He assured Connor he did *all* the work, and cousin Millie hadn't helped at all.

She loved to watch her husband interact with their son. It was like watching her most wished-for dream develop before her eyes.

A gathering of family and friends were enjoying

this special day at Sithig Manor which was alive with conversation, laughter, and it seemed, dozens of children. In fact there were eleven rascals in all, and they swarmed everywhere. There were Maeve and Dougal's three children, Millie the eldest and ringleader in most things; Megahn and Alick's four, the youngest two, twins; Connor and Dougal's long time friend, Tannan, his wife Fiona and their two. Tannan had taken over much of the company business in Europe for Connor and Dougal.

Mrs. Mac, as Eva was affectionately called, cooked up a storm in the kitchen. Connor asked her to join them, but she insisted on remaining in the kitchen where all knew she was happiest.

June, the guest of honour, sat at the kitchen table bouncing a baby girl on her lap. June and Eva met four years ago at Connor and Jo's wedding and were now old comrades. June was Aunty June to most of the children, though Davie Haig copied Jonathon and called her Nana. June didn't mind in the least.

Although a great distance separated them, June looked upon these people as family. Scotland was her second home and she visited every year for three months.

Connor and Jo exited the cellar carrying the bottles of fine red wine they selected. Their son already scampered back through the conservatory and into the garden where a small marquee was erected for the weekend festivities. This was one Scottish clan needing no real reason to celebrate; June's annual arrival was more than enough for the gathering.

Entering the kitchen, she could see the look of love on June's face as the older woman cuddled Jonathon's baby sister. The baby was four months old now and June had received DVDs, photos, and emails since the birth of Connor and Jo's second child. However, they were not the same as holding the child to her heart, and she had four months to catch up on.

"I don't suppose you want me to take Kathryn yet!" Jo asked.

"When she's hungry; that is the only thing I can't give her, dear. You go and mingle. Eva and I have everything under control here. Don't we, my friend?"

"Aye, that we do, that we do. Ye young ones go and play. Leave us old lassies be, we know a thing or two aboot bairns." Eva winked at June.

Before she and Connor left the kitchen, Connor leaned over and kissed June on the forehead. "It's so good ta have ye back with us," he said.

The two old friends loved to monopolise the babies whenever they were given the opportunity.

Connor and Jo stood beside the glass door of the new conservatory overlooking the back garden. They stopped at the same time, in sync with each other's feelings, and surveyed the scene before them; family, friends as close as blood, uncles, aunts, cousins—they were all here.

"Could life be any more perfect than this?" she spoke almost to herself. Connor turned her to face him, his eyes were dark and penetrating. They alone had the ability to arouse her.

"Nae. It could not." He looped his arms around her. "Have I told ye taday wife, that I love ye?"

"Stretch marks and all?"

"Oh, aye. Especially those!" Connor cut off her giggle with a kiss. "Hmmm, ye taste like spring. Good enough ta eat," he whispered into her mouth.

"Fer Christ's sake, man. Where's the bloody wine? Everyone's parched waiting fer ye two."

Dougal. Some things never changed.

"Mind yer manners, Dougal," Megahn scolded. "Can ye no see he is occupied?" she said with a twinkle in her eye.

"Aye. But that kind of occupation leads ta..."

"All right husband," scolded Maeve. "There are children aboot."

Maeve continued with the teasing, "If they disappear for a time...it's the walk that will give them away!"

Meg choked on a biscuit and Alick patted her on the back, with little affect.

Jo's face went red with the taunt. Connor just laughed. Nothing fazed him.

"Ooh. Is that nae grand?" teased Maeve. "After all these years she can still blush."

"All right, all right, you lot. Cut it out," said Jo. "There are children about." She knew where this conversation was going. Downhill, all the way!

"Weel, man. Are ye going ta hold onto them bottles, or are ye going ta open them? Taday would be fine!" Dougal was never a patient man.

Connor smiled, leaned in and gave Jo a possessive, lingering kiss, and a look of later promise.

This of course, caused more jeering from the spectators as he drew away from his wife and sauntered down the stone steps into the garden.

Jo stood back, happy to observe the banter as they opened the bottles of Connor's special vintage. Whether in the seventeenth or twenty-first century, Connor MacKay stood out in a crowd. His physique and dark imposing looks could not be matched by any other man—not in Jo's opinion. And she liked him in denims as much as his kilt.

Sometimes she pinched herself to make sure this was not some incredible dream. But it was real; this man, children, family, friends, and Scottish home, all of it real.

She also felt a sense of peace. Their lives in this time would always be so different from the fragile existence of the past. Here, they were safe and protected.

The others knew nothing about living life in the seventeenth century; but Jo did.

Maeve accepted it as fact, and so did Connor. Dougal, well, Dougal was Dougal. Only the immediate family knew how Connor and Jo met and it prompted much discussion and research. However, no historical information was found concerning a Clan MacKay of Shreave though not all clan records survived through the centuries.

Incredibly, by chance, they discovered a family connection between Maeve and June.

It was a small world after all. Jo descended the stones steps, a smile of contentment on her lips and her heart full of timeless love.

A word about the author...

Gail Symmonds loves to be swept away by a good read. She believes unless a book is too hard to put down, it doesn't deserve to be picked up in the first place! Her love of writing started as a child, but her diverse career path, including marketing and education, lead her in a different direction. She recommends at some stage in your life you should stop and ask yourself this: 'Is there something in this life I'd like to achieve but haven't?' Her answer was to write novels that swept people away just as many wonderful authors had done to her over the years.

Gail lives with her husband and two children on a small property in Australia. She loves the rural lifestyle; cows in the paddock, chairs on the veranda, space and peace to dream.

Thank you for purchasing
this Wild Rose Press publication.
For other wonderful stories of romance,
please visit our on-line bookstore at
www.thewildrosepress.com.

For questions or more information,
contact us at info@thewildrosepress.com.

The Wild Rose Press
www.TheWildRosePress.com

LaVergne, TN USA
07 July 2010
188617LV00006B/36/P